Charles Dickens, Adelaide Anne Procter

The complete Poetical Works

Charles Dickens, Adelaide Anne Procter

The complete Poetical Works

ISBN/EAN: 9783337400613

Printed in Europe, USA, Canada, Australia, Japan

Cover: Foto ©Andreas Hilbeck / pixelio.de

More available books at **www.hansebooks.com**

THE COMPLETE POETICAL WORKS OF ADELAIDE ANNE PROCTER

Cabinet Edition

WITH AN INTRODUCTION BY
CHARLES DICKENS

BOSTON AND NEW YORK
HOUGHTON, MIFFLIN AND COMPANY
The Riverside Press, Cambridge

PUBLISHERS' NOTE.

THE few personal items to be gleaned regarding the life and work of the author of the poems contained in this volume were affectionately recorded by Charles Dickens in an article printed in *The Atlantic Monthly* for December, 1865, and reprinted herewith as an introduction. The collection of poems is believed to be complete, including as it does *A Chaplet of Verses*, with Miss Procter's special introduction to that group.

Autumn, 1899.

CONTENTS.

———◆———

		Page
INTRODUCTION	. . . .	xiii

LEGENDS AND LYRICS. A BOOK OF VERSES.

FIRST SERIES.

	Page
THE ANGEL'S STORY	1
ECHOES	5
A FALSE GENIUS	6
MY PICTURE	6
JUDGE NOT	7
FRIEND SORROW	8
ONE BY ONE	8
TRUE HONORS	9
A WOMAN'S QUESTION	14
THE THREE RULERS	15
A DEAD PAST	16
A DOUBTING HEART	16
A STUDENT	17
A KNIGHT-ERRANT	18
LINGER, O GENTLE TIME	19
HOMEWARD BOUND	19
LIFE AND DEATH	24
NOW	25
CLEANSING FIRES	25
THE VOICE OF THE WIND	26
TREASURES	27
SHINING STARS	28
WAITING	28
THE CRADLE-SONG OF THE POOR	29

Be Strong	30
God's Gifts	31
A Tomb in Ghent	32
The Angel of Death	39
A Dream	40
The Present	41
Changes	41
Strive, Wait, and Pray	41
A Lament for the Summer	42
The Unknown Grave	42
Give me thy Heart	43
The Wayside Inn	45
Voices of the Past	48
The Dark Side	48
A First Sorrow	49
Murmurs	49
Give	50
My Journal	50
A Chain	52
The Pilgrims	53
Incompleteness	53
A Legend of Bregenz	54
A Farewell	57
Sowing and Reaping	57
The Storm	58
Words	59
A Love Token	60
A Tryst with Death	60
Fidelis	61
A Shadow	62
The Sailor Boy	62
A Crown of Sorrow	71
The Lesson of the War	71
The Two Spirits	72
A Little Longer	74
Grief	75
The Triumph of Time	77
A Parting	78
The Golden Gate	79
Phantoms	80
Thankfulness	80

CONTENTS.

Home-Sickness	81
Wishes	82
The Peace of God	83
Life in Death and Death in Life	83
Recollections	86
Illusion	87
A Vision	88
Pictures in the Fire	89
The Settlers	90
Hush!	91
Hours	92
The Two Interpreters	93
Comfort	94
Home at Last	95
Unexpressed	96
Because	97
Rest at Evening	97
A Retrospect	98
True or False	99
Golden Words	101

LEGENDS AND LYRICS. A BOOK OF VERSES.
Second Series.

A Legend of Provence	105
Envy	114
Over the Mountain	114
Beyond	115
A Warning	116
Maximus	117
Optimus	118
A Lost Chord	119
Too Late	119
The Requital	120
Returned — "Missing"	121
In the Wood	122
Two Worlds	123
A New Mother	124
Give Place	131
My Will	132
King and Slave	133

A Chant 133
Dream-Life 135
Rest 135
The Tyrant and the Captive 137
The Carver's Lesson 138
Three Roses 139
My Picture Gallery 140
Sent to Heaven 142
Never Again 143
Listening Angels 144
Golden Days 145
Philip and Mildred 146
Borrowed Thoughts.
    I. From "Lavater" 153
    II. From "Phantastes" 153
    III. From "Lost Alice" 154
    IV. From * * * 154
Light and Shade 155
A Changeling 157
Discouraged 158
If thou couldst know 159
The Warrior to his Dead Bride 159
A Letter 160
A Comforter 162
Unseen 164
A Remembrance of Autumn 165
Three Evenings in a Life 165
The Wind 172
Expectation 173
An Ideal 174
Our Dead 175
A Woman's Answer 176
The Story of the Faithful Soul 178
A Contrast 179
The Bride's Dream 181
The Angel's Bidding 182
Spring 183
Evening Hymn 184
The Inner Chamber 185
Hearts 185
Two Loves 187
A Woman's Last Word 187

Past and Present 188
For the Future 189

A CHAPLET OF VERSES. .

Introduction 195
The Army of the Lord 199
The Star of the Sea 202
The Sacred Heart 202
The Names of Our Lady 204
A Chaplet of Flowers 205
Kyrie Eleison 207
The Annunciation 208
An Appeal 208
The Jubilee of 1850 210
Christmas Flowers 211
A Desire 212
Our Daily Bread 214
Threefold 214
Confido et Conquiesco 215
Ora pro Me 215
The Church in 1849 216
Fishers of Men 216
The Old Year's Blessing 217
Evening Chant 218
A Christmas Carol 219
Our Titles 220
Ministering Angels 221
The Shrines of Mary 222
The Homeless Poor 226
Milly's Expiation 231
A Castle in the Air 239
Per Pacem ad Lucem 240
A Legend 240
Birthday Gifts 241
A Beggar 244
Links with Heaven 245
Homeless 246
Index of First Lines 249
Index of Titles 255

AN INTRODUCTION.

BY CHARLES DICKENS.

In the spring of the year 1853, I observed, as conductor of the weekly journal, HOUSEHOLD WORDS, a short poem among the proffered contributions, very different, as I thought, from the shoal of verses perpetually setting through the office of such a periodical, and possessing much more merit. Its authoress was quite unknown to me. She was one MISS MARY BERWICK, whom I had never heard of; and she was to be addressed by letter, if addressed at all, at a circulating library in the western district of London. Through this channel, Miss Berwick was informed that her poem was accepted, and was invited to send another. She complied, and became a regular and frequent contributor. Many letters passed between the journal and Miss Berwick, but Miss Berwick herself was never seen.

How we came gradually to establish, at the office of Household Words, that we knew all about Miss Berwick, I have never discovered. But, we settled somehow, to our complete satisfaction, that she was governess in a family; that she went to Italy in that capacity, and returned; and that she had long been in the same family. We really knew nothing whatever of her, except that she was remarkably business-like, punctual, self-reliant, and reliable: so I suppose we insensibly invented the rest. For myself, my mother was not a more real personage to me, than Miss Berwick the governess became.

This went on until December 1854, when the Christmas number, entitled The Seven Poor Travellers, was sent to press. Happening to be going to dine that day with an old and dear friend, distinguished in literature as BARRY CORNWALL, I took with me an early proof of that number, and remarked, as I

laid it on the drawing-room table, that it contained a very
pretty poem, written by a certain Miss Berwick. Next day
brought me the disclosure that I
had so spoken of the poem to
the mother of its writer, in its
writer's presence; that I had no
such correspondent in existence
as Miss Berwick; and that the
name had been assumed by Barry Cornwall's eldest daughter,
Miss ADELAIDE ANNE PROC-
TER.

The anecdote I have here noted down, besides serving to ex-
plain why the parents of the late
Miss Procter have looked to me
for these poor words of remembrance of their lamented child,
strikingly illustrates the hon-
esty, independence, and quiet
dignity of the lady's character.
I had known her when she was
very young; I had been honored with her father's friendship
when I was myself a young as-
pirant; and she had said at
home, "If I send him, in my
own name, verses that he does
not honestly like, either it will be
very painful to him to return
them, or he will print them for
papa's sake, and not for their
own. So I have made up my
mind to take my chance fairly
with the unknown volunteers"

Perhaps it requires an edi-
tor's experience of the profound-
ly unreasonable grounds on
which he is often urged to ac-
cept unsuitable articles — such
as having been to school with
the writer's husband's broth-
er-in-law, or having lent an al-
penstock in Switzerland to the
writer's wife's nephew, when
that interesting stranger had
broken his own — fully to appre-
ciate the delicacy and the self-
respect of this resolution.

Some verses by Miss Procter
had been published in the BOOK
OF BEAUTY, ten years before
she became Miss Berwick. With
the exception of two poems in
the CORNHILL MAGAZINE, two
in GOOD WORDS, and others in
a little book called A CHAPLET
OF VERSES (issued in 1862 for
the benefit of a Night Refuge),
her published writings first appeared in HOUSEHOLD WORDS,
or ALL THE YEAR ROUND.
The present edition contains
the whole of her Legends and
Lyrics, and originates in the
great favor with which they
have been received by the public.

Miss Procter was born in Bed-
ford Square, London, on the
30th of October, 1825. Her
love of poetry was conspicuous
at so early an age, that I have
before me a tiny album made
of small note-paper, into which
her favorite passages were copied for her by her mother's hand
before she herself could write

It looks as if she had carried it about as another little girl might have carried a doll. She soon displayed a remarkable memory, and great quickness of apprehension. When she was quite a young child, she learnt with facility several of the problems of Euclid. As she grew older, she acquired the French, Italian, and German languages, became a clever piano-forte player, and showed a true taste and sentiment in drawing. But, as soon as she had completely vanquished the difficulties of any one branch of study, it was her way to lose interest in it, and pass to another. While her mental resources were being trained, it was not at all suspected in her family that she had any gift of authorship, or any ambition to become a writer. Her father had no idea of her having ever attempted to turn a rhyme, until her first little poem saw the light in print.

When she attained to womanhood, she had read an extraordinary number of books, and throughout her life she was always largely adding to the number. In 1853 she went to Turin and its neighborhood, on a visit to her aunt, a Roman Catholic lady. As Miss Procter had herself professed the Roman Catholic faith two years before, she entered with the greater ardor

on the study of the Piedmontese dialect, and the observation of the habits and manners of the peasantry. In the former, she soon became a proficient. On the latter head, I extract from her familiar letters, written home to England at the time, two pleasant pieces of description.

A BETROTHAL.

" We have been to a ball, of which I must give you a description. Last Tuesday we had just done dinner at about seven, and stepped out into the balcony to look at the remains of the sunset behind the mountains, when we heard very distinctly a band of music, which rather excited my astonishment, as a solitary organ is the utmost that toils up here. I went out of the room for a few minutes, and, on my returning, Emily said, ' Oh ! that band is playing at the farmer's near here. The daughter is *fiancée* to-day, and they have a ball.' I said, ' I wish I was going ! ' ' Well,' replied she, ' the farmer's wife did call to invite us.' ' Then I shall certainly go,' I exclaimed. I applied to Madame B., who said she would like it very much, and we had better go, children and all. Some of the servants were already gone. We rushed away to put on some shawls, and put off any shred of black we might have about us (as the people would have been quite annoyed if we had appeared on such an occasion with any black), and we started. When we reached the farmer's, which is a stone's throw above our house, we were received with great enthusiasm; the only drawback being that no one spoke French, and we did not yet speak Piedmontese. We were placed on a bench against the wall, and the people went on dancing. The room was a large white-washed kitchen (I suppose), with several large pictures in black frames, and very smoky. I distinguished the Martyrdom of Saint Sebastian, and the others appeared equally lively and appropriate subjects. Whether they were Old Masters or not, and if so, by whom, I could not ascertain. The band were seated opposite us. Five men, with wind-instruments, part of the band of the National Guard, to which the farmer's sons belong. They played really admirably, and I began to be afraid that some idea of our dignity would prevent my getting a partner; so, by Madame B.'s advice, I went up to the bride, and offered to dance with her. Such a handsome young woman! Like one of Uwins's pictures. Very dark, with a quantity of black hair,

and on an immense scale. The children were already dancing, as well as the maids. After we came to an end of our dance, which was what they call a Polka-Mazourka, I saw the bride trying to screw up the courage of her *fiancé* to ask me to dance, which after a little hesitation he did. And admirably he danced, as indeed they all did, — in excellent time, and with a little more spirit than one sees in a ball-room. In fact, they were very like one's ordinary partners, except that they wore ear-rings and were in their shirt-sleeves, and truth compels me to state that they decidedly smelt of garlic. Some of them had been smoking, but threw away their cigars when we came in. The only thing that did not look cheerful was, that the room was only lighted by two or three oil-lamps, and that there seemed to be no preparation for refreshments. Madame B., seeing this, whispered to her maid, who disengaged herself from her partner, and ran off to the house; she and the kitchen-maid presently returning with a large tray covered with all kinds of cakes (of which we are great consumers and always have a stock), and a large hamper full of bottles of wine, with coffee and sugar. This seemed all very acceptable. The *fiancée* was requested to distribute the eatables, and a bucket of water being produced to wash the glasses in, the wine disappeared very quickly, — as fast as they could open the bottles. But, elated I suppose by this, the floor was sprinkled with water, and the musicians played a Monferrino, which is a Piedmontese dance. Madame B. danced with the farmer's son, and Emily with another distinguished member of the company. It was very fatiguing, — something like a Scotch reel. My partner was a little man, like Perrot, and very proud of his dancing. He cut in the air and twisted about, until I was out of breath, though my attempts to imitate him were feeble in the extreme. At last, after seven or eight dances, I was obliged to sit down. We stayed till nine, and I was so dead beat with the heat that I could hardly crawl about the house, and in an agony with the cramp, it is so long since I have danced."

A Marriage.

" The wedding of the farmer's daughter has taken place. We had hoped it would have been in the little chapel of our house, but it seems some special permission was necessary, and they applied for it too late. They all said, ' This is the Constitution.

There would have been no difficulty before ! ' the lower classes making the poor Constitution the scape-goat for everything they don't like. So, as it was impossible for us to climb up to the church where the wedding was to be, we contented ourselves with seeing the procession pass. It was not a very large one, for, it requiring some activity to go up, all the old people remained at home. It is not the etiquette for the bride's mother to go, and no unmarried woman can go to a wedding, — I suppose for fear of its making her discontented with her own position. The procession stopped at our door, for the bride to receive our congratulations. She was dressed in a shot silk, with a yellow handkerchief, and rows of a large gold chain. In the afternoon they sent to request us to go there. On our arrival we found them dancing out of doors, and a most melancholy affair it was. All the bride's sisters were not to be recognized, they had cried so. The mother sat in the house, and could not appear. And the bride was sobbing so she could hardly stand ! The most melancholy spectacle of all to my mind was, that the bridegroom was decidedly tipsy. He seemed rather affronted at all the distress. We danced a Monferrino ; I with the bridegroom, and the bride crying the whole time. The company did their utmost to enliven her by firing pistols, but without success, and at last they began a series of yells which reminded me of a set of savages. But even this delicate method of consolation failed, and the wishing good-by began. It was altogether so melancholy an affair that Madame B. dropped a few tears, and I was very near it, particularly when the poor mother came out to see the last of her daughter, who was finally dragged off between her brother and uncle, with a last explosion of pistols. As she lives quite near, makes an excellent match, and is one of nine children, it really was a most desirable marriage, in spite of all the show of distress. Albert was so discomfited by it, that he forgot to kiss the bride as he had intended to do, and therefore went to call upon her yesterday, and found her very smiling in her new house, and supplied the omission. The cook came home from the wedding, declaring she was cured of any wish to marry; but I would not recommend any man to act upon that threat and make her an offer. In a couple of days we had some rolls of the bride's first baking, which they call Madonna's. The musicians, it seems, were in the same state

as the bridegroom, for, in escorting her home, they all fell down in the mud. My wrath against the bridegroom is somewhat calmed by finding that it is considered bad luck if he does not get tipsy at his wedding."

Those readers of Miss Procter's poems who should suppose from their tone that her mind was of a gloomy or despondent cast would be curiously mistaken. She was exceedingly humorous, and had a great delight in humor. Cheerfulness was habitual with her, she was very ready at a sally or a reply, and in her laugh (as I remember well) there was an unusual vivacity, enjoyment, and sense of drollery. She was perfectly unconstrained and unaffected: as modestly silent about her productions as she was generous with their pecuniary results. She was a friend who inspired the strongest attachments; she was a finely sympathetic woman, with a great accordant heart and a sterling noble nature. No claim can be set up for her, thank God, to the possession of any of the conventional poetical qualities. She never by any means held the opinion that she was among the greatest of human beings; she never suspected the existence of a conspiracy on the part of mankind against her; she never recognized in her best friends her worst enemies; she never cultivated the luxury of being misunderstood and unappreciated; she would far rather have died without seeing a line of her composition in print, than that I should have maundered about her, here, as "the Poet," or "the Poetess."

With the recollection of Miss Procter as a mere child and as a woman fresh upon me, it is natural that I should linger on my way to the close of this brief record, avoiding its end. But, even as the close came upon her, so must it come here.

Always impelled by an intense conviction that her life must not be dreamed away, and that her indulgence in her favorite pursuits must be balanced by action in the real world around her, she was indefatigable in her endeavors to do some good. Naturally enthusiastic, and conscientiously impressed with a deep sense of her Christian duty to her neighbor, she devoted herself to a variety of benevolent objects. Now, it was the visitation of the sick that had possession of her; now, it was the sheltering of the houseless; now, it was the elementary teaching of the densely ignorant; now, it was the raising up of those who had wandered and got trodden under foot; now, it was the wider employ-

ment of her own sex in the general business of life; now, it was all these things at once. Perfectly unselfish, swift to sympathize and eager to relieve, she wrought at such designs with a flushed earnestness that disregarded season, weather, time of day or night, food, rest. Under such a hurry of the spirits, and such incessant occupation, the strongest constitution will commonly go down. Hers, neither of the strongest nor the weakest, yielded to the burden, and began to sink.

To have saved her life, then, by taking action on the warning that shone in her eyes and sounded in her voice, would have been impossible without changing her nature. As long as the power of moving about in the old way was left to her, she must exercise it, or be killed by the restraint. And so the time came when she could move about no longer, and took to her bed.

All the restlessness gone then, and all the sweet patience of her natural disposition purified by the resignation of her soul, she lay upon her bed through the whole round of changes of the seasons. She lay upon her bed through fifteen months. In all that time, her old cheerfulness never quitted her. In all that time, not an impatient or a querulous minute can be remembered.

At length, at midnight on the 2d of February, 1864, she turned down a leaf of a little book she was reading, and shut it up.

The ministering hand that had copied the verses into the tiny album was soon around her neck, and she quietly asked, as the clock was on the stroke of one: "Do you think I am dying, mamma?"

"I think you are very, very ill to-night, my dear."

"Send for my sister. My feet are so cold. Lift me up!"

Her sister entering as they raised her, she said: "It has come at last!" And with a bright and happy smile looked upward, and departed.

Well had she written: —

Why shouldst thou fear the beautiful
    angel, Death,
Who waits thee at the portals of the
    skies,
Ready to kiss away thy struggling
    breath,
Ready with gentle hand to close thine
    eyes?

Oh, what were life, if life were all?
    Thine eyes
Are blinded by their tears, or thou
    wouldst see
Thy treasures wait thee in the far-off
    skies,
And Death, thy friend, will give them
    all to thee.

LEGENDS AND LYRICS.

A BOOK OF VERSES.

FIRST SERIES.

𝔇𝔢𝔡𝔦𝔠𝔞𝔱𝔢𝔡

TO

MATILDA M. HAYS.

"Our tokens of love are for the most part barbarous. Cold and lifeless, because they do not represent our life. The only gift is a portion of thyself. Therefore let the farmer give his corn; the miner, a gem; the sailor, coral and shells; the painter, his picture; and the poet, his poem." — EMERSON'S *Essays*.

A. A. P.

May, 1858.

LEGENDS AND LYRICS.

THE ANGEL'S STORY.

THROUGH the blue and frosty
heavens
   Christmas stars were shining
bright;
Glistening lamps throughout the
City
   Almost matched their gleam-
ing light;
While the winter snow was ly-
ing,
And the winter winds were
sighing,
   Long ago, one Christmas
night.

While, from every tower and
steeple,
   Pealing bells were sounding
clear,
(Never with such tones of gladness,
   Save when Christmas time is
near,)
Many a one that night was
merry
   Who had toiled through all
the year.

That night saw old wrongs forgiven,
   Friends, long parted, recon-
ciled;
Voices all unused to laughter,
   Mournful eyes that rarely
smiled,
Trembling hearts that feared the
morrow,
   From their anxious thoughts
beguiled.

Rich and poor felt love and
blessing
   From the gracious season fall;
Joy and plenty in the cottage,
   Peace and feasting in the hall;
And the voices of the children
   Ringing clear above it all!

Yet one house was dim and dark-
ened;
   Gloom, and sickness, and de-
spair,
Dwelling in the gilded chambers,
   Creeping up the marble stair,
Even stilled the voice of mourn-
ing, —
   For a child lay dying there.

Silken curtains fell around him,
  Velvet carpets hushed the
    tread,
Many costly toys were lying,
  All unheeded, by his bed ;
And his tangled golden ringlets
  Were on downy pillows spread.

The skill of that mighty City
  To save one little life was
    vain, —
One little thread from being
    broken,
One fatal word from being spo-
    ken ;
  Nay, his very mother's pain,
And the mighty love within her,
  Could not give him health
    again.

So she knelt there still beside
    him,
  She alone with strength to
    smile,
Promising that he should suffer
  No more in a little while,
Murmuring tender song and
    story
  Weary hours to beguile.

Suddenly an unseen Presence
  Checked those constant moan-
    ing cries,
Stilled the little heart's quick
    fluttering,
  Raised those blue and won-
    dering eyes,
Fixed on some mysterious vision,
  With a startled sweet sur-
    prise.

For a radiant angel hovered,
  Smiling, o'er the little bed ;
White his raiment, from his
    shoulders
  Snowy dove - like pinions
    spread,
And a starlike light was shining
  In a Glory round his head.

While, with tender love, the an-
    gel,
  Leaning o'er the little nest,
In his arms the sick child fold-
    ing,
  Laid him gently on his breast,
Sobs and wailings told the moth-
    er
  That her darling was at rest.

So the angel, slowly rising,
  Spread his wings, and through
    the air
Bore the child, and, while he
    held him
  To his heart with loving care,
Placed a branch of crimson
    roses
  Tenderly beside him there.

While the child, thus clinging,
    floated
  Towards the mansions of the
    Blest,
Gazing from his shining guar-
    dian
  To the flowers upon his breast,
Thus the angel spake, still smil-
    ing
  On the little heavenly guest :

"Know, dear little one, that
    Heaven
Does no earthly thing disdain,
Man's poor joys find there an
    echo
Just as surely as his pain ;
Love, on earth so feebly striv.
    ing,
Lives divine in Heaven again !

"Once in that great town below
    us,
In a poor and narrow street,
Dwelt a little sickly orphan ;
Gentle aid, or pity sweet,
Never in life's rugged pathway
    Guided his poor tottering feet.

" All the striving anxious fore-
    thought
That should only come with
    age
Weighed upon his baby spirit,
Showed him soon life's stern-
    est page ;
Grim Want was his nurse, and
    Sorrow
Was his only heritage.

"All too weak for childish pas-
    times,
Drearily the hours sped ;
On his hands so small and trem-
    bling
Leaning his poor aching head,
Or, through dark and painful
    hours,
Lying sleepless on his bed.

"Dreaming strange and longing
    fancies
Of cool forests far away ;
And of rosy, happy children,
    Laughing merrily at play,
Coming home through green
    lanes, bearing
Trailing boughs of blooming
    May.

"Scarce a glimpse of azure heav-
    en
Gleamed above that narrow
    street,
And the sultry air of summer
    (That you call so warm and
    sweet)
Fevered the poor orphan, dwell-
    ing
In the crowded alley's heat.

"One bright day, with feeble
    footsteps
Slowly forth he tried to crawl,
Through the crowded city's path-
    ways,
Till he reached a garden-wall,
Where 'mid princely halls and
    mansions
Stood the lordliest of all.

" There were trees with giant
    branches,
Velvet glades where shadows
    hide ;
There were sparkling fountains
    glancing,
Flowers, which in luxuriant
    pride

Even wafted breaths of perfume
  To the child who stood out-
    side.

" He against the gate of iron
  Pressed his wan and wistful
    face,
Gazing with an awe-struck pleas-
    ure
  At the glories of the place ;
Never had his brightest day-
    dream
  Shone with half such won-
    drous grace.

" You were playing in that gar-
    den,
  Throwing blossoms in the air,
Laughing when the petals floated
  Downwards on your golden
    hair ;
And the fond eyes watching o'er
    you,
And the splendor spread before
    you,
  Told a House's Hope was
    there.

"When your servants, tired of
    seeing
  Such a face of want and woe,
Turning to the ragged orphan,
  Gave him coin, and bade him
    go,
Down his cheeks so thin and
    wasted
  Bitter tears began to flow.

" But that look of childish sor-
    row
  On your tender child-heart
    fell,
And you plucked the reddest
    roses
  From the tree you loved so
    well
Passed them through the stern
    cold grating,
  Gently bidding him ' Fare-
    well ! '

" Dazzled by the fragrant treas-
    ure
  And the gentle voice he heard,
In the poor forlorn boy's spirit,
  Joy, the sleeping Seraph,
    stirred ;
In his hand he took the flowers,
  In his heart the loving word.

" So he crept to his poor garret ;
  Poor no more, but rich and
    bright,
For the holy dreams of child-
    hood —
  Love, and Rest, and Hope,
    and Light —
Floated round the orphan's pil-
    low
  Through the starry summer
    night.

" Day dawned, yet the visions
    lasted ;
  All too weak to rise he lay ;
Did he dream that none spake
    harshly, —

All were strangely kind that
day ?
Surely then his treasured roses
Must have charmed all ills
away.

" And he smiled, though they
were fading ;
One by one their leaves were
shed ;
' Such bright things could never
perish,
They would bloom again,' he
said.
When the next day's sun had
risen
Child and flowers both were
dead.

" Know, dear little one! our
Father
Will no gentle deed disdain :
Love on the cold earth begin-
ning
Lives divine in Heaven again,
While the angel hearts that beat
there
Still all tender thoughts re-
tain "

So the angel ceased, and gently
O'er his little burden leant ;
While the child gazed from the
shining,
Loving eyes that o'er him
bent,
To the blooming roses by him,
Wondering what that mystery
meant.

Thus the radiant angel answered,
And with tender meaning
smiled :
" Ere your childlike, loving
spirit,
Sin and the hard world defiled,
God has given me leave to seek
you, —
I was once that little child ! "

* * * *

In the churchyard of that city
Rose a tomb of marble rare,
Decked, as soon as Spring awak-
ened,
With her buds and blossoms
fair, —
And a humble grave beside it, —
No one knew who rested there.

ECHOES.

STILL the angel stars are shining,
Still the rippling waters flow,
But the angel-voice is silent
That I heard so long ago.
Hark ! the echoes murmur
low,
Long ago !

Still the wood is dim and lonely,
Still the plashing fountains
play,
But the past and all its beauty,
Whither has it fled away ?
Hark ! the mournful echoes
say,
Fled away !

Still the bird of night complain-
eth,
(Now, indeed, her song is
pain,)
Visions of my happy hours,
Do I call and call in vain?
Hark! the echoes cry again,
All in vain!

Cease, O echoes, mournful echoes!
Once I loved your voices well;
Now my heart is sick and weary —
Days of old, a long farewell!
Hark! the echoes sad and
dreary
Cry farewell, farewell!

———

A FALSE GENIUS.

I SEE a Spirit by thy side,
Purple-winged and eagle-eyed,
Looking like a heavenly guide.

Though he seem so bright and
fair,
Ere thou trust his proffered care,
Pause a little, and beware!

If he bid thee dwell apart,
Tending some ideal smart
In a sick and coward heart;

In self-worship wrapped alone,
Dreaming thy poor griefs are
grown
More than other men have known;

Dwelling in some cloudy sphere,
Though God's work is waiting
here,
And God deigneth to be near;

If his torch's crimson glare
Show the evil everywhere,
Tainting all the wholesome air;

While with strange distorted
choice,
Still disdaining to rejoice,
Thou *wilt* hear a wailing voice;

If a simple, humble heart
Seem to thee a meaner part
Than thy noblest aim and art;

If he bid thee bow before
Crownéd Mind and nothing more,
The great idol men adore;

And with starry veil enfold
Sin, the trailing serpent old,
Till his scales shine out like gold;

Though his words seem true and
wise,
Soul, I say to thee, Arise,
He is a Demon in disguise!

———

MY PICTURE.

STAND this way — more near the
window —
By my desk — you see the
light
Falling on my picture better —
Thus I see it while I write!

Who the head may be I know
   not,
But it has a student air;
With a look half sad, half stately,
   Grave sweet eyes and flowing
   hair.

Little care I who the painter,
   How obscure a name he bore;
Nor, when some have named
   Velasquez,
   Did I value it the more.

As it is, I would not give it
   For the rarest piece of art;
It has dwelt with me, and lis-
   tened
   To the secrets of my heart.

Many a time, when to my garret,
   Weary, I returned at night,
It has seemed to look a wel-
   come
   That has made my poor room
   bright.

Many a time, when ill and sleep-
   less,
   I have watched the quivering
   gleam
Of my lamp upon that picture,
   Till it faded in my dream.

When dark days have come, and
   friendship
   Worthless seemed, and life in
   vain,
That bright friendly smile has
   sent me
   Boldly to my task again.

Sometimes when hard need has
   pressed me
To bow down where I despise,
I have read stern words of coun-
   sel
   In those sad, reproachful eyes.

Nothing that my brain imagined,
   Or my weary hand has
   wrought,
But it watched the dim Idea
   Spring forth into arméd
   Thought.

It has smiled on my successes,
   Raised me when my hopes
   were low,
And by turns has looked upon
   me
   With all the loving eyes I
   know.

Do you wonder that my picture
   Has become so like a friend?—
It has seen my life's beginnings,
   It shall stay and cheer the
   end!

JUDGE NOT.

JUDGE not; the workings of his
   brain
   And of his heart thou canst
   not see;
What looks to thy dim eyes a
   stain,
   In God's pure light may only
   be

A scar, brought from some well-
    won field,
Where thou wouldst only faint
    and yield.

The look, the air, that frets thy
    sight,
  May be a token, that below
The soul has closed in deadly
    fight
  With some infernal fiery foe,
Whose glance would scorch thy
    smiling grace,
And cast thee shuddering on thy
    face !

The fall thou darest to despise —
  Maybe the angel's slackened
    hand
Has suffered it, that he may rise
  And take a firmer, surer stand ;
Or, trusting less to earthly things,
May henceforth learn to use his
    wings.

And judge none lost ; but wait
    and see,
  With hopeful pity, not disdain ;
The depth of the abyss may be
  The measure of the height of
    pain
And love and glory that may
    raise
This soul to God in after days !

FRIEND SORROW.

Do not cheat thy Heart and tell
    her,
  " Grief will pass away,

Hope for fairer times in future,
  And forget to-day." —
Tell her, if you will, that sorrow
  Need not come in vain ;
Tell her that the lesson taught
    her
  Far outweighs the pain.

Cheat her not with the old com-
    fort,
  " Soon she will forget," —
Bitter truth, alas ! but matter
  Rather for regret ;
Bid her not " Seek other pleas-
    ures,
  Turn to other things " ; —
Rather nurse her cagéd sorrow
  Till the captive sings.

Rather bid her go forth bravely,
  And the stranger greet ;
Not as foe, with spear and buckler,
  But as dear friends meet :
Bid her with a strong clasp hold
    her,
  By her dusky wings,
Listening for the murmured
    blessing
  Sorrow always brings.

ONE BY ONE.

One by one the sands are flow-
    ing,
  One by one the moments fall ;
Some are coming, some are go-
    ing ;
  Do not strive to grasp them
    all.

One by one thy duties wait
thee,
  Let thy whole strength go to
each,
Let no future dreams elate thee,
  Learn thou first what these
can teach.

One by one (bright gifts from
Heaven)
  Joys are sent thee here be-
low ;
Take them readily when given,
  Ready too to let them go.

One by one thy griefs shall meet
thee, ·
  Do not fear an arméd band ;
One will fade as others greet
thee ;
  Shadows passing through the
land.

Do not look at life's long sorrow ;
  See how small each moment's
pain,
God will help thee for to-morrow,
  So each day begin again.

Every hour that fleets so slowly
  Has its task to do or bear ;
Luminous the crown, and holy,
  When each gem is set with
care.

Do not linger with regretting,
  Or for passing hours despond ;

Nor, the daily toil forgetting,
  Look too eagerly beyond.

Hours are golden links, God's
token,
  Reaching heaven ; but one by
one
Take them, lest the chain be
broken
  Ere the pilgrimage be done.

TRUE HONORS.

Is my darling tired already,
  Tired of her day of play ?
Draw your little stool beside me,
  Smooth this tangled hair away.
Can she put the logs together,
  Till they make a cheerful
blaze ?
Shall her blind old Uncle tell
her
  Something of his youthful
days ?

Hark ! The wind among the
cedars
  Waves their white arms to and
fro ;
I remember how I watched them
  Sixty Christmas Days ago :
Then I dreamt a glorious vision
  Of great deeds to crown each
year ;
Sixty Christmas Days have found
me
  Useless, helpless, blind — and
here !

Yes, I feel my darling stealing
  Warm soft fingers into mine :
Shall I tell her what I fancied
  In that strange old dream of
    mine ?
I was kneeling by the window,
  Reading how a noble band,
With the red cross on their
  breastplates,
  Went to gain the Holy Land.

While with eager eyes of wonder
  Over the dark page I bent,
Slowly twilight shadows gath-
  ered
  Till the letters came and went ;
Slowly, till the night was round
  me ;
  Then my heart beat loud and
    fast,
For I felt before I saw it
  That a spirit near me passed.

Then I raised my eyes, and,
  shining
  Where the moon's first ray
    was bright,
Stood a wingéd Angel-warrior
  Clothed and panoplied in
    light :
So, with Heaven's love upon him,
  Stern in calm and resolute will,
Looked St. Michael, — does the
  picture
  Hang in the old cloister still ?

Threefold were the dreams of
  honor
  That absorbed my heart and
    brain ;

Threefold crowns the Angel
  promised,
  Each one to be bought by pain :
While he spoke, a threefold bless-
  ing
  Fell upon my soul like rain.
HELPER OF THE POOR AND SUF-
  FERING ;
  VICTOR IN A GLORIOUS
    STRIFE ;
SINGER OF A NOBLE POEM :
  Such the honors of my life.

Ah, that dream ! Long years
  that gave me
  Joy and grief as real things
Never touched the tender memory
  Sweet and solemn that it
    brings, —
Never quite effaced the feeling
  Of those white and shadowing
    wings.

Do those blue eyes open wider ?
  Does my faith too foolish
    seem ?
Yes, my darling, years have
  taught me
  It was nothing but a dream.
Soon, too soon, the bitter knowl-
  edge
  Of a fearful trial rose,
Rose to crush my heart, and
  sternly
  Bade my young ambition close.

More and more my eyes were
  clouded,
  Till at last God's glorious
    light

Passed away from me forever,
　And I lived and live in night.
Dear, I will not dim your pleasure,
　Christmas should be only
　　gay : —
In my night the stars have risen,
　And I wait the dawn of day.

Spite of all I could be happy ;
　For my brothers' tender care
In their boyish pastimes ever
　Made me take, or feel a share.
Philip, even then so thoughtful,
　Max so noble, brave, and tall,
And your father, little Godfrey,
　The most loving of them all.

Philip reasoned down my sorrow,
　Max would laugh my gloom
　　away,
Godfrey's little arms put round
　me
　Helped me through my drea-
　　riest day ;
While the promise of my Angel,
　Like a star, now bright, now
　　pale,
Hung in blackest night above me,
　And I felt it could not fail.

Years passed on, my brothers
　left me,
　Each went out to take his
　　share
In the struggle of life ; my por-
　tion
　Was a humble one — to bear.
Here I dwelt, and learnt to wan-
　der
　Through the woods and fields
　　alone,

Every cottage in the village
　Had a corner called my own

Old and young, all brought their
　troubles,
　Great or small, for me to
　　hear ;
I have often blessed my sorrow
　That drew others' grief so
　　near.
Ah, the people needed helping —
　Needed love — (for Love and
　　Heaven
Are the only gifts not bartered,
　They alone are freely given) —-

And I gave it. Philip's bounty
　(We were orphans, dear) made
　　toil
Prosper, and want never fastened
　On the tenants of the soil.
Philip's name (O, how I gloried,
　He so young, to see it rise !)
Soon grew noted among states-
　men
　As a patriot true and wise.

And his people all felt honored
　To be ruled by such a name ;
I was proud too that they loved
　me ;
　Through their pride in him it
　　came.
He had gained what I had longed
　for,
　I meanwhile grew glad and
　　gay,
'Mid his people, to be serving
　Him and them, in some poor
　　way.

How his noble earnest speeches
  With untiring fervor came!
HELPER OF THE POOR AND
  SUFFERING ;
  Truly he deserved the name!
Had my Angel's promise failed
  me ?
  Had that word of hope grown
    dim ?
Why, my Philip had fulfilled
  it,
  And I loved it best in him !

Max meanwhile — ah, you, my
  darling,
  Can his loving words recall —
'Mid the bravest and the no-
  blest,
  Braver, nobler, than them
    all.
How I loved him ! how my heart
  thrilled
  When his sword clanked by
    his side,
When I touched his gold em-
  broidery,
  Almost *saw* him in his pride !

So we parted ; he all eager
  To uphold the name he bore,
Leaving in my charge — he
  loved me —
  Some one whom he loved still
    more :
I must tend this gentle flower,
  I must speak to her of him,
For he feared — Love still is
  fearful —
  That his memory might grow
    dim.

I must guard her from all sorrow,
  I must play a brother's part,

Shield all grief and trial from
  her,
  If it need be, with my heart.
Years passed, and his name
  grew famous ;
  We were proud, both she
    and I ;
And we lived upon his let-
  ters,
  While the slow days fleeted by.

Then at last — you know the
  story,
  How a fearful rumor spread,
Till all hope had slowly faded,
  And we heard that he was
    dead.
Dead ! O, those were bitter
  hours ;
  Yet within my soul there
    dwelt
A warning, and while others
  mourned him,
  Something like a hope I felt.

His was no weak life as mine
  was,
  But a life, so full and strong —
No, I could not think he per-
  ished
  Nameless, 'mid a conquered
    throng.
How she drooped ! Years pass-
  ed ; no tidings
  Came, and yet that little flame
Of strange hope within my
  spirit
  Still burnt on, and lived the
    same.

Ah ! my child, our hearts will
  fail us,
  When to us they strongest
    seem :

I can look back on those hours
As a fearful, evil dream.
She had long despaired; what
wonder
That her heart had turned to
mine ?
Earthly loves are deep and ten-
der,
Not eternal and divine !

Can I say how bright a future
Rose before my soul that day ?
O, so strange, so sweet, so tender !
And I had to turn away.
Hard and terrible the struggle,
For the pain not mine alone ;
I called back my Brother's spirit,
And I bade him claim his own.

Told her — now I dared to do
it —
That I felt the day would rise
When he would return to glad-
den
My weak heart and her bright
eyes.
And I pleaded — pleaded stern-
ly —
In his name, and for his sake :
Now, I can speak calmly of it,
Then, I thought my heart
would break.

Soon — ah, Love had not de-
ceived me,
(Love's true instincts never
err,)
Wounded, weak, escaped from
prison,
He returned to me, — to her.

I could thank God that bright
morning,
When I felt my Brother's
gaze,
That my heart was true and
loyal,
As in our old boyish days.

Bought by wounds and deeds of
daring,
Honors he had brought away ;
Glory crowned his name — my
Brother's ;
Mine too ! — we were one that
day.
Since the crown on him had
fallen,
"VICTOR IN A NOBLE STRIFE,"
I could live and die contented
With my poor ignoble life.

Well, my darling, almost weary
Of my story ? Wait awhile ;
For the rest is only joyful ;
I can tell it with a smile.
One bright promise still was left
me,
Wound so close about my soul,
That, as one by one had failed me,
This dream now absorbed the
whole.

"SINGER OF A NOBLE POEM,"—
Ah, my darling, few and rare
Burn the glorious names of
Poets,
Like stars in the purple air.
That too, and I glory in it,
That great gift my Godfrey
won ;

I have my dear share of honor,
  Gained by that belovéd one.

One day shall my darling read
    it;
  Now she cannot understand
All the noble thoughts that
    lighten
  Through the genius of the
    land.
I am proud to be his brother,
  Proud to think that hope was
    true;
Though I longed and strove so
    vainly,
  What I failed in, he could do.

I was long before I knew it,
  Longer ere I felt it so;
Then I strung my rhymes to-
    gether
  Only for the poor and low.
And, it pleases me to know it,
  (For I love them well indeed,)
They care for my humble verses,
  Fitted for their humble need.

And, it cheers my heart to hear
    it,
  Where the far-off settlers roam,
My poor words are sung and
    cherished,
  Just because they speak of
    Home.
And the little children sing them,
  (That, I think, has pleased me
    best,)
Often, too, the dying love them,
  For they tell of Heaven and
    rest.

So my last vain dream has faded;
  (Such as I to think of fame!)
Yet I will not say it failed me,
  For it crowned my Godfrey's
    name.
No; my Angel did not cheat me,
  For my long life *has* been
    blest;
He did give me Love and Sor-
    row,
  He will bring me Light and
    Rest.

A WOMAN'S QUESTION.

BEFORE I trust my Fate to thee,
  Or place my hand in thine,
Before I let thy Future give
  Color and form to mine,
Before I peril all for thee, question
  thy soul to-night for me.

I break all slighter bonds, nor
    feel
  A shadow of regret:
Is there one link within the Past
  That holds thy spirit yet?
Or is thy Faith as clear and free
  as that which I can pledge to
  thee?

Does there within thy dimmest
    dreams
  A possible future shine,
Wherein thy life could hence-
    forth breathe,
  Untouched, unshared by mine?
If so, at any pain or cost, O, tell
  me before all is lost.

Look deeper still. If thou canst
   feel
  Within my inmost soul,
That thou hast kept a portion
   back,
  While I have staked the
   whole;
Let no false pity spare the blow,
  but in true mercy tell me so.

Is there within thy heart a need
  That mine cannot fulfil?
One chord that any other hand
  Could better wake or still?
Speak now — lest at some fu-
   ture day my whole life
   wither and decay.

Lives there within thy nature
   hid
  The demon-spirit Change,
Shedding a passing glory still
  On all things new and
   strange? —
It may not be thy fault alone —
   but shield my heart against
   thy own.

Couldst thou withdraw thy hand
   one day
  And answer to my claim,
That Fate, and that to-day's mis-
   take —
  Not thou — had been to
   blame?
Some soothe their conscience
   thus; but thou wilt surely warn and save me now.

Nay, answer *not*, — I dare not
   hear,
  The words would come too
   late;
Yet I would spare thee all remorse,
  So, comfort thee, my Fate —
Whatever on my heart may fall
  — remember, I *would* risk
  it all!

THE THREE RULERS.

I saw a Ruler take his stand,
And trample on a mighty land;
The People crouched before his
   beck,
His iron heel was on their neck,
His name shone bright through
   blood and pain,
His sword flashed back their
   praise again.

I saw another Ruler rise:
His words were noble, good, and
   wise;
With the calm sceptre of his pen
He ruled the minds and thoughts
   of men:
Some scoffed, some praised, —
   while many heard,
Only a few obeyed his word.

Another Ruler then I saw:
Love and sweet Pity were his
   law;
The greatest and the least had
   part.

(Yet most the unhappy) in his
  heart:
The People, in a mighty band,
Rose up, and drove him from
  the land !

A DEAD PAST.

SPARE her at least: look, you
  have taken from me
The Present, and I murmur not,
  nor moan ;
The Future too, with all her
  glorious promise ;
But do not leave me utterly
  alone.

Spare me the Past: for, see, she
  cannot harm you,
She lies so white and cold,
  wrapped in her shroud ;
All, all my own ! and, trust me,
  I will hide her
Within my soul, nor speak to
  her aloud.

I folded her soft hands upon her
  bosom,
And strewed my flowers upon
  her, — *they* still live :
Sometimes I like to kiss her
  closed white eyelids,
And think of all the joy she
  used to give.

Cruel indeed it were to take her
  from me ;
She sleeps, she will not wake —
  no fear — again :

And so I laid her, such a gentle
  burden,
Quietly on my heart to still its
  pain.

I do not think that any smiling
  Present,
Any vague Future, spite of all
  her charms,
Could ever rival her. You know
  you laid her,
Long years ago, then living, in
  my arms.

Leave her at least: while my
  tears fall upon her,
I dream she smiles, just as she
  did of yore ;
As dear as ever to me, — nay, it
  may be,
Even dearer still, — since I have
  nothing more.

A DOUBTING HEART.

WHERE are the swallows fled ?
  Frozen and dead,
Perchance upon some bleak and
  stormy shore.
  O doubting heart !
  Far over purple seas,
  They wait, in sunny ease,
  The balmy southern breeze,
To bring them to their northern
  homes once more.

Why must the flowers die ?
  Prisoned they lie

In the cold tomb, heedless of
    tears or rain.
    O doubting heart!
  They only sleep below
  The soft white ermine snow,
  While winter winds shall
    blow,
To breathe and smile upon you
    soon again.

The sun has hid its rays
    These many days;
Will dreary hours never leave
    the earth?
    O doubting heart!
  The stormy clouds on high
  Veil the same sunny sky,
  That soon (for spring is
    nigh)
Shall wake the summer into
    golden mirth.

Fair hope is dead, and light
    Is quenched in night.
What sound can break the si-
    lence of despair?
    O doubting heart!
  Thy sky is overcast,
  Yet stars shall rise at last,
  Brighter for darkness past,
And angels' silver voices stir the
    air.

A STUDENT.

Over an ancient scroll I bent,
Steeping my soul in wise con-
    tent,

Nor paused a moment, save to
    chide
A low voice whispering at my
    side.

I wove beneath the stars' pale
    shine
A dream, half human, half divine;
And shook off (not to break the
    charm)
A little hand laid on my arm.

I read; until my heart would
    glow
With the great deeds of long
    ago;
Nor heard, while with those
    mighty dead,
Pass to and fro a faltering tread.

On the old theme I pondered
    long, —
The struggle between right and
    wrong;
I could not check such visions
    high,
To soothe a little quivering sigh.

I tried to solve the problem —
    Life;
Dreaming of that mysterious
    strife,
How could I leave such reason-
    ings wise,
To answer two blue pleading
    eyes?

I strove how best to give, and
    when,
My blood to save my fellow-
    men, —

How could I turn aside, to look
At snowdrops laid upon my
book ?

Now Time has fled — the world
is strange,
Something there is of pain and
change;
My books lie closed upon the
shelf;
I miss the old heart in myself.

I miss the sunbeams in my
room, —
It was not always wrapped in
gloom :
I miss my dreams, — they fade
so fast,
Or flit into some trivial past.

The great stream of the world
goes by ;
None care, or heed, or question,
why
I, the lone student, cannot raise
My voice or hand as in old days.

No echo seems to wake again
My heart to anything but pain,
Save when a dream of twilight
brings
The fluttering of an angel's
wings !

A KNIGHT-ERRANT.

THOUGH he lived and died among
us,
Yet his name may be enrolled
With the knights whose deeds of
daring
Ancient chronicles have told.

Still a stripling, he encountered
Poverty, and struggled long,
Gathering force from every effort,
Till he knew his arm was
strong.

Then his heart and life he of-
fered
To his radiant mistress, —
Truth ;
Never thought, or dream, or fal-
tering,
Marred the promise of his
youth.

So he rode forth to defend her,
And her peerless worth pro-
claim ;
Challenging each recreant doubter
Who aspersed her spotless
name.

First upon his path stood Igno-
rance,
Hideous in his brutal might;
Hard the blows and long the
battle
Ere the monster took to flight.

Then, with light and fearless
spirit,
Prejudice he dared to brave ;
Hunting back the lying craven
To her black sulphurous
cave.

Followed by his servile minions,
　Custom, the old Giant, rose;
Yet he, too, at last was conquered
　By the good Knight's weighty
　　blows.

Then he turned, and, flushed with
　　victory,
　Struck upon the brazen shield
Of the world's great king, Opin-
　　ion,
　And defied him to the field.

Once again he rose a conqueror,
　And, though wounded in the
　　fight,
With a dying smile of triumph
　Saw that Truth had gained
　　her right.

On his failing ear re-echoing
　Came the shouting round her
　　throne;
Little cared he that no future
　With her name would link his
　　own.

Spent with many a hard-fought
　　battle,
　Slowly ebbed his life away,
And the crowd that flocked to
　　greet her
　Trampled on him where he
　　lay.

Gathering all his strength, he
　　saw her
　Crowned and reigning in her
　　pride;
Looked his last upon her beauty,
　Raised his eyes to God, and
　　died.

LINGER, O GENTLE TIME.

Linger, O gentle Time,
Linger, O radiant grace of bright
　　To-day!
　Let not the hours' chime
　　Call thee away,
But linger near me still with
　　fond delay.

Linger, for thou art mine!
What dearer treasures can the
　　future hold?
　What sweeter flowers than
　　thine
　　Can she unfold?
What secrets tell my heart thou
　　hast not told?

O, linger in thy flight!
For shadows gather round, and
　　should we part,
　A dreary, starless night
　　May fill my heart, —
Then pause and linger yet ere
　　thou depart.

Linger, I ask no more, —
Thou art enough forever — thou
　　alone;
　What future can restore,
　　When thou art flown,
All that I hold from thee and call
　　my own?

HOMEWARD BOUND.

I have seen a fiercer tempest,
　Known a louder whirlwind
　　blow;

I was wrecked off red Algiers,
  Six-and-thirty years ago.
Young I was, and yet old sea-
  men
Were not strong or calm as I;
While life held such treasures for
  me,
  I felt sure I could not die.

Life I struggled for, — and saved
  it;
  Life alone, — and nothing
  more;
Bruised, half dead, alone and
  helpless
  I was cast upon the shore.
I feared the pitiless rocks of
  Ocean;
  So the great sea rose, — and
  then
Cast me from her friendly bosom,
  On the pitiless hearts of men.

Gaunt and dreary ran the moun-
  tains,
  With black gorges, up the
  land;
Up to where the lonely Desert
  Spreads her burning, dreary
  sand:
In the gorges of the mountains,
  On the plain beside the sea,
Dwelt my stern and cruel mas-
  ters,
  The black Moors of Barbary.

Ten long years I toiled among
  them,
  Hopeless — as I used to say;

Now I know Hope burnt within
  me
  Fiercer, stronger, day by day:
Those dim years of toil and sor-
  row
  Like one long, dark dream ap-
  pear;
One long day of weary wait-
  ing, —
  Then each day was like a year.

How I cursed the land, — my pris-
  on;
  How I cursed the serpent sea,
And the Demon Fate that show-
  ered
  All her curses upon me;
I was mad, I think — God pardon
  Words so terrible and wild —
This voyage would have been my
  last one,
  For I left a wife and child.

Never did one tender vision
  Fade away before my sight,
Never once through all my slav-
  ery,
  Burning day or dreary night;
In my soul it lived, and kept me,
  Now I feel, from black despair,
And my heart was not quite
  broken,
  While they lived and blest me
  there.

When at night my task was over,
  I would hasten to the shore;
(All was strange and foreign in-
  land,
  Nothing I had known before;)

Strange looked the bleak moun-
    tain passes,
  Strange the red glare and black
    shade,
And the Oleanders, waving
  To the sound the fountains
    made.

Then I gazed at the great Ocean,
  Till she grew a friend again ;
And because she knew old Eng-
    land,
  I forgave her all my pain :
So the blue still sky above me,
  With its white clouds' fleecy
    fold,
And the glimmering stars (though
    brighter),
Looked like home and days of
    old

And a calm would fall upon me,
  Worn perhaps with work and
    pain,
The wild, hungry longing left
    me,
  And I was myself again :
Looking at the silver waters,
  Looking up at the far sky,
Dreams of home and all I left
    there
  Floated sorrowfully by.

A fair face, but pale with sor-
    row,
  With blue eyes, brimful of
    tears,
And the little red mouth, quiver-
    ing
  With a smile, to hide its fears ;

Holding out her baby towards me,
  From the sky she looked on
    me ;
So it was that last I saw her,
  As the ship put out to sea.

Sometimes (and a pang would
    seize me
  That the years were floating
    on)
I would strive to paint her, al-
    tered,
  And the little baby gone :
She no longer young and girlish,
  The child standing by her
    knee,
And her face more pale and
    saddened
  With the weariness for me.

Then I saw, as night grew darker,
  How she taught my child to
    pray,
Holding its small hands together,
  For its father, far away ;
And I felt her sorrow, weighing
  Heavier on me than my own,
Pitying her blighted spring-time,
  And her joy so early flown.

Till upon my hands (now hard-
    ened
  With the rough, harsh toil of
    years)
Bitter drops of anguish falling,
  Woke me from my dream, to
    tears ;
Woke me as a slave, an outcast,
  Leagues from home, across the
    deep ;

So — though you may call it
　　childish —
So I sobbed myself to sleep.

Well, the years sped on, — my
　　Sorrow,
　　Calmer, and yet stronger
　　grown,
Was my shield against all suffer-
　　ing,
Poorer, meaner than her own.
Thus my cruel master's harsh-
　　ness
Fell upon me all in vain,
Yet the tale of what we suffered
　　Echoed back from main to
　　main.

You have heard in a far country
Of a self-devoted band,
Vowed to rescue Christian cap-
　　tives
Pining in a foreign land.
And these gentle-hearted stran-
　　gers
　　Year by year go forth from
　　Rome,
In their hands the hard-earned
　　ransom,
To restore some exiles home.

I was freed: they broke the
　　tidings
　　Gently to me: but indeed
Hour by hour sped on, I knew
　　not
　　What the words meant — I
　　was freed!
Better so, perhaps; while sorrow
　　(More akin to earthly things)

Only strains the sad heart's
　　fibres,
　　Joy, bright stranger, breaks
　　the strings.

Yet at last it rushed upon me,
　　And my heart beat full and
　　fast;
What were now my years of
　　waiting,
　　What was all the dreary past?
Nothing — to the impatient
　　throbbing
I must bear across the sea:
Nothing — to the eternal hours
　　Still between my home and
　　me!

How the voyage passed, I know
　　not;
　　Strange it was once more to
　　stand
With my countrymen around me,
　　And to clasp an English hand.
But, through all, my heart was
　　dreaming
　　Of the first words I should
　　hear,
In the gentle voice that echoed,
　　Fresh as ever, on my ear.

Should I see her start of wonder,
　　And the sudden truth arise,
Flushing all her face and light-
　　ening
　　The dimmed splendor of her
　　eyes?
Oh! to watch the fear and
　　doubting
　　Stir the silent depths of pain,

And the rush of joy — then
  melting
Into perfect peace again.

And the child! — but why re-
  member
Foolish fancies that I thought?
Every tree and every hedge-row
From the well-known past I
  brought;
I would picture my dear cottage,
See the crackling wood-fire
  burn,
And the two beside it seated,
Watching, waiting, my return.

So, at last we reached the harbor.
I remember nothing more
Till I stood, my sick heart throb-
  bing,
With my hand upon the door.
There I paused — I heard her
  speaking;
Low, soft, murmuring words
  she said;
Then I first knew the dumb
  terror
I had had lest she were dead.

It was evening in late autumn,
And the gusty wind blew chill;
Autumn leaves were falling round
  me,
And the red sun lit the hill.
Six-and-twenty years are van-
  ished
Since then, — I am old and
  gray, —
But I never told to mortal
What I saw, until this day.

She was seated by the fire,
In her arms she held a child,
Whispering baby-words caress-
  ing,
And then, looking up, she
  smiled;
Smiled on him who stood beside
  her —
Oh! the bitter truth was told,
In her look of trusting fondness —
I had seen the look of old!

But she rose and turned towards
  me
(Cold and dumb I waited
  there)
With a shriek of fear and terror,
And a white face of despair.
He had been an ancient com-
  rade, —
Not a single word we said,
While we gazed upon each other,
He the living: I the dead!

I drew nearer, nearer to her,
And I took her trembling hand,
Looking on her white face, look-
  ing
That her heart might under-
  stand
All the love and all the pity
That my lips refused to say, —
I thank God no thought save
  sorrow
Rose in our crushed hearts
  that day.

Bitter tears that desolate moment,
Bitter, bitter tears we wept,

We three broken hearts together,
  While the baby smiled and
    slept.
Tears alone — no words were
    spoken,
  Till he — till her husband said
That my boy, (I had forgotten
  The poor child,) that he was
    dead.

Then at last I rose, and, turning,
  Wrung his hand, but made no
    sign ;
And I stooped and kissed her
    forehead
Once more, as if she were mine.
Nothing of farewell I uttered,
  Save in broken words to pray
That God would ever guard and
  bless her, —
  Then in silence passed away.

Over the great restless ocean
  Six-and-twenty years I roam ;
All my comrades, old and weary,
  Have gone back to die at home.
Home ! yes, I shall reach a
    haven,
  I, too, shall reach home and
    rest ;
I shall find her waiting for me
  With our baby on her breast.

LIFE AND DEATH.

" What is Life, father ? "
        " A Battle, my child,
  Where the strongest lance may
    fail,
Where the wariest eyes may be
    beguiled,
  And the stoutest heart may
    quail.
Where the foes are gathered on
  every hand,
  And rest not day or night,
And the feeble little ones must
    stand
  In the thickest of the fight."

" What is Death, father ? "
        " The rest, my child,
  When the strife and the toil are
    o'er ;
The angel of God, who, calm
    and mild,
  Says we need fight no more ;
Who, driving away the demon
    band,
  Bids the din of the battl
    cease ;
Takes banner and spear from
  our failing hand,
  And proclaims an eternal
    peace."

" Let me die, father ! I tremble,
    and fear
  To yield in that terrible
    strife ! "

" The crown must be won for
    Heaven, dear,
  In the battle-field of life :
My child, though thy foes are
  strong and tried,
He loveth the weak and small :
The angels of heaven are on thy
    side,
  And God is over all ! "

NOW.

RISE ! for the day is passing,
  And you lie dreaming on ;
The others have buckled their
    armor,
  And forth to the fight are
    gone :
A place in the ranks awaits
    you,
  Each man has some part to
    play;
The Past and the Future are
    nothing,
  In the face of the stern To-
    day.

Rise from your dreams of the
    Future, —
  Of gaining some hard-fought
    field ;
Of storming some airy fortress,
  Or bidding some giant yield ;
Your Future has deeds of glory,
  Of honor (God grant it may !)
But your arm will never be
    stronger,
  Or the need so great as To-day.

Rise ! if the Past detains you,
  Her sunshine and storms
    forget ;
No chains so unworthy to hold
    you
  As those of a vain regret :
Sad or bright, she is lifeless ever ;
  Cast her phantom arms away,
Nor look back, save to learn the
    lesson
  Of a nobler strife To-day.

Rise ! for the day is passing ;
  The sound that you scarcely
    hear
Is the enemy marching to bat-
    tle : —
  Arise ! for the foe is here !
Stay not to sharpen your weap-
    ons,
  Or the hour will strike at last,
When, from dreams of a coming
    battle,
  You may wake to find it past !

CLEANSING FIRES.

LET thy gold be cast in the fur-
    nace,
  Thy red gold, precious and
    bright ;
Do not fear the hungry fire,
  With its caverns of burning
    light ;
And thy gold shall return more
    precious,
  Free from every spot and
    stain ;
For gold must be tried by fire,
  As a heart must be tried by
    pain.

In the cruel fire of Sorrow
  Cast thy heart, do not faint or
    wail ;
Let thy hand be firm and steady,
  Do not let thy spirit quail :
But wait till the trial is over,
  And take thy heart again ;

For as gold is tried by fire,
  So a heart must be tried by
    pain !
I shall know by the gleam and
    glitter
  Of the golden chain you wear,
By your heart's calm strength
    in loving,
  Of the fire they have had to
    bear.
Beat on, true heart, forever ;
  Shine bright, strong golden
    chain ;
And bless the cleansing fire,
  And the furnace of living pain !

THE VOICE OF THE WIND.

Let us throw more logs on the
    fire !
We have need of a cheerful
    light,
And close round the hearth to
    gather,
  For the wind has risen to-night.
With the mournful sound of its
    wailing
  It has checked the children's
    glee,
And it calls with a louder clamor
  Than the clamor of the sea.
      Hark to the voice of
        the wind !

Let us listen to what it is saying,
  Let us hearken to where it has
    been ;

For it tells, in its terrible crying,
  The fearful sights it has seen.
It clatters loud at the casements,
  Round the house it hurries on,
And shrieks with redoubled fury
  When we say, " The blast is
    gone ! "
      Hark to the voice of
        the wind !

It has been on the field of battle,
  Where the dying and wounded
    lie ;
And it brings the last groan they
    uttered,   ·
  And the ravenous vulture's
    cry.
It has been where the icebergs
    were meeting,
  And closed with a fearful
    crash :
On shores where no foot has
    wandered
  It has heard the waters dash.
      Hark to the voice of
        the wind !

It has been on the desolate ocean
  When the lightning struck the
    mast ;
It has heard the cry of the
    drowning,
  Who sank as it hurried past ;
The words of despair and an-
    guish,
  That were heard by no living
    ear,
The gun that no signal answered,
  It brings them all to us here.
      Hark to the voice of
        the wind !

It has been on the lonely moor-
land,
  Where the treacherous snow-
    drift lies,
Where the traveller, spent and
weary,
  Gasped fainter and fainter
    cries ;
It has heard the bay of the blood-
hounds
  On the track of the hunted
    slave,
The lash and the curse of the
master,
  And the groan that the cap-
    tive gave.
        Hark to the voice of
        the wind !

It has swept through the gloomy
forest,
  Where the sledge was urged
    to its speed,
Where the howling wolves were
rushing
  On the track of the panting
    steed.
Where the pool was black and
lonely,
  It caught up a splash and a
    cry, —
Only the bleak sky heard it,
  And the wind as it hurried by.
        Hark to the voice of
        the wind !

Then throw more logs on the
fire,
  Since the air is bleak and
    cold,

And the children are drawing
nigher,
  For the tales that the wind
    has told.
So closer and closer gather
  Round the red and crackling
    light ;
And rejoice (while the wind is
blowing)
  We are safe and warm to-
    night.
        Hark to the voice of
        the wind !

TREASURES.

LET me count my treasures,
  All my soul holds dear,
Given me by dark spirits
  Whom I used to fear.

Through long days of anguish,
  And sad nights, did Pain
Forge my shield, Endurance,
  Bright and free from stain !

Doubt, in misty caverns,
  'Mid dark horrors sought,
Till my peerless jewel, .
  Faith, to me she brought.

Sorrow, that I wearied
  Should remain so long,
Wreathed my starry glory,
  The bright Crown of Song.

Strife, that racked my spirit
  Without hope or rest,

Left the blooming flower,
  Patience, on my breast.

Suffering, that I dreaded,
  Ignorant of her charms,
Laid the fair child, Pity,
  Smiling, in my arms.

So I count my treasures,
  Stored in days long past, —
And I thank the givers,
  Whom I know at last!

SHINING STARS.

SHINE, ye stars of heaven,
  On a world of pain!
See old Time destroying
  All our hoarded gain;
All our sweetest flowers,
  Every stately shrine,
All our hard-earned glory,
  Every dream divine!

Shine, ye stars of heaven,
  On the rolling years!
See how Time, consoling,
  Dries the saddest tears,
Bids the darkest storm-clouds
  Pass in gentle rain,
While upspring in glory
  Flowers and dreams again!

Shine, ye stars of heaven,
  On a world of fear!
See how Time, avenging,
  Bringeth judgment here:
Weaving ill-won honors
  To a fiery crown;

Bidding hard hearts perish;
  Casting proud hearts down.

Shine, ye stars of heaven,
  On the hours' slow flight!
See how Time, rewarding,
  Gilds good deeds with light;
Pays with kingly measure;
  Brings earth's dearest prize;
Or, crowned with rays diviner,
  Bids the end arise!

WAITING.

" WHEREFORE dwell so sad and
      lonely
  By the desolate sea-shore,
With the melancholy surges
  Beating at your cottage door?

" You shall dwell beside the
      castle
  Shadowed by our ancient
      trees;
And your life shall pass on
      gently,
  Cared for, and in rest and
      ease."

" Lady, one who loved me dearly
  Sailed for distant lands away;
And I wait here his returning
  Hopefully from day to day.

" To my door I bring my spin-
      ning,
  Watching every ship I see;
Waiting, hoping, till the sunset
  Fades into the western sea.

" After sunset, at my casement,
 Still I place a signal light;
He will see its well-known shin-
 ing
 Should his ship return at
 night.

" Lady, see your infant smiling,
 With its flaxen curling hair, —
I remember when your mother
 Was a baby just as fair.

" I was watching then, and hoping:
 Years have brought great
 change to all;
To my neighbors in their cottage,
 To you nobles at the hall.

" Not to me, — for I am waiting,
 And the years have fled so
 fast,
I must look at you to tell me
 That a weary time has past!

" When I hear a footstep coming
 On the shingle — years have
 fled —
Yet amid a thousand others,
 I shall know his quick, light
 tread.

" When I hear (to-night it may
 be)
 Some one pausing at my door,
I shall know the gay, soft accents,
 Heard and welcomed oft before !

" So each day I am more hopeful,
 He may come before the night;
Every sunset I feel surer
 He must come ere morning
 light.

" Then I thank you, noble lady,
 But I cannot do your will:
Where he left me he must find
 me,
 Waiting, watching, hoping,
 still ! "

THE CRADLE-SONG OF THE POOR.

Hush ! I cannot bear to see thee
 Stretch thy tiny hands in vain ;
Dear, I have no bread to give
 thee,
 Nothing, child, to ease thy
 pain !
When God sent thee first to bless
 me,
 Proud, and thankful too, was
 I ;
Now, my darling, I, thy mother,
 Almost long to see thee die.
 Sleep, my darling, thou
 art weary ;
 God is good, but life is
 dreary.

I have watched thy beauty fading,
 And thy strength sink day by
 day,
Soon, I know, will Want and
 Fever
 Take thy little life away.

Famine makes thy father reckless,
  Hope has left both him and
  me;
We could suffer all, my baby,
  Had we but a crust for thee.
    Sleep, my darling, thou
    art weary;
    God is good, but life is
    dreary.

Better thou shouldst perish early,
  Starve so soon, my darling
  one,
Than in helpless sin and sorrow
  Vainly live, as I have done.
Better that thy angel spirit
  With my joy, my peace, were
  flown,
Than thy heart grew cold and
  careless,
  Reckless, hopeless, like my
  own.
    Sleep, my darling, thou
    art weary;
    God is good, but life is
    dreary.

I am wasted, dear, with hunger,
  And my brain is all opprest,
I have scarcely strength to press
  thee,
  Wan and feeble, to my breast.
Patience, baby, God will help us,
  Death will come to thee and
  me,
He will take us to his heaven,
  Where no want or pain can be.
    Sleep, my darling, thou
    art weary;
    God is good, but life is
    dreary.

Such the plaint that, late and
  early,
Did we listen, we might hear
Close beside us, — but the thun-
  der
Of a city dulls our ear.
Every heart, as God's bright
  Angel,
  Can bid one such sorrow cease;
God has glory when his children
  Bring his poor ones joy and
  peace!
    Listen, nearer while she
    sings
    Sounds the fluttering of
    wings!

BE STRONG.

Be strong to *hope*, O Heart!
  Though day is bright,
The stars can only shine
  In the dark night.
Be strong, O Heart of mine,
  Look towards the light!

Be strong to *bear*, O Heart!
  Nothing is vain:
Strive not, for life is care,
  And God sends pain;
Heaven is above, and there
  Rest will remain!

Be strong to *love*, O Heart!
  Love knows not wrong;
Didst thou love — creatures
  even,
  Life were not long;
Didst thou love God in heaven,
  Thou wouldst be strong!

GOD'S GIFTS.

Gon gave a gift to Earth : a child,
Weak, innocent, and undefiled,
Opened its ignorant eyes and
  smiled.

It lay so helpless, so forlorn,
Earth took it coldly and in scorn,
Cursing the day when it was
  born.

She gave it first a tarnished
  name,
For heritage, a tainted fame,
Then cradled it in want and
  shame.

All influence of Good or Right,
All ray of God's most holy light,
She curtained closely from its
  sight.

Then turned her heart, her eyes
  away,
Ready to look again, the day
Its little feet began to stray.

In dens of guilt the baby played,
Where sin, and sin alone, was
  made
The law that all around obeyed.

With ready and obedient care,
He learnt the tasks they taught
  him there ;
Black sin for lesson, — oaths for
  prayer.

Then Earth arose, and, in her
  might,

To vindicate her injured right,
Thrust him in deeper depths of
  night ;

Branding him with a deeper
  brand
Of shame, he could not understand,
The felon outcast of the land.

God gave a gift to Earth : a child,
Weak, innocent, and undefiled,
Opened its ignorant eyes and
  smiled.

And Earth received the gift, and
  cried
Her joy and triumph far and
  wide,
Till echo answered to her pride.

She blessed the hour when first
  he came
To take the crown of pride and
  fame,
Wreathed through long ages for
  his name.

Then bent her utmost art and
  skill
To train the supple mind and
  will,
And guard it from a breath of ill.

She strewed his morning path
  with flowers,
And Love, in tender dropping
  showers,
Nourished the blue and dawning
  hours.

She shed, in rainbow hues of
    light,
A halo round the Good and
    Right,
To tempt and charm the baby's
    sight.

And every step, of work or play,
Was lit by some such dazzling ray,
Till morning brightened into
    day.

And then the World arose, and
    said,
Let added honors now be shed
On such a noble heart and head!

O World, both gifts were pure
    and bright,
Holy and sacred in God's sight:—
God will judge them and thee
    aright!

A TOMB IN GHENT.

A SMILING look she had, a figure
    slight,
With cheerful air, and step both
    quick and light;
A strange and foreign look the
    maiden bore,
That suited the quaint Belgian
    dress she wore;
Yet the blue, fearless eyes in her
    fair face,
And her soft voice, told her of
    English race;
And ever, as she flitted to and
    fro,

She sang, (or murmured, rather,)
    soft and low,
Snatches of song, as if she did
    not know
That she was singing, but the
    happy load
Of dream and thought thus from
    her heart o'erflowed:
And while on household cares
    she passed along,
The air would bear me fragments
    of her song;
Not such as village maidens sing,
    and few
The framers of her changing
    music knew;
Chants such as heaven and earth
    first heard of when
The master Palestrina held the
    pen.
But I with awe had often turned
    the page,
Yellow with time, and half de-
    faced by age,
And listened, with an ear not
    quite unskilled,
While heart and soul to the
    grand echo thrilled;
And much I marvelled, as her
    cadence fell
From the Laudate, that I knew
    so well,
Into Scarlatti's minor fugue,
    how she
Had learned such deep and sol-
    emn harmony.
But what she told I set in rhyme,
    as meet
To chronicle the influence, dim
    and sweet,

'Neath which her young and innocent life had grown :
Would that my words were simple as her own.

Many years since, an English
workman went
Over the seas, to seek a home in
Ghent,
Where English skill was prized;
nor toiled in vain ;
Small, yet enough, his hard-
earned daily gain.
He dwelt alone, — in sorrow, or
in pride.
He mixed not with the workers
by his side ;
He seemed to care but for one
present joy, —
To tend, to watch, to teach his
sickly boy.
Severe to all beside, yet for the
child
He softened his rough speech to
soothings mild;
For him he smiled, with him each
day he walked
Through the dark, gloomy
streets ; to him he talked
Of home, of England, and
strange stories told
Of English heroes in the days of
old;
And (when the sunset gilded
roof and spire)
The marvellous tale which never
seemed to tire :
How the gilt dragon, glaring
fiercely down

From the great belfry, watching
all the town,
Was brought, a trophy of the
wars divine,
By a Crusader from far Palestine,
And given to Bruges ; and how
Ghent arose,
And how they struggled long as
deadly foes,
Till Ghent, one night, by a brave
soldier's skill,
Stole the great dragon ; and she
keeps it still.
One day the dragon — so 't is
said — will rise,
Spread his bright wings, and
glitter in the skies,
And over desert lands and azure
seas
Will seek his home 'mid palm
and cedar trees.
So, as he passed the belfry every
day,
The boy would look if it were
flown away ;
Each day surprised to find it
watching there,
Above him, as he crossed the
ancient square,
To seek the great cathedral, that
had grown
A home for him — mysterious
and his own.

Dim with dark shadows of
the ages past,
St. Bavon stands, solemn and
rich and vast;
The slender pillars, in long
vistas spread,

Like forest arches meet and close
   o'erhead ;
So high that, like a weak and
   doubting prayer,
Ere it can float to the carved
   angels there,
The silver clouded incense faints
   in air :
Only the organ's voice, with peal
   on peal,
Can mount to where those far-off
   angels kneel.
Here the pale boy, beneath a low
   side-arch,
Would listen to its solemn chant
   or march ;
Folding his little hands, his simple prayer
Melted in childish dreams, and
   both in air :
While the great organ over all
   would roll,
Speaking strange secrets to his
   innocent soul,
Bearing on eagle-wings the great
   desire
Of all the kneeling throng, and
   piercing higher
Than aught but love and prayer
   can reach, until
Only the silence seemed to listen
   still ;
Or gathering like a sea still more
   and more,
Break in melodious waves at
   heaven's door,
And then fall, slow and soft, in
   tender rain,
Upon the pleading, longing
   hearts again.

Then he would watch the rosy
   sunlight glow,
That crept along the marble floor
   below,
Passing, as life does, with the
   passing hours,
Now by a shrine all rich with
   gems and flowers,
Now on the brazen letters of a
   tomb,
Then, leaving it again to shade
   and gloom,
And creeping on, to show, dis-
   tinct and quaint,
The kneeling figure of some
   marble saint :
Or lighting up the carvings
   strange and rare,
That told of patient toil, and
   reverent care ;
Ivy that trembled on the spray,
   and ears
Of heavy corn, and slender bul-
   rush spears,
And all the thousand tangled
   weeds that grow
In summer, where the silver rivers flow ;
And demon - heads grotesque,
   that seemed to glare
In impotent wrath on all the
   beauty there :
Then the gold rays up pillared
   shaft would climb,
And so be drawn to heaven, at
   evening time.
And deeper silence, darker shadows flowed
On all around, only the windows
   glowed

With blazoned glory, like the
shields of light
Archangels bear, who, armed
with love and might,
Watch upon heaven's battlements at night.
Then all was shade ; the silver
lamps that gleamed,
Lost in the daylight, in the darkness seemed
Like sparks of fire in the dim
aisles to shine,
Or trembling stars before each
separate shrine.
Grown half afraid, the child
would leave them there,
And come out, blinded by the
noisy glare
That burst upon him from the
busy square.

The church was thus his home
for rest or play ;
And as he came and went again
each day,
The pictured faces that he knew
so well
Seemed to smile on him welcome
and farewell.
But holier, and dearer far than all,
One sacred spot his own he loved
to call ;
Save at mid-day, half hidden by
the gloom ;
The people call it The White
Maiden's Tomb :
For there she stands ; her folded
hands are pressed
Together, and laid softly on her
breast,

As if she waited but a word to
rise
From the dull earth, and pass to
the blue skies ;
Her lips expectant part, she holds
her breath,
As listening for the angel voice
of death.
None know how many years have
seen her so,
Or what the name of her who
sleeps below.
And here the child would come,
and strive to trace,
Through the dim twilight, the
pure, gentle face
He loved so well, and here he oft
would bring
Some violet-blossom of the early
spring,
And, climbing softly by the fret-
ted stand,
Not to disturb her, lay it in her
hand ;
Or, whispering a soft, loving
message sweet,
Would stoop and kiss the little
marble feet.
So, when the organ's pealing
music rang,
He thought amid the gloom the
Maiden sang ;
With reverent, simple faith by
her he knelt,
And fancied what she thought,
and what she felt ;
" Glory to God," re-echoed from
her voice,
And then his little spirit would
rejoice ;

Or when the Requiem sobbed
  upon the air,
His baby tears dropped with her
  mournful prayer.

So years fled on, while childish
  fancies past,
The childish love and simple faith
  could last.
The artist-soul awoke in him, the
  flame
Of genius, like the light of Heaven,
  came
Upon his brain, and (as it will,
  if true)
It touched his heart and lit his
  spirit, too.
His father saw, and with a proud
  content
Let him forsake the toil where
  he had spent
His youth's first years, and on
  one happy day
Of pride, before the old man
  passed away,
He stood with quivering lips, and
  the big tears
Upon his cheek, and heard the
  dream of years
Living and speaking to his very
  heart, —
The low, hushed murmur at the
  wondrous art
Of him who with young, trembling fingers made
The great church-organ answer
  as he played ;
And, as the uncertain sound grew
  full and strong,

Rush with harmonious spirit-
  wings along,
And thrill with master-power
  the breathless throng.

The old man died, and years
  passed on, and still
The young musician bent his
  heart and will
To his dear toil. St. Bavon now
  had grown
More dear to him, and even more
  his own ;
And as he left it every night he
  prayed
A moment by the archway in the
  shade,
Kneeling once more within the
  sacred gloom
Where the White Maiden
  watched upon her tomb.
His hopes of travel and a world-
  wide fame,
Cold Time had sobered, and his
  fragile frame ;
Content at last only in dreams
  to roam,
Away from the tranquillity of
  home ;
Content that the poor dwellers
  by his side
Saw in him but the gentle friend
  and guide,
The patient counsellor in the
  poor strife
And petty details of their common life,
Who comforted where woe and
  grief might fall,

Nor slighted any pain or want as
   small,
But whose great heart took in
   and felt for all.

   Still he grew famous;—many
   came to be
His pupils in the art of harmony.
One day a voice floated so pure
   and free
Above his music, that he turned
   to see
What angel sang, and saw before
   his eyes,
What made his heart leap with
   a strange surprise,
His own White Maiden, calm,
   and pure, and mild,
As in his childish dreams she
   sang and smiled;
Her eyes raised up to Heaven,
   her lips apart,
And music overflowing from her
   heart.
But the faint blush that tinged
   her cheek betrayed
No marble statue, but a living
   maid ;
Perplexed and startled at his
   wondering look,
Her rustling score of Mozart's
   Sanctus shook ;
The uncertain notes, like birds
   within a snare,
Fluttered and died upon the
   trembling air.

   Days passed; each morning
   saw the maiden stand,
Her eyes cast down, her lesson in
   her hand,

Eager to study, never weary,
   while
Repaid by the approving word
   or smile
Of her kind master; days and
   months fled on ;
One day the pupil from the choir
   was gone ;
Gone to take light, and joy, and
   youth once more
Within the poor musician's hum
   ble door ;
And to repay, with gentle, hap•
   py art,
The debt so many owed his generous heart.
And now, indeed, was one who
   knew and felt
That a great gift of God within
   him dwelt ;
One who could listen, who could
   understand,
Whose idle work dropped from
   her slackened hand,
While with wet eyes entranced
   she stood, nor knew
How the melodious wingéd hours
   flew ;
Who loved his art as none had
   loved before,
Yet prized the noble, tender spirit
   more.
While the great organ brought
   from far and near
Lovers of harmony to praise and
   hear,
Unmarked by aught save what
   filled every day,
Duty, and toil, and rest, years
   passed away :

And now by the low archway in
the shade
Beside her mother knelt a little
maid,
Who through the great cathedral
learned to roam,
Climb to the choir, and bring her
father home;
And stand, demure and solemn
by his side,
Patient till the last echo softly
died;
Then place her little hand in his,
and go
Down the dark winding stair to
where below
The mother knelt, within the
gathering gloom
Waiting and praying by the
Maiden's Tomb.

So their life went, until, one
winter's day,
Father and child came there
alone to pray, —
The mother, gentle soul, had fled
away!
Their life was altered now, and
yet the child
Forgot her passionate grief in
time, and smiled,
Half wondering why, when
spring's fresh breezes came,
To see her father was no more
the same.
Half guessing at the shadow of
his pain,
And then contented if he smiled
again,

A sad, cold smile, that passed in
tears away,
As reassured she ran once more
to play.
And now each year that added
grace to grace,
Fresh bloom and sunshine to the
young girl's face,
Brought a strange light in the
musician's eyes,
As if he saw some starry hope
arise,
Breaking upon the midnight of
sad skies.
It might be so: more feeble
year by year,
The wanderer to his resting-place
drew near.
One day the Gloria he could
play no more,
Echoed its grand rejoicing as of
yore;
His hands were clasped, his weary
head was laid,
Upon the tomb where the White
Maiden prayed;
Where the child's love first
dawned, his soul first spoke,
The old man's heart there
throbbed its last and broke.
The grave cathedral that had
nursed his youth,
Had helped his dreaming, and
had taught him truth,
Had seen his boyish grief and
baby tears,
And watched the sorrows and
the joys of years,
Had lit his fame and hope with
sacred rays,

And consecrated sad and happy days,
Had blessed his happiness, and soothed his pain,
Now took her faithful servant home again.

He rests in peace : some travellers mention yet
An organist whose name they all forget.
He has a holier and a nobler fame
By poor men's hearths, who love and bless the name
Of a kind friend; and in low tones to-day
Speak tenderly of him who passed away.
Too poor to help the daughter of their friend,
They grieved to see the little pittance end ;
To see her toil and strive with cheerful heart,
To bear the lonely orphan's struggling part;
They grieved to see her go at last alone
To English kinsmen she had never known :
And here she came ; the foreign girl soon found
Welcome, and love, and plenty all around,
And here she pays it back with earnest will,
By well-taught housewife watchfulness and skill ;
Deep in her heart she holds her father's name,

And tenderly and proudly keeps his fame ;
And while she works with thrifty Belgian care,
Past dreams of childhood float upon the air ;
Some strange old chant, or solemn Latin hymn,
That echoed through the old cathedral dim,
When as a little child each day she went
To kneel and pray by an old tomb in Ghent.

———

THE ANGEL OF DEATH.

Why shouldst thou fear the beautiful angel, Death,
  Who waits thee at the portals of the skies,
Ready to kiss away thy struggling breath,
  Ready with gentle hand to close thine eyes ?

How many a tranquil soul has passed away,
  Fled gladly from fierce pain and pleasures dim,
To the eternal splendor of the day ;
  And many a troubled heart still calls for him.

Spirits too tender for the battle here
  Have turned from life, its hopes, its fears, its charms ;

And children, shuddering at a
    world so drear,
    Have smiling passed away
      into his arms.

He whom thou fearest will, to
    ease its pain,
    Lay his cold hand upon thy
      aching heart:
Will soothe the terrors of thy
    troubled brain,
    And bid the shadow of earth's
      grief depart.

He will give back what neither
    time, nor might,
    Nor passionate prayer, nor
      longing hope restore,
(Dear as to long-blind eyes re-
    covered sight,)
    He will give back those who
      are gone before.

O, what were life, if life were
    all? Thine eyes
    Are blinded by their tears, or
      thou wouldst see
Thy treasures wait thee in the
    far-off skies,
    And Death, thy friend, will
      give them all to thee.

A DREAM.

ALL yesterday I was spinning,
    Sitting alone in the sun;
And the dream that I spun was
    so lengthy,
    It lasted till day was done.

I heeded not cloud or shadow
    That flitted over the hill,
Or the humming-bees, or the
    swallows,
    Or the trickling of the rill.

I took the threads for my spin-
    ning,
    All of blue summer air,
And a flickering ray of sunlight
    Was woven in here and there.

The shadows grew longer and
    longer,
    The evening wind passed by,
And the purple splendor of
    sunset
    Was flooding the western sky.

But I could not leave my spin-
    ning,
    For so fair my dream had
      grown,
I heeded not, hour by hour,
    How the silent day had flown.

At last the gray shadows fell
    round me,
    And the night came dark and
      chill,
And I rose and ran down the
    valley,
    And left it all on the hill.

I went up the hill this morning
    To the place where my spin-
      ning lay,—
There was nothing but glistening
    dew-drops
    Remained of my dream to-day.

THE PRESENT.

Do not crouch to-day, and wor-
ship
  The old Past, whose life is
  fled ;
Hush your voice to tender rever-
ence ;
  Crowned he lies, but cold and
  dead :
For the Present reigns our mon-
arch,
  With an added weight of
  hours ;
Honor her, for she is mighty!
  Honor her, for she is ours !

See the shadows of his heroes
  Girt around her cloudy
  throne ;
Every day the ranks are strength-
ened
  By great hearts to him un-
  known ;
Noble things the great Past
promised,
  Holy dreams, both strange and
  new ;
But the Present shall fulfil them,
  What he promised she shall do.

She inherits all his treasures,
  She is heir to all his fame,
And the light that lightens round
  her
  Is the lustre of his name ;
She is wise with all his wisdom,
  Living on his grave she stands,
On her brow she bears his laurels,
  And his harvest in her hands.

Coward, can she reign and con-
quer
  If we thus her glory dim ?
Let us fight for her as nobly
  As our fathers fought for him.
God, who crowns the dying ages,
  Bids her rule, and us obey, —
Bids us cast our lives before her,
  Bids us serve the great To-day.

CHANGES.

Mourn, O rejoicing heart !
  The hours are flying ;
Each one some treasure takes,
Each one some blossom breaks,
  And leaves it dying ;
The chill dark night draws near,
  Thy sun will soon depart,
  And leave thee sighing ;
Then mourn, rejoicing heart,
  The hours are flying !

Rejoice, O grieving heart !
  The hours fly fast ;
With each some sorrow dies,
With each some shadow flies,
  Until at last
The red dawn in the east
  Bids weary night depart,
  And pain is past.
Rejoice then, grieving heart,
  The hours fly fast !

STRIVE, WAIT, AND PRAY.

Strive ; yet I do not promise
  The prize you dream of to-day

Will not fade when you think
  to grasp it,
And melt in your hand away;
But another and holier treasure,
  You would now perchance dis-
    dain,
Will come when your toil is over,
  And pay you for all your pain.

Wait; yet I do not tell you
  The hour you long for now
Will not come with its radiance
  vanished,
  And a shadow upon its brow;
Yet far through the misty future,
  With a crown of starry light,
An hour of joy you know not
  Is winging her silent flight.

Pray; though the gift you ask for
  May never comfort your fears,
May never repay your pleading,
  Yet pray, and with hopeful
    tears;
An answer, not that you long for,
  But diviner, will come one
    day;
Your eyes are too dim to see it,
  Yet strive, and wait, and pray.

A LAMENT FOR THE SUMMER.

Moan, O ye Autumn Winds!
  Summer has fled,
The flowers have closed their
  tender leaves and die;

  The lily's gracious head
All low must lie,
  Because the gentle Summer
    now is dead.

  Grieve, O ye Autumn Winds!
    Summer lies low;
The rose's trembling leaves will
    soon be shed,
  For she that loved her so,
Alas! is dead,
  And one by one her loving
    children go.

  Wail, O ye Autumn Winds!
    She lives no more,
The gentle Summer, with her
    balmy breath,
  Still sweeter than before
When nearer death,
  And brighter every day the
    smile she wore!

  Mourn, mourn, O Autumn
    Winds,
    Lament and mourn;
How many half-blown buds must
    close and die;
  Hopes with the Summer born
All faded lie,
  And leave us desolate and
    Earth forlorn!

THE UNKNOWN GRAVE.

No name to bid us know
  Who rests below,
No word of death or birth,

Only the grass's wave,
Over a mound of earth,
Over a nameless grave.

Did this poor wandering heart
In pain depart?
Longing, but all too late,
For the calm home again,
Where patient watchers wait,
And still will wait in vain.

Did mourners come in scorn,
And thus forlorn
Leave him, with grief and shame,
To silence and decay,
And hide the tarnished name
Of the unconscious clay?

It may be from his side
His loved ones died,
And, last of some bright band,
(Together now once more,)
He sought his home, the land
Where they had gone before.

No matter, — limes have made
As cool a shade,
And lingering breezes pass
As tenderly and slow,
As if beneath the grass
A monarch slept below.

No grief, though loud and deep,
Could stir that sleep;
And earth and heaven tell
Of rest that shall not cease,
Where the cold world's farewell
Fades into endless peace.

GIVE ME THY HEART.

WITH echoing steps the wor-
shippers
Departed one by one;
The organ's pealing voice was
stilled,
The vesper hymn was done;
The shadows fell from roof and
arch,
Dim was the incensed air,
One lamp alone, with trembling
ray,
Told of the Presence there!

In the dark church she knelt
alone;
Her tears were falling fast;
" Help, Lord," she cried, " the
shades of death
Upon my soul are cast!
Have I not shunned the path of
sin,
And chosen the better part?" —
What voice came through the
sacred air? —
" *My child, give me thy Heart!* "

" Have I not laid before Thy
shrine
My wealth, O Lord?" she
cried;
" Have I kept aught of gems or
gold,
To minister to pride?
Have I not bade youth's joys retire,
And vain delights depart?" —
But sad and tender was the
voice, —
" *My child give me thy Heart!* "

" Have I not, Lord, gone day by
   day
   Where   Thy   poor   children
   dwell ;
And carried help, and gold, and
   food ?
O Lord, Thou knowest it well !
From many a house, from many
   a soul,
   My hand bids care depart " : —
More sad, more tender was the
   voice, —
   " My child, give me thy Heart !"

" Have I not worn my strength
   away
   With fast and penance sore ?
Have I not watched and wept ?"
   she cried ;
   " Did Thy dear Saints do
   more ?
Have I not gained Thy grace,
   O Lord,
   And   won   in   Heaven   my
   part ? " —
It echoed louder in her soul, —
   " My child, give me thy Heart !

" For I have loved thee with a
   love
 . No mortal heart can show ;
A love so deep, my Saints in
   heaven
   Its depths can never know :
When pierced and wounded on
   the Cross,
   Man's   sin   and   doom   were
   mine,
I loved thee with undying love,
   Immortal and divine !

" I loved thee ere the skies were
   spread ;
   My soul bears all thy pains ;
To gain thy love my sacred
   Heart
   In earthly shrines remains :
Vain are thy offerings, vain thy
   sighs,
   Without one gift divine ;
Give it, my child, thy Heart to
   me,
   And it shall rest in mine !' "

In awe she listened, and the
   shade
   Passed from her soul away ;
In low and trembling voice she
   cried, —
   " Lord, help me to obey !
Break Thou the chains of earth,
   O Lord,
   That bind and hold my heart ;
Let it be Thine, and Thine
   alone,
   Let none with Thee have part.

" Send down, O Lord, Thy sa-
   cred fire !
   Consume and cleanse the sin
That lingers still within its
   depths :
   Let heavenly love begin.
That sacred flame Thy Saints
   have known,
   Kindle, O Lord, in me,
Thou above all the rest forever,
   And all the rest in Thee."

The blessing fell upon her soul ;
   Her angel by her side

Knew that the hour of peace was
  come ;
Her soul was purified :
The shadows fell from roof and
  arch,
Dim was the incensed air, —
But Peace went with her as she
  left
The sacred Presence there !

———

THE WAYSIDE INN.

A LITTLE past the village
  The Inn stood, low and white ;
Green shady trees behind it,
  And an orchard on the right ;
Where over the green paling
  The red-cheeked apples hung,
As if to watch how wearily
  The sign-board creaked and
  swung.

The heavy-laden branches, ˙
  Over the road hung low,
Reflected fruit or blossom
  From the wayside well below ;
Where children, drawing water,
  Looked up and paused to see,
Amid the apple-branches,
  A purple Judas-Tree.

The road stretched winding on-
  ward
  For many a weary mile, —
So dusty, foot-sore wanderers
  Would pause and rest awhile ;
And panting horses halted,
  And travellers loved to tell

The quiet of the wayside inn,
  The orchard, and the well.

Here Maurice dwelt ; and often
  The sunburnt boy would stand
Gazing upon the distance,
  And shading with his hand
His eyes, while watching vainly
  For travellers, who might need
His aid to loose the bridle,
  And tend the weary steed.

And once (the boy remembered
  That morning many a day, —
The dew lay on the hawthorn,
  The bird sang on the spray)
A train of horsemen, nobler
  Than he had seen before,
Up from the distance galloped,
  And halted at the door.

Upon a milk-white pony,
  Fit for a faery queen,
Was the loveliest little damsel
  His eyes had ever seen :
A serving-man was holding
  The leading rein, to guide
The pony and its mistress,
  Who cantered by his side.

Her sunny ringlets round her
  A golden cloud had made,
While her large hat was keeping
  Her calm blue eyes in shade ;
One hand held fast the silken
  reins
  To keep her steed in check,
The other pulled his tangled
  mane,
  Or stroked his glossy neck.

And as the boy brought water,
  And loosed the rein, he heard
The sweetest voice that thanked him
  In one low gentle word ;
She turned her blue eyes from him,
  Looked up, and smiled to see
The hanging purple blossoms
  Upon the Judas-Tree ;

And showed it with a gesture,
  Half pleading, half command,
Till he broke the fairest blossom,
  And laid it in her hand ;
And she tied it to her saddle
  With a ribbon from her hair,
While her happy laugh rang gayly,
  Like silver on the air.

But the champing steeds were rested, —
  The horsemen now spurred on,
And down the dusty highway
  They vanished and were gone.
Years passed, and many a traveller
  Paused at the old inn-door,
But the little milk-white pony
  And the child returned no more.

Years passed, the apple-branches
  A deeper shadow shed ;
And many a time the Judas-Tree,
  Blossom and leaf, lay dead ;
When on the loitering western breeze
  Came the bells' merry sound,

And flowery arches rose, and flags
  And banners waved around.

Maurice stood there expectant :
  The bridal train would stay
Some moments at the inn-door,
  The eager watchers say ;
They come, — the cloud of dust draws near, —
  'Mid all the state and pride,
He only sees the golden hair
  And blue eyes of the bride.

The same, yet, ah, still fairer ;
  He knew the face once more
That bent above the pony's neck
  Years past at that inn-door :
Her shy and smiling eyes looked round,
  Unconscious of the place,
Unconscious of the eager gaze
  He fixed upon her face.

He plucked a blossom from the tree, —
  The Judas-Tree, — and cast
Its purple fragrance towards the Bride,
  A message from the Past.
The signal came, the horses plunged, —
  Once more she smiled around :
The purple blossom in the dust
  Lay trampled on the ground.

Again the slow years fleeted,
  Their passage only known
By the height the Passion-flower
  Around the porch had grown ;

And many a passing traveller
  Paused at the old inn-door,
But the bride, so fair and bloom-
    ing,
  The bride returned no more.

One winter morning, Maurice,
  Watching the branches bare,
Rustling and waving dimly
  In the gray and misty air,
Saw blazoned on a carriage
  Once more the well-known
    shield,
The stars and azure fleurs-de-lis
  Upon a silver field.

He looked — was that pale wo-
    man,
  So grave, so worn, so sad,
The child, once young and smiling,
  The bride, once fair and glad?
What grief had dimmed that
    glory,
  And brought that dark eclipse
Upon her blue eyes' radiance,
  And paled those trembling lips?

What memory of past sorrow,
  What stab of present pain,
Brought that deep look of an-
    guish,
  That watched the dismal rain,
That watched (with the absent
    spirit
  That looks, yet does not see)
The dead and leafless branches
  Upon the Judas-Tree?

The slow dark months crept on-
    ward
  Upon their icy way,

Till April broke in showers,
  And Spring smiled forth in
    May;
Upon the apple-blossoms
  The sun shone bright again,
When slowly up the highway
  Came a long funeral train.

The bells tolled slowly, sadly,
  For a noble spirit fled;
Slowly, in pomp and honor,
  They bore the quiet dead.
Upon a black-plumed charger
  One rode, who held a shield,
Where stars and azure fleurs-de-
    lis
  Shone on a silver field.

'Mid all that homage given
  To a fluttering heart at rest,
Perhaps an honest sorrow
  Dwelt only in one breast.
One by the inn-door standing
  Watched with fast-dropping
    tears
The long procession passing,
  And thought of bygone years.

The boyish, silent homage
  To child and bride unknown,
The pitying, tender sorrow
  Kept in his heart alone,
Now laid upon the coffin
  With a purple flower, might
    be
Told to the cold, dead sleep
    er; —
  The rest could only see
A fragrant purple blossom,
  Plucked from a Judas-Tree.

VOICES OF THE PAST.

You wonder that my tears should
    flow
  In listening to that simple
    strain;
That those unskilful sounds
  should fill
My soul with joy and pain:
How can you tell what thoughts
    it stirs
  Within my heart again?

You wonder why that common
    phrase,
  So all unmeaning to your ear,
Should stay me in my merriest
    mood,
  And thrill my soul to hear:
How can you tell what ancient
    charm
  Has made me hold it dear?

You marvel that I turn away
  From all those flowers so fair
    and bright,
And gaze at this poor herb, till
    tears
  Arise and dim my sight:
You cannot tell how every leaf
  Breathes of a past delight.

You smile to see me turn and
    speak
  With one whose converse you
    despise;
You do not see the dreams of old
  That with his voice arise:
How can you tell what links have
    made
  Him sacred in my eyes?

O, these are Voices of the Past,
  Links of a broken chain,
Wings that can bear me back to
    Times
  Which cannot come again;
Yet God forbid that I should lose
  The echoes that remain!

THE DARK SIDE.

Thou hast done well, perhaps,
  To lift the bright disguise,
And lay the bitter truth
  Before our shrinking eyes;
When evil crawls below
  What seems so pure and fair,
Thine eyes are keen and true
  To find the serpent there:
And yet—I turn away;
  Thy task is not divine,—
The evil angels look
  On earth with eyes like thine.

Thou hast done well, perhaps,
  To show how closely wound
Dark threads of sin and self
  With our best deeds are found,
How great and noble hearts,
  Striving for lofty aims,
Have still some earthly chord
  A meaner spirit claims;
And yet—although thy task
  Is well and fairly done—
Methinks for such as thou
  There is a holier one.

Shadows there are, who dwell
  Among us, yet apart,

Deaf to the claim of God,
  Or kindly human heart;
Voices of earth and heaven
  Call, but they turn away,
And Love, through such black
    night
  Can see no hope of day;
And yet — our eyes are dim,
  And thine are keener far:
Then gaze till thou canst see
  The glimmer of some star.

The black stream flows along
  Whose waters we despise, —
Show us reflected there
  Some fragment of the skies;
'Neath tangled thorns and briers,
  (The task is fit for thee,)
Seek for the hidden flowers,
  We are too blind to see;
Then will I thy great gift
  A crown and blessing call;
Angels look thus on men,
  And God sees good in all!

A FIRST SORROW.

ARISE! this day shall shine,
  Forevermore,
To thee a star divine,
  On Time's dark shore.

Till now thy soul has been
  All glad and gay:
Bid it awake and look
  At grief to-day!

No shade has come between
  Thee and the sun;

Like some long childish dream
  Thy life has run:

But now the stream has reached
  A dark, deep sea,
And Sorrow, dim and crowned,
  Is waiting thee.

Each of God's soldiers bears
  A sword divine:
Stretch out thy trembling hands
  To-day for thine!

To each anointed Priest
  God's summons came:
O Soul, he speaks to-day,
  And calls thy name.

Then, with slow reverent step,
  And beating heart,
From out thy joyous days
  Thou must depart.

And, leaving all behind,
  Come forth alone,
To join the chosen band
  Around the throne.

Raise up thine eyes — be strong,
  Nor cast away
The crown that God has given
  Thy soul to-day!

MURMURS.

WHY wilt thou make bright
    music
  Give forth a sound of pain?
Why wilt thou weave fair flowers
  Into a weary chain?

Why turn each cool gray shadow
  Into a world of fears?
Why say the winds are wailing?
  Why call the dew-drops tears?

The voices of happy nature,
  And the Heaven's sunny
    gleam,
Reprove thy sick heart's fancies,
  Upbraid thy foolish dream.

Listen, and I will tell thee
  The song Creation sings,
From the humming of bees in
  the heather,
To the flutter of angels' wings.

An echo rings forever,
  The sound can never cease;
It speaks to God of glory,
  It speaks to Earth of peace.

Not alone did angels sing it
  To the poor shepherds' ear;
But the spheréd Heavens chant it,
  While listening ages hear.

Above thy peevish wailing
  Rises that holy song;
Above Earth's foolish clamor,
  Above the voice of wrong.

No creature of God 's too lowly
  To murmur peace and praise:
When the starry nights grow
  silent,
  Then speak the sunny days.

So leave thy sick heart's fancies,
  And lend thy little voice
To the silver song of glory
  That bids the world rejoice.

GIVE.

See the rivers flowing
  Downwards to the sea,
Pouring all their treasures
  Bountiful and free:
Yet to help their giving
  Hidden springs arise;
Or, if need be, showers
  Feed them from the skies\

Watch the princely flowers
  Their rich fragrance spread,
Load the air with perfumes,
  From their beauty shed:
Yet their lavish spending
  Leaves them not in dearth,
With fresh life replenished
  By their mother earth!

Give thy heart's best treasures, —
  From fair Nature learn;
Give thy love — and ask not,
  Wait not a return!
And the more thou spendest
  From thy little store,
With a double bounty,
  God will give thee more.

———

MY JOURNAL.

It is a dreary evening;
  The shadows rise and fall:
With   strange   and   ghostly
    changes,
  They flicker on the wall.

Make the charred logs burn
  brighter;
I will show you, by their blaze,

The half-forgotten record
 Of bygone things and days.

Bring here the ancient volume;
 The clasp is old and worn,
The gold is dim and tarnished,
 And the faded leaves are torn.

The dust has gathered on it, —
 There are so few who care
To read what Time has written
 Of joy and sorrow there.

Look at the first fair pages;
 Yes, I remember all:
The joys now seem so trivial,
 The griefs so poor and small.

Let us read the dreams of glory
 That childish fancy made;
Turn to the next few pages,
 And see how soon they fade.

Here, where still waiting, dream-
  ing,
 For some ideal Life,
The young heart all unconscious
 Had entered on the strife.

See how this page is blotted:
 What, could those tears be
  mine?
How coolly I can read you
 Each blurred and trembling
  line!

Now I can reason calmly,
 And, looking back again,
Can see divinest meaning
 Threading each separate pain.

Here strong resolve — how bro-
  ken;
 Rash hope, and foolish fear,
And prayers, which God in pity
 Refused to grant or hear.

Nay, I will turn the pages
 To where the tale is told
Of how a dawn diviner
 Flushed the dark clouds with
  gold.

And see, that light has gilded
 The story, — nor shall set;
And, though in mist and shadow,
 You know I see it yet.

Here — well, it does not matter,
 I promised to read all;
I know not why I falter,
 Or why my tears should fall;

You see each grief is noted;
 Yet it was better so —
I can rejoice to-day — the pain
 Was over, long ago.

I read — my voice is failing,
 But you can understand
How the heart beat that guided
 This weak and trembling hand.

Pass over that long struggle,
 Read where the comfort came,
Where the first time is written
 Within the book your name.

Again it comes, and oftener,
 Linked, as it now must be,
With all the joy or sorrow
 That Life may bring to me.

So all the rest — you know it :
　Now shut the clasp again,
And put aside the record
　Of bygone hours of pain.

The dust shall gather on it,
　I will not read it more :
Give me your hand — what was it
　We were talking of before ?

I know not why — but tell me
　Of something gay and bright.
It is strange — my heart is heavy,
　And my eyes are dim to-night.

―――――

A CHAIN.

THE bond that links our souls
　together ;
Will it last through stormy
　weather ?
Will it moulder and decay
As the long hours pass away ?
Will it stretch if Fate divide us,
When dark and weary hours
　have tried us ?
O, if it look too poor and slight,
Let us break the links to-night !

It was not forged by mortal
　hands,
Or clasped with golden bars and
　bands ;
Save thine and mine, no other
　eyes
The slender link can recognize :
In the bright light it seems to
　fade —

And it is hidden in the shade ;
While Heaven nor Earth have
　never heard,
Or solemn vow, or plighted word.

Yet what no mortal hand could
　make,
No mortal power can ever break ;
What words or vows could never
　do,
No words or vows can make un-
　true ;
And if to other hearts unknown
The dearer and the more our own,
Because too sacred and divine
For other eyes, save thine and
　mine.

And see, though slender, it is
　made
Of Love and Trust, and can they
　fade ?
While, if **too** slight it seem, to
　bear
The breathings of the summer
　air,
We know that it could bear the
　weight
Of a most heavy heart of late,
And as each day and hour flew
The stronger for its burden grew.

And, too, we know and feel again
It has been sanctified by pain,
For what God deigns to try with
　sorrow
He means not to decay to-mor-
　row ;
But through that fiery trial last
When earthly ties and bonds are
　past ;

What slighter things dare not
  endure
Will make our Love more safe
  and pure.

Love shall be purified by Pain,
And Pain be soothed by Love
  again :
So let us now take heart and go
Cheerfully on, through joy and
  woe ;
No change the summer sun can
  bring,
Or the inconstant skies of spring,
Or the bleak winter's stormy
  weather,
For we shall meet them, Love,
  together!

THE PILGRIMS.

THE way is long and dreary,
The path is bleak and bare ;
Our feet are worn and weary,
But we will not despair.
More heavy was Thy burden,
More desolate Thy way ; —
O Lamb of God who takest
The sin of the world away,
  Have mercy on us.

The snows lie thick around us
In the dark and gloomy night ;
And the tempest wails above us,
And the stars have hid their
  light ;
But blacker was the darkness
Round Calvary's Cross that
  day ; —

O Lamb of God who takest
The sin of the world away,
  Have mercy on us.

Our hearts are faint with sorrow,
Heavy and hard to bear ;
For we dread the bitter morrow,
But we will not despair :
Thou knowest all our anguish,
And Thou wilt bid it cease, —
O Lamb of God who takest
The sin of the world away,
  Give us Thy Peace!

INCOMPLETENESS.

NOTHING resting in its own
  completeness
Can have worth or beauty : but
  alone
Because it leads and tends to
  further sweetness,
Fuller, higher, deeper than its
  own.

Spring's real glory dwells not
  in the meaning,
Gracious though it be, of her
  blue hours ;
But is hidden in her tender leaning
To the Summer's richer wealth
  of flowers.

Dawn is fair, because the mists
  fade slowly
Into Day, which floods the world
  with light ;

Twilight's mystery is so sweet
and holy
Just because it ends in starry
Night.

Childhood's smiles unconscious
graces borrow
From Strife, that in a far-off future lies ;
And angel glances (veiled now
by Life's sorrow)
Draw our hearts to some belovéd
eyes.

Life is only bright when it pro-
ceedeth
Towards a truer, deeper Life
above ;
Human Love is sweetest when it
leadeth
To a more divine and perfect
Love.

Learn the mystery of Progression
duly :
Do not call each glorious change,
Decay ;
But know we only hold our
treasures truly,
When it seems as if they passed
away.

Nor dare to blame God's gifts
for incompleteness ;
In that want their beauty lies :
they roll
Towards some infinite depth of
love and sweetness,
Bearing onward man's reluctant
soul.

A LEGEND OF BREGENZ.

GIRT round with rugged moun-
tains
The fair Lake Constance lies ;
In her blue heart reflected
Shine back the starry skies ;
And, watching each white cloud
let
Float silently and slow,
You think a piece of Heaven
Lies on our earth below !

Midnight is there : and Silence,
Enthroned in Heaven, looks
down
Upon her own calm mirror,
Upon a sleeping town :
For Bregenz, that quaint city
Upon the Tyrol shore,
Has stood above Lake Constance
A thousand years and more.

Her battlements and towers,
From off their rocky steep,
Have cast their trembling shadow
For ages on the deep :
Mountain, and lake, and valley,
A sacred legend know,
Of how the town was saved, one
night,
Three hundred years ago.

Far from her home and kindred.
A Tyrol maid had fled,
To serve in the Swiss valleys,
And toil for daily bread ;
And every year that fleeted
So silently and fast,
Seemed to bear farther from her
The memory of the Past.

She served kind, gentle masters,
Nor asked for rest or change;
Her friends seemed no more new
ones,
Their speech seemed no more
strange;
And when she led her cattle
To pasture every day,
She ceased to look and wonder
On which side Bregenz lay.

She spoke no more of Bregenz,
With longing and with tears;
Her Tyrol home seemed faded
In a deep mist of years;
She heeded not the rumors
Of Austrian war and strife;
Each day she rose, contented,
To the calm toils of life.

Yet, when her master's children
Would clustering round her
stand,
She sang them ancient ballads
Of her own native land;
And when at morn and evening
She knelt before God's throne,
The accents of her childhood
Rose to her lips alone.

And so she dwelt: the valley
More peaceful year by year;
When suddenly strange portents
Of some great deed seemed
near.
The golden corn was bending
Upon its fragile stock,
While farmers, heedless of their
fields,
Paced up and down in talk.

The men seemed stern and al-
tered,
With looks cast on the ground;
With anxious faces, one by one,
The women gathered round;
All talk of flax, or spinning,
Or work, was put away;
The very children seemed afraid
To go alone to play.

One day, out in the meadow
With strangers from the town,
Some secret plan discussing,
The men walked up and down.
Yet now and then seemed watch-
ing
A strange uncertain gleam,
That looked like lances 'mid the
trees,
That stood below the stream.

At eve they all assembled,
Then care and doubt were fled;
With jovial laugh they feasted;
The hoard was nobly spread.
The elder of the village
Rose up, his glass in hand,
And cried, " We drink the down-
fall
Of an accursed land !

" The night is growing darker,
Ere one more day is flown,
Bregenz, our foemen's strong-
hold,
Bregenz shall be our own ! "
The women shrank in terror,
(Yet Pride, too, had her part,)
But one poor Tyrol maiden
Felt death within her heart.

Before her stood fair Bregenz ;
　Once more her towers arose ;
What were the friends beside her ?
　Only her country's foes !
The faces of her kinsfolk,
　The days of childhood flown,
The echoes of her mountains,
　Reclaimed her as their own !

Nothing she heard around her,
　(Though shouts rang forth
　　again,)
Gone were the green Swiss val-
　leys,
The pasture, and the plain ;
Before her eyes one vision,
　And in her heart one cry,
That said, " Go forth, save Bre-
　genz,
　And then, if need be, die ! "

With trembling haste and breath-
　less,
　With noiseless step, she sped ;
Horses and weary cattle
　Were standing in the shed ;
She loosed the strong, white
　charger,
　That fed from out her hand,
She mounted, and she turned
　his head
　Towards her native land.

Out — out into the darkness —
　Faster, and still more fast ;
The smooth grass flies behind her,
　The chestnut wood is past ;
She looks up ; clouds are heavy :
　Why is her steed so slow ? —
Scarcely the wind beside them
　Can pass them as they go.

" Faster ! " she cries, " O fast-
　er ! "
　Eleven the church-bells chime :
" O God," she cries, help Bre-
　genz,
　And bring me there in time ! "
But louder than bells' ringing,
　Or lowing of the kine,
Grows nearer in the midnight
　The rushing of the Rhine.

Shall not the roaring waters
　Their headlong gallop check ?
The steed draws back in terror,
　She leans upon his neck
To watch the flowing darkness ;
　The bank is high and steep ;
One pause — he staggers for-
　ward,
　And plunges in the deep.

She strives to pierce the blackness,
　And looser throws the rein ;
Her steed must breast the waters
　That dash above his mane.
How gallantly, how nobly,
　He struggles through the foam,
And see — in the far distance
　Shine out the lights of home !

Up the steep banks he bears her,
　And now, they rush again
Towards the heights of Bregenz
　That tower above the plain.
They reach the gate of Bregenz,
　Just as the midnight rings,
And out comes serf and soldier
　To meet the news she brings.

Bregenz is saved ! Ere daylight
　Her battlements are manned ;

Defiance greets the army
  That marches on the land.
And if to deeds heroic
  Should endless fame be paid,
Bregenz does well to honor
  The noble Tyrol maid.

Three hundred years are van-
    ished,
  And yet upon the hill
An old stone gateway rises,
  To do her honor still.
And there, when Bregenz women
  Sit spinning in the shade,
They see in quaint old carving
  The Charger and the Maid.

And when, to guard old Bregenz,
  By gateway, street, and tower,
The warder paces all night long
  And calls each passing hour;
"Nine," "ten," "eleven," he
    cries aloud,
  And then (O crown of Fame !)
When midnight pauses in the
    skies,
  He calls the maiden's name !

FAREWELL.

Farewell, O dream of mine !
  I dare not stay ;
The hour is come, and time
  Will not delay :
Pleasant and dear to me
  Wilt thou remain ;
No future hour
  Brings thee again.

She stands, the Future dim,
  And draws me on,
And shows me dearer joys, —
  But thou art gone !
Treasures and Hopes more fair
  Bears she for me,
And yet I linger,
  O dream, with thee !

Other and brighter days
  Perhaps she brings ;
Deeper and holier songs
  Perchance she sings ;
But thou and I, fair time,
  We too must sever : —
O dream of mine,
  Farewell forever !

SOWING AND REAPING.

Sow with a generous hand ;
  Pause not for toil or pain ;
Weary not through the heat of
    summer,
  Weary not through the cold
    spring rain ;
But wait till the autumn comes
  For the sheaves of golden
    grain.

Scatter the seed, and fear not,
  A table will be spread ;
What matter if you are too weary
  To eat your hard - earned
    bread !
Sow, while the earth is broken,
  For the hungry must be fed.

Sow;—while the seeds are lying
  In the warm earth's bosom
      deep,
And your warm tears fall upon
      it, —
  They will stir in their quiet
      sleep;
And the green blades rise the
      quicker,
  Perchance, for the tears you
      weep.

Then sow; — for the hours are
      fleeting,
  And the seed must fall to-day;
And care not what hands shall
      reap it,
  Or if you shall have passed
      away
Before the waving cornfields
  Shall gladden the sunny day.

Sow; and look onward, upward,
  Where the starry light ap-
      pears, —
Where, in spite of the coward's
      doubting,
  Or your own heart's trembling
      fears,
You shall reap in joy the harvest
  You have sown to-day in tears.

THE STORM.

THE tempest rages wild and
      high,
The waves lift up their voice and
      cry

Fierce answers to the angry
      sky, —
            Miserere Domine.

Through the black night and
      driving rain
A ship is struggling, all in
      vain,
To live upon the stormy main ; —
            Miserere Domine.

The thunders roar, the light-
      nings glare,
Vain is it now to strive or dare ;
A cry goes up of great despair, —
            Miserere Domine.

The stormy voices of the main,
The moaning wind and pelting
      rain
Beat on the nursery window
      pane : —
            Miserere Domine.

Warm curtained was the little
      bed,
Soft pillowed was the little
      head ;
"The storm will wake the child,"
      they said : —
            Miserere Domine.

Cowering among his pillow
      white
He prays, his blue eyes dim with
      fright,
"Father, save those at sea to-
      night!" —
            Miserere Domine.

The morning shone all clear and
gay,
On a ship at anchor in the bay,
And on a little child at play, —
 Gloria tibi Domine!

WORDS.

Words are lighter than the
 cloud-foam
Of the restless ocean spray ;
Vainer than the trembling shad-
 ow
 That the next hour steals
 away.
By the fall of summer rain-drops
Is the air as deeply stirred ;
And the rose-leaf that we tread
 on
 Will outlive a word.

Yet, on the dull silence breaking
With a lightning flash, a Word,
Bearing endless desolation
 On its blighting wings, I
 heard :
Earth can forge no keener
 weapon,
Dealing surer death and pain,
And the cruel echo answered
 Through long years again.

I have known one word hang
 starlike
O'er a dreary waste of years,
And it only shone the brighter
 Looked at through a mist of
 tears ;

While a weary wanderer gath-
 ered
Hope and heart on Life's dark
 way,
By its faithful promise, shining
 Clearer day by day.

I have known a spirit, calmer
 Than the calmest lake, and
 clear
As the heavens that gazed upon
 it,
 With no wave of hope or fear ;
But a storm had swept across
 it,
 And its deepest depths were
 stirred,
(Never, never more to slumber,)
 Only by a word.

I have known a word more gentle
 Than the breath of summer
 air ;
In a listening heart it nestled,
 And it lived forever there.
Not the beating of its prison
 Stirred it ever, night or day ;
Only with the heart's last throb-
 bing
 Could it fade away.

Words are mighty, words are
 living :
Serpents with their venomous
 stings,
Or bright angels, crowding round
 us,
With heaven's light upon their
 wings :
Every word has its own spirit,

True or false, that never dies;
Every word man's lips have ut-
tered
Echoes in God's skies.

A LOVE TOKEN.

Do you grieve no costly offer-
ing
To the Lady you can make?
One there is, and gifts less worthy
Queens have stooped to take.

Take a Heart of virgin silver,
Fashion it with heavy blows,
Cast it into Love's hot furnace
When it fiercest glows.

With Pain's sharpest point trans-
fix it,
And then carve, in letters fair,
Tender dreams and quaint de-
vices,
Fancies sweet and rare.

Set within it Hope's blue sap-
phire,
Many-changing opal fears,
Blood-red ruby-stones of daring,
Mixed with pearly tears.

And when you have wrought and
labored
Till the gift is all complete,
You may humbly lay your offer-
ing
At the Lady's feet.

Should her mood perchance be
gracious,
With disdainful, smiling pride,
She will place it with the trinkets
Glittering at her side.

A TRYST WITH DEATH.

I AM footsore and very weary,
But I travel to meet a Friend:
The way is long and dreary,
But I know that it soon must
end.

He is travelling fast like the
whirlwind,
And though I creep slowly on
We are drawing nearer, nearer,
And the journey is almost done

Through the heat of many sum
mers,
Through many a springtime
rain,
Through long autumns and weary
winters,
I have hoped to meet him, in
vain.

I know that he will not fail me,
So I count every hour chime,
Every throb of my own heart's
beating,
That tells of the flight of Time,

On the day of my birth he
plighted
His kingly word to me : —

I have seen him in dreams so often,
That I know what his smile
must be.

have toiled through the sunny
woodland,
Through fields that basked in
the light;
And through the lone paths in
the forest
I crept in the dead of night.

I will not fear at his coming,
Although I must meet him
alone ;
He will look in my eyes so gently,
And take my hand in his own.

Like a dream all my toil will
vanish,
When I lay my head on his
breast :
But the journey is very weary,
And he only can give me rest !

FIDELIS.

You have taken back the promise
That you spoke so long ago ;
Taken back the heart you gave
me, —
I must even let it go.
Where Love once has breathed,
Pride dieth :
So I struggled, but in vain,
First to keep the links together,
Then to piece the broken chain.

But it might not be — so freely
All your friendship I restore,
And the heart that I had taken
As my own forevermore.
No shade of reproach shall touch
you,
Dread no more a claim from
me :
But I will not have you fancy
That I count myself as free.

I am bound by the old promise ;
What can break that golden
chain ?
Not even the words that you have
spoken,
Or the sharpness of my pain :
Do you think, because you fail
me
And draw back your hand to-
day,
That from out the heart I gave
you
My strong love can fade away ?

It will live. No eyes may see it ;
In my soul it will lie deep,
Hidden from all ; but I shall feel
it
Often stirring in its sleep.
So remember, that the friendship,
Which you now think poor
and vain,
Will endure in hope and patience,
Till you ask for it again.

Perhaps in some long twilight
hour,
Like those we have known of
old,

When past shadows gather round
    you,
And your present friends grow
    cold,
You may stretch your hands out
    towards me, —
    Ah! you will — I know not
    when —
I shall nurse my love and keep it
    Faithfully, for you, till then.

A SHADOW.

WHAT lack the valleys and
    mountains
That once were green and gay?
What lack the babbling foun-
    tains? ·
    Their voice is sad to-day.
      Only the sound of a voice,
      Tender and sweet and low,
      That made the earth rejoice,
      A year ago!

What lack the tender flowers?
    A shadow is on the sun:
What lack the merry hours,
    That I long that they were
    done?
      Only two smiling eyes,
      That told of joy and mirth;
      They are shining in the skies,
      I mourn on earth!

What lacks my heart, that makes
    it
So weary and full of pain,
That trembling Hope forsakes it,
    Never to come again?

Only another heart,
Tender and all mine own,
In the still grave it lies;
    I weep alone!

THE SAILOR BOY.

MY Life you ask of? why, you
    know
Full soon my little Life is told;
It has had no great joy or woe,
For I am only twelve years old.
Erelong I hope I shall have been
On my first voyage, and wonders
    seen.
Some princess I may help to free
From pirates on a far-off sea;
Or, on some desert isle be left,
Of friends and shipmates all bereft

    For the first time I venture
    forth
From our blue mountains of the
    north.
My kinsman kept the lodge that
    stood
Guarding the entrance near the
    wood,
By the stone gateway gray and
    old,
With quaint devices carved about,
And broken shields; while drag-
    ons bold
Glared on the common world
    without:
And the long trembling ivy spray
Half hid the centuries' decay.
In solitude and silence grand

The castle towered above the
  land :
The castle of the Earl, whose
  name
(Wrapped in old bloody legends)
  came
Down through the times when
  Truth and Right
Bent down to arméd Pride and
  Might.
He owned the country far and
  near ;
And, for some weeks in every
  year,
(When the brown leaves were
  falling fast
And the long, lingering autumn
  past,)
He would come down to hunt
  the deer,
With hound and horse in splen-
  did pride.
The story lasts the live-long year,
The peasant's winter evening
  fills,
When he is gone and they abide
In the lone quiet of their hills.

  I longed, too, for the happy
  night,
When, all with torches flaring
  bright,
The crowding villagers would
  stand,
A patient, eager, waiting band,
Until the signal ran like flame,
" They come ! " and, slackening
  speed, they came.
Outriders first, in pomp and
  state,

Pranced on their horses through
  the gate ;
Then the four steeds as black as
  night,
All decked with trappings blue
  and white,
Drew through the crowd that
  opened wide,
The Earl and Countess side by
  side.
The stern grave Earl, with for
  mal smile
And glistening eyes and stately
  pride,
Could ne'er my childish gaze be-
  guile
From the fair presence by his
  side.
The lady's soft sad glance, her
  eyes,
(Like stars that shone in sum-
  mer skies,)
Her pure white face so calmly bent,
With gentle greetings round her
  sent ;
Her look, that always seemed to
  gaze
Where the blue past had closed
  again
Over some happy shipwrecked
  days,
With all their freight of love and
  pain :
She did not even seem to see
The little lord upon her knee.
And yet he was like angel fair,
With rosy cheeks and golden
  hair,
That fell on shoulders white as
  snow :

But the blue eyes that shone below
His clustering rings of auburn
　curls
Were not his mother's, but the
　Earl's.

I feared the Earl, so cold and
　grim,
I never dared be seen by him.
When through our gate he used
　to ride,
My kinsman Walter bade me
　hide;
He said he was so stern.
So, when the hunt came past
　our way,
I always hastened to obey,
Until I heard the bugles play
　The notes of their return.
But she, — my very heart-strings
　stir
Whene'er I speak or think of
　her, —
The whole wide world could
　never see
A noble lady such as she,
　So full of angel charity.

Strange things of her our
　neighbors told
In the long winter evenings cold,
Around the fire. They would
　draw near
And speak half-whispering, as in
　fear;
As if they thought the Earl
　could hear
　Their treason 'gainst his name.
They thought the story that his
　pride

Had stooped to wed a low-born
　bride,
　A stain upon his fame.
Some said 't was false; there
　could not be
Such blot on his nobility:
But others vowed that they had
　heard
The actual story word for word,
From one who well my lady
　knew,
And had declared the story true.

In a far village, little known
She dwelt — so ran the tale —
　alone.
A widowed bride, yet, oh! so
　bright,
Shone through the mist of grief
　her charms;
They said it was the loveliest
　sight —
She with her baby in her arms
The Earl, one summer morning,
　rode
By the sea-shore where she
　abode;
Again he came — that vision
　sweet
Drew him reluctant to her feet.
Fierce must the struggle in his
　heart
Have been, between his love and
　pride,
Until he chose that wondrous
　part,
To ask her to become his bride.
Yet, ere his noble name she bore,
He made her vow that nevermore
She would behold her child again,

But hide his name and hers from men.
The trembling promise duly spoken,
All links of the low past were broken ;
And she arose to take her stand
Amid the nobles of the land.
Then all would wonder — could it be
That one so lowly born as she,
Raised to such height of bliss, should seem
Still living in some weary dream?
'T is true she bore with calmest grace
The honors of her lofty place,
Yet never smiled, in peace or joy,
Not even to greet her princely boy.
She heard, with face of white despair,
The cannon thunder through the air,
That she had given the Earl an heir.
Nay, even more, (they whispered low,
As if they scarce durst fancy so,)
That, through her lofty wedded life,
No word, no tone, betrayed the wife.
Her look seemed ever in the past ;
Never to him it grew more sweet ;
The self-same weary glance she cast
Upon the greyhound at her feet,

As upon him, who bade her claim
The crowning honor of his name.

This gossip, if old Walter heard,
He checked it with a scornful word :
I never durst such tales repeat ;
He was too serious and discreet
To speak of what his lord might do ;
Besides, he loved my lady too.
And many a time, I recollect,
They were together in the wood ;
He, with an air of grave respect,
And earnest look, uncovered stood.
And though their speech I never heard,
(Save now and then a louder word,)
I saw he spake as none but one
She loved and trusted durst have done ;
For oft I watched them in the shade
That the close forest branches made,
Till slanting golden sunbeams came
And smote the fir-trees into flame,
A radiant glory round her lit,
Then down her white robes seemed to flit,
Gilding the brown leaves on the ground,
And all the waving ferns around.

While by some gloomy pine she
leant
And he in earnest talk would
stand,
I saw the tear-drops, as she bent,
Fall on the flowers in her
hand. —
Strange as it seemed and seems
to be,
That one so sad, so cold as she,
Could love a little child like me,
Yet so it was. I never heard
Such tender words as she would
say,
And murmurs, sweeter than a
word,
Would breathe upon me as I lay.
While I, in smiling joy, would
rest,
For hours, my head upon her
breast.
Our neighbors said that none
could see
In me the common childish
charms,
(So grave and still I used to be,)
And yet she held me in her arms,
In a fond clasp, so close, so tight,
I often dream of it at night.
She bade me tell her all, — no
other
My childish thoughts e'er cared
to know :
For I — I never knew my moth-
er ;
I was an orphan long ago.
And I could all my fancies pour,
That gentle, loving face before.
She liked to hear me tell her
all ;

How that day I had climbed the
tree,
To make the largest fir-cones
fall ;
And how one day I hoped to be
A sailor on the deep blue sea, —
She loved to hear it all !

Then wondrous things she
used to tell,
Of the strange dreams that she
had known.
I used to love to hear them
well,
If only for her sweet low tone,
Sometimes so sad, although I
knew
That such things never could be
true.
One day she told me such a tale
It made me grow all cold and pale,
The fearful thing she told !
Of a poor woman mad and wild
Who coined the life-blood of her
child,
And, tempted by a fiend, had
sold
The heart out of her breast for
gold.
But when she saw me frightened
seem,
She smiled, and said it was a
dream.
When I look back and think of
her,
My very heart-strings seem to
stir ;
How kind, how fair she was, how
good,
I cannot tell you. If I could,

You, too, would love her.   The
  mere thought
Of her great love for me has
  brought
Tears in my eyes : though far
  away,
It seems as it were yesterday.
And just as when I look on high,
Through the blue silence of the
  sky,
Fresh stars shine out, and more
  and more,
Where I could see so few before ;
So, the more steadily I gaze
Upon those far-off misty days,
Fresh words, fresh tones, fresh
  memories start
Before my eyes and in my heart.
I can remember how one day
(Talking in silly childish way)
I said how happy I should be
If I were like her son, — as fair,
With just such bright blue eyes
  as he,
And such long locks of golden
  hair.
A strange smile on her pale face
  broke,
And in strange, solemn words
  she spoke :
  " My own, my darling one, —
  no, no !
I love you, far, far better so.
I would not change the look you
  bear,
Or one wave of your dark brown
  hair.
The mere glance of your sunny
  eyes,
Deep in my deepest soul I prize

Above that baby fair !
Not one of all the Earl's proud
  line
In beauty ever matched with
  thine ;
And, 't is by thy dark locks thou
  art
Bound even faster round 'my
  heart,
And made more wholly mine ! "
And then she paused, and weep-
  ing said,
" You are like one who now is
  dead, —
Who sleeps in a far-distant grave.
O, may God grant that you may
  be
As noble and as good as he,
As gentle and as brave ! "
Then in my childish way I cried,
" The one you tell me of who died,
Was he as noble as the Earl ? "
I see her red lips scornful curl,
I feel her hold my hand again,
So tightly, that I shrink in
  pain, —
I seem to hear her say,
" He whom I tell you of, who
  died,
He was so noble and so gay,
So generous and so brave,
That the proud Earl by his dear
  side
Would look a craven slave."
She paused ; then, with a quiv-
  ering sigh,
She laid her hand upon my
  brow :
' Live like him, darling, and so
  die.

Remember that he tells you now,
True peace, real honor, and con-
  tent,
In cheerful, pious toil abide;
That gold and splendor are but
  sent
To curse our vanity and pride."

One day some childish fever
  pain
Burnt in my veins and fired my
  brain.
Moaning, I turned from side to
  side;
And, sobbing in my bed, I cried,
Till night in calm and darkness
  crept
Around me, and at last I slept.
When suddenly I woke to see
The Lady bending over me.
The drops of cold November rain
Were falling from her long, damp
  hair;
Her anxious eyes were dim with
  pain;
Yet she looked wondrous fair.
Arrayed for some great feast she
  came,
With stones that shone and burnt
  like flame;
Wound round her neck, like some
  bright snake,
And set like stars within her hair,
They sparkled so, they seemed
  to make
A glory everywhere.
I felt her tears upon my face,
Her kisses on my eyes;
And a strange thought I could
  not trace

I felt within my heart arise;
And, half in feverish pain, I
  said:
"O if my mother were not
  dead!"
And Walter bade me sleep; but
  she
Said, "Is it not the same to thee
That *I* watch by thy bed?"
I answered her, "I love you,
  too;
But it can never be the same;
She was no Countess like to you,
Nor wore such sparkling stones
  of flame."
O the wild look of fear and
  dread!
The cry she gave of bitter woe!
I often wonder what I said
To make her moan and shudder
  so.
Through the long night she tend-
  ed me
With such sweet care and charity.
But I should weary you to tell
All that I know and love so well:
Yet one night more stands out
  alone
With a sad sweetness all its own.

The wind blew loud that drea-
  ry night:
Its wailing voice I well remem-
  ber;
The stars shone out so large and
  bright
Upon the frosty fir-boughs white,
That dreary night of cold Decem-
  ber.
I saw old Walter silent stand,

Watching the soft, white flakes
of snow
With looks I could not under-
stand,
Of strange perplexity and woe.
At last he turned and took my
hand,
And said the Countess just had
sent
To bid us come ; for she would
fain
See me once more, before she
went
Away — never to come again.
We came in silence through the
wood
(Our footfall was the only sound)
To where the great white castle
stood,
With darkness shadowing it
around.
Breathless, we trod with cautious
care
Up the great echoing marble
stair ;
Trembling, by Walter's hand I
held,
Scared by the splendors I be-
held :
Now thinking, "Should the Earl
appear ! "
Now looking up with giddy fear
To the dim, vaulted roof that
spread
Its gloomy arches overhead.
Long corridors we softly passed,
(My heart was beating loud and
fast,)
And reached the Lady's room at
last :

A strange, faint odor seemed to
weigh
Upon the dim and darkened air ;
One shaded lamp, with softened
ray,
Scarce showed the gloomy splen-
dor there.
The dull red brands were burn-
ing low,
And yet a fitful gleam of light
Would now and then, with sud-
den glow,
Start forth, then sink again in
night.
I gazed around, yet half in fear,
Till Walter told me to draw
near :
And in the strange and flicker-
ing light,
Towards the Lady's bed I crept ;
All folded round with snowy
white,
She lay ; (one would have said
she slept ;)
So still the look of that white face,
It seemed as it were carved in
stone,
I paused before I dared to place
Within her cold white hand my
own.
But, with a smile of sweet sur-
prise,
She turned to me her dreamy
eyes ;
And slowly, as if life were pain,
She drew me in her arms to lie:
She strove to speak, and strove
in vain ;
Each breath was like a long
drawn sigh.

The throbs that seemed to shake
her breast,
The trembling clasp, so loose
and weak,
At last grew calmer, and at rest;
And then she strove once more
to speak:
" My God, I thank thee, that my
pain
Of day by day, and year by year,
Has not been suffered all in vain,
And I may die while he is near.
I will not fear but that Thy
grace
Has swept away my sin and woe,
And sent this little angel face,
In my last hour, to tell me so."
(And here her voice grew faint
and low,)
" My child, where'er thy life may
go,
To know that thou art brave and
true,
Will pierce the highest heavens
through,
And even there my soul shall be
More joyful for this thought of
thee."
She folded her white hands, and
stayed;
All cold and silently she lay:
I knelt beside the bed, and
prayed
The prayer she used to make
me say.
I said it many times, and then
She did not move, but seemed
to be
In a deep sleep, nor stirred again.
No sound woke in the silent room,

Or broke the dim and solemn
gloom,
Save when the brands that burnt
so low,
With noisy, fitful gleam of light,
Would spread around a sudden
glow,
Then sink in silence and in
night.
How long I stood I do not know:
At last poor Walter came, and
said
(So sadly) that we now must
go,
And whispered, she we loved
was dead.
He bade me kiss her face once
more,
Then led me sobbing to the door.
I scarcely knew what dying
meant,
Yet a strange grief, before un-
known,
Weighed on my spirit as we
went
And left her lying all alone.

We went to the far North once
more,
To seek the well-remembered
home
Where my poor kinsman dwelt
before,
Whence now he was too old to
roam;
And there six happy years we
past,
Happy and peaceful till the last;
When poor old Walter died, and
he

Blessed me and said I now might
    be
A sailor on the deep blue sea.
And so I go ; and yet in spite
Of all the joys I long to know,
Though I look onward with de-
    light,
With something of regret I go ;
And young or old, on land or
    sea,
One guiding memory I shall
    take, —
Of what She prayed that I might
    be,
And what I will be for her
    sake !

A CROWN OF SORROW.

A SORROW, wet with early tears
    Yet bitter, had been long with
    me ;
I wearied of this weight of years,
    And would be free.

I tore my Sorrow from my heart,
    I cast it far away in scorn ;
Right joyful that we two could
    part,
        Yet most forlorn.

I sought (to take my Sorrow's
    place)
    Over the world for flower or
    gem ;
But she had had an ancient grace
    Unknown to them.

I took once more with strange
    delight
    My slighted Sorrow ; proudly
    now
I wear it, set with stars of light,
    Upon my brow.

THE   LESSON   OF   THE
            WAR.

1855.

THE feast is spread through
    England
    For rich and poor to-day ;
Greetings and laughter may be
    there,
    But thoughts are far away ;
Over the stormy ocean,
    Over the dreary track,
Where some are gone, whom
    England
    Will never welcome back.

Breathless she waits, and listens
    For every eastern breeze
That bears upon its bloody wings
    News from beyond the seas.
The leafless branches stirring
    Make many a watcher start ;
The distant tramp of steed may
    send
    A throb from heart to heart.

The rulers of the nation,
    The poor ones at their gate,
With the same eager wonder
    The same great news await.
The poor man's stay and comfort,
    The rich man's joy and pride,

Upon the bleak Crimean shore
   Are fighting side by side.

The bullet comes — and either
   A desolate hearth may see;
And God alone to-night knows
     where
   The vacant place may be!
The dread that stirs the peasant
   Thrills nobles' hearts with
     fear;
Yet above selfish sorrow
   Both hold their country dear.

The rich man who reposes
   In his ancestral shade,
The peasant at his ploughshare,
   The worker at his trade,
Each one his all has perilled,
   Each has the same great stake,
Each soul can but have patience,
   Each heart can only break!

Hushed is all party clamor;
   One thought in every heart,
One dread in every household,
   Has bid such strife depart.
England has called her children;
   Long silent — the word came
That lit the smouldering ashes
   Through all the land to flame.

O you who toil and suffer,
   You gladly heard the call;
But those you sometimes envy,
   Have they not given their all?
O you who rule the nation,
   Take now the toil-worn hand:
Brothers you are in sorrow,
   In duty to your land.

Learn but this noble lesson
   Ere Peace returns again,
And the life-blood of Old Eng-
     land
   Will not be shed in vain.

————

THE TWO SPIRITS.

1855.

Last night, when weary silence
   fell on all,
   And starless skies arose so dim
     and vast,
I heard the Spirit of the Present
   call
   Upon the sleeping Spirit of
     the Past.
Far off and near, I saw their
   radiance shine,
And listened while they spoke
   of deeds divine.

The Spirit of the Past.

My deeds are writ in iron;
   My glory stands alone;
A veil of shadowy honor
   Upon my tombs is thrown;
The great names of my heroes
   Like gems in history lie;
To live they deemed ignoble,
   Had they the chance to die!

The Spirit of the Present.

My children, too, are honored;
   Dear shall their memory be
To the proud lands that own
   them;
   Dearer than thine to thee;

For, though they hold that sa-
cred
Is God's great gift of life,
At the first call of duty
They rush into the strife!

The Spirt of the Past !

Then, with all valiant precepts
Woman's soft heart was
fraught ;
" Death, not dishonor," echoed
The war-cry she had taught.
Fearless and glad, those mothers,
At bloody deaths elate,
Cried out they bore their chil-
dren
Only for such a fate !

The Spirit of the Present.

Though such stern laws of honor
Are faded now away,
Yet many a mourning mother,
With nobler grief than they,
Bows down in sad submission :
The heroes of the fight
Learnt at her knee the lesson,
" For God and for the Right! "

The Spirit of the Past.

No voice there spake of sorrow :
They saw the noblest fall
With no repining murmur ;
Stern Fate was lord of all.
And when the loved ones per-
ished,
One cry alone arose,
Waking the startled echoes,
" Vengeance upon our foes ! "

The Spirit of the Present.

Grief dwells in France and Eng-
land
For many a noble son ;
Yet louder than the sorrow,
" Thy will, O God, be done ! "
From desolate homes is rising
One prayer, — " Let carnage
cease !
On friends and foes have mercy,
O Lord, and give us peace ! "

The Spirit of the Past.

Then, every hearth was honored
That sent its children forth,
To spread their country's glory,
And gain her south or north.
Then, little recked they numbers,
No band would ever fly,
But stern and resolute they stood
To conquer or to die.

The Spirit of the Present.

And now from France and Eng-
land
Their dearest and their best
Go forth to succor freedom,
To help the much oppressed;
Now, let the far-off Future
And Past bow down to-day,
Before the few young hearts that
hold
Whole armaments at bay.

The Spirit of the Past.

Then, each one strove for honor,
Each for a deathless name ;

Love, home, rest, joy, were
offered
  As sacrifice to Fame.
They longed that in far ages
  Their deeds might still be
told,
And distant times and nations
  Their names in honor hold.

The Spirit of the Present.

Though nursed by such old
legends,
  Our heroes of to-day
Go cheerfully to battle
  As children go to play;
They gaze with awe and won-
der
  On your great names of pride,
Unconscious that their own will
shine
  In glory side by side!

Day dawned; and as the Spirits
passed away,
Methought I saw, in the dim
morning gray,
The Past's bright diadem had
paled before
The starry crown the glorious
Present wore.

A LITTLE LONGER.

A LITTLE longer yet — a little
longer,
Shall violets bloom for thee, and
sweet birds sing;

And the lime-branches, where
soft winds are blowing,
Shall murmur the sweet promise
of the Spring!

A little longer yet — a little
longer,
Thou shalt behold the quiet of
the morn;
While tender grasses and awak-
ening flowers
Send up a golden mist to greet
the dawn!

A little longer yet — a little
longer,
The tenderness of twilight shall
be thine,
The rosy clouds that float o'er
dying daylight,
Nor fade till trembling stars begin to shine.

A little longer yet — a little
longer,
Shall starry night be beautiful
for thee;
And the cold moon shall look
through the blue silence,
Flooding her silver path upon the
sea.

A little longer yet — a little
longer,
Life shall be thine; life with its
power to will;
Life with its strength to bear, to
love, to conquer,
Bringing its thousand joys thy
heart to fill.

A little longer yet — a little
longer,
The voices thou hast loved shall
charm thine ear ;
And thy true heart, that now
beats quick to hear them,
A little longer yet shall hold them
dear.

A little longer yet — joy while
thou mayest ;
Love and rejoice ! for time has
naught in store :
And soon the darkness of the
grave shall bid thee
Love and rejoice and feel and
know no more.

———————

A little longer still — Patience,
Belovéd :
A little longer still, ere Heaven
unroll
The Glory, and the Brightness,
and the Wonder,
Eternal, and divine, that waits
thy Soul !

A little longer ere Life true, im-
mortal,
(Not this our shadowy Life,) will
be thine own ;
And thou shalt stand where
winged Archangels worship,
And trembling bow before the
Great White Throne.

A little longer still, and Heaven
awaits thee,
And fills thy spirit with a great
delight ;

Then our pale joys will seem a
dream forgotten,
Our Sun a darkness, and our
Day a Night.

A little longer, and thy Heart,
Belovéd,
Shall beat forever with a Love
divine ;
And joy so pure, so mighty, so
eternal,
No creature knows and lives, will
then be thine.

A little longer yet — and angel
voices
Shall ring in heavenly chant
upon thine ear ;
Angels and Saints await thee,
and God needs thee :
Belovéd, can we bid thee linger
here !

———————

GRIEF.

An ancient enemy have I,
And either he or I must die ;
For he never leaveth me,
Never gives my soul relief,
Never lets my sorrow cease,
Never gives my spirit peace, —
For mine enemy is Grief !
Pale he is, and sad and stern ;
And whene'er he cometh nigh,
Blue and dim the torches burn,
Pale and shrunk the roses turn ;
While my heart that he has pierced
Many a time with fiery lance,
Beats and trembles at his glance :

Clad in burning steel is he,
All my strength he can defy;
For he never leaveth me —
And one of us must die !

I have said, " Let ancient sages
Charm me from my thoughts of
    pain ! "
So I read their deepest pages,
And I strove to think — in vain !
Wisdom's cold, calm words I
    tried,
But he was seated by my side ; —
Learning I have won in vain ;
She cannot rid me of my pain.

When at last soft sleep comes
    o'er me,
A cold hand is on my heart;
Stern sad eyes are there before
    me ;
Not in dreams will he depart :
And when the same dreary vision
From my weary brain has fled,
Daylight brings the living phan-
    tom,
He is seated by my bed,
Bending o'er me all the while,
With his cruel, bitter smile,
Ever with me, ever nigh ; —
And either he or I must die !

Then I said, long time ago,
" I will flee to other climes,
I will leave mine ancient foe ! "
Though I wandered far and
    wide —
Still he followed at my side.

And I fled where the blue waters
Bathe the sunny isles of Greece ;

Where Thessalian mountains rise
Up against the purple skies ;
Where a haunting memory liv-
eth
In each wood and cave and rill ;
But no dream of gods could help
    me, —
He went with me still !

I have been where Nile's broad
    river
Flows upon the burning sand ;
Where the desert monster brood-
eth,
Where the Eastern palm-trees
    stand ;
I have been where pathless forests
Spread a black eternal shade ;
Where the lurking panther hiding
Glares from every tangled glade ;
But in vain I wandered wide,
He was always by my side !

Then I fled where snows eternal
Cold and dreary ever lie ;
Where the rosy lightnings gleam,
Flashing through the northern
    sky ;
Where the red sun turns again
Back upon his path of pain ; —
But a shadowy form was with
    me, —
I had fled in vain !

I have thought, " If I can gaze
Sternly on him he will fade,
For I know that he is nothing
But a dim ideal shade."
As I gazed at him the more,
He grew stronger than before !

Then I said, "Mine arm is strong,
I will make him turn and flee";
I have struggled with him long —
But that could never be!

Once I battled with him so
That I thought I laid him low;
Then in trembling joy I fled,
While again and still again
Murmuring to myself I said,
"Mine old enemy is dead!"
And I stood beneath the stars,
When a chill came on my frame,
And a fear I could not name,
And a sense of quick despair,
And, lo! — mine enemy was
    there!

Listen, for my soul is weary,
Weary of its endless woe;
I have called on one to aid me
Mightier even than my foe.
Strength and hope fail day by
    day;
I shall cheat him of his prey;
Some day soon, I know not when,
He will stab me through and
    through;
He has wounded me before,
But my heart can bear no
    more;
Pray that hour may come to
    me,
Only then shall I be free;
Death alone has strength to take
    me
Where my foe can never be;
Death, and Death alone, has
    power
To conquer mine old enemy!

THE TRIUMPH OF TIME.

THE tender, delicate Flow-
    ers,
I saw them fanned by a warm
    western wind,
Fed by soft summer show-
    ers,
Shielded by care, and yet, (O
    Fate unkind!)
Fade in a few short hours.

The gentle and the gay,
Rich in a glorious Future of
    bright deeds,
Rejoicing in the day,
Are met by Death, who sternly,
    sadly leads
Them far away.

And Hopes, perfumed and
    bright,
So lately shining, wet with dew
    and tears,
Trembling in morning light;
I saw them change to dark and
    anxious fears
Before the night!

I wept that all must die
"Yet Love," I cried, "doth live,
    and conquer death — "
And time passed by,
And breathed on Love, and
    killed it with his breath
Ere Death was nigh.

More bitter far than all
It was to know that Love could
    change and die! —

Hush! for the ages call,
"The Love of God lives through
    eternity,
    And conquers all!"

A PARTING.

WITHOUT one bitter feeling let
    us part, —
And for the years in which
    your love has shed
A radiance like a glory round
    my head,
I thank you, yes, I thank you
    from my heart.

I thank you for the cherished
    hope of years,
A starry future, dim and yet
    divine,
Winging its way from Heaven
    to be mine,
Laden with joy, and ignorant of
    tears.

I thank you, yes, I thank you
    even more
That my heart learnt not with-
    out love to live,
But gave and gave, and still
    had more to give,
From an abundant and exhaust-
    less store.

I thank you, and no grief is in
    these tears;
I thank you, not in bitterness
    but truth,

For the fair vision that adorned
    my youth
And glorified so many happy
    years.

Yet how much more I thank you
    that you tore
At length the veil your hand
    had woven away,
Which hid my idol was a thing
    of clay,
And false the altar I had knelt
    before.

I thank you that you taught me
    the stern truth,
(None other could have told
    and I believed,)
That vain had been my life,
    and I deceived,
And wasted all the purpose of
    my youth.

I thank you that your hand
    dashed down the shrine,
Wherein my idol worship I
    had paid ;
Else had I never known a soul
    was made
To serve and worship only the
    Divine.

I thank you that the heart I cast
    away
On such as you, though bro
    ken, bruised, and crushed.
Now that its fiery throbbing is
    all hushed,
Upon a worthier altar I can lay

I thank you for the lesson that
  such love
  Is a perverting of God's royal
  right,
  That it is made but for the
  Infinite,
And all too great to live except
  above.

I thank you for a terrible awak-
  ing,
  And if reproach seemed nidden
  in my pain,

And sorrow seemed to cry on
  your disdain,
Know that my blessing lay in
  your forsaking.

Farewell forever now: in peace
  we part;
  And should an idle vision of
  my tears
  Arise before your soul in after
  years,
Remember that I thank you from
  my heart!

THE GOLDEN GATE.

Dim shadows gather thickly round, and up the misty stair they climb,
The cloudy stair that upward leads to where the closéd portals shine,
Round which the kneeling spirits wait the opening of the Golden Gate.

And some with eager longing go, still pressing forward, hand in hand,
And some, with weary step and slow, look back where their Belovéd
  stand :
Yet up the misty stair they climb, led onward by the Angel Time.

As unseen hands roll back the doors, the light that floods the very air
Is but the shadow from within, of the great glory hidden there :
And morn and eve, and soon and late, the shadows pass within the gate.

As one by one they enter in, and the stern portals close once more,
The halo seems to linger round those kneeling closest to the door :
The joy that lightened from that place shines still upon the watcher's
  face.

The faint low echo that we hear of far-off music seems to fill
The silent air with love and fear, and the world's clamors all grow still,
Until the portals close again, and leave us toiling on in pain.

Complain not that the way is long: what road is weary that leads there?
But let the Angel take thy hand, and lead thee up the misty stair,
And then with beating heart await the opening of the Golden Gate

PHANTOMS.

Back, ye Phantoms of the Past;
  In your dreary caves remain :
What have I to do with memories
  Of a long-forgotten pain ?

For my Present is all peaceful,
  And my Future nobly planned :
Long ago Time's mighty billows
  Swept your footsteps from the
    sand.

Back into your caves; nor haunt
  me
  With your voices full of woe;
I have buried grief and sorrow
  In the depths of Long-ago.

See the glorious clouds of morning
  Roll away, and clear and
    bright
Shine the rays of cloudless daylight : —
    Wherefore will ye moan of
    night ?

Never shall my heart be burdened
  With its ancient woe and
    fears ;
I can drive them from my presence,
    I can check these foolish
    tears.

Back, ye Phantoms; leave, O
  leave me,
  To a new and happy lot;

Speak no more of things departed ;
  Leave me — for I know ye
  not.

Can it be that 'mid my gladness
  I must ever hear you wail,
Of the grief that wrung my
  spirit,
  And that made my cheek so
  pale ?

Joy is mine; but your sad
  voices
  Murmur ever in mine ear :
Vain is all the Future's promise,
  While the dreary Past is here.

Vain, O worse than vain, the
  Visions
  That my heart, my life, would
  fill,
If the Past's relentless phantoms
  Call upon me still !

———

✓ THANKFULNESS.

My God, I thank Thee who hast
  made
  The Earth so bright;
So full of splendor and of joy,
  Beauty and light;
So many glorious things are here,
  Noble and right !

I thank Thee, too, that Thou
  hast made
  Joy to abound;

So many gentle thoughts and deeds
  Circling us round,
That in the darkest spot of Earth
  Some love is found.

I thank Thee *more* that all our joy
  Is touched with pain ;
That shadows fall on brightest hours ;
  That thorns remain ;
So that Earth's bliss may be our guide,
  And not our chain.

For Thou who knowest, Lord, how soon
  Our weak heart clings,
Hast given us joys, tender and true,
  Yet all with wings,
So that we see, gleaming on high,
  Diviner things !

I thank Thee, Lord, that Thou hast kept
  The best in store ;
We have enough, yet not too much
  To long for more :
A yearning for a deeper peace,
  Not known before.

I thank Thee, Lord, that here our souls,
  Though amply blest,
Can never find, although they seek,
  A perfect rest, —
Nor ever shall, until they lean
  On Jesus' breast !

HOME-SICKNESS.

WHERE I am, the halls are gilded,
  Stored with pictures bright and rare ;
Strains of deep melodious music
  Float upon the perfumed air : —
Nothing stirs the dreary silence
  Save the melancholy sea,
Near the poor and humble cottage,
  Where I fain would be !

Where I am, the sun is shining,
  And the purple windows glow,
Till their rich armorial shadows
  Stain the marble floor below : —
Faded autumn leaves are trembling
  On the withered jasmine-tree,
Creeping round the little casement,
  Where I fain would be !

Where I am, the days are passing
  O'er a pathway strewn with flowers ;
Song and joy and starry pleasures
  Crown the happy, smiling hours : —
Slowly, heavily, and sadly,
  Time with weary wings must flee,
Marked by pain, and toil, and sorrow,
  Where I fain would be !

Where I am, the great and noble
　Tell me of renown and fame,
And the red wine sparkles highest,
　To do honor to my name : —
Far away a place is vacant,
　By a humble hearth, for me,
Dying embers dimly show it,
　Where I fain would be !

Where I am are glorious dream-
　　ings,
　Science, genius, art divine ;
And the great minds whom all
　　honor
　Interchange their thoughts
　　with mine : —
A few simple hearts are waiting,
　Longing, wearying, for me,
Far away where tears are falling,
　Where I fain would be !

Where I am, all think me happy,
　For so well I play my part,
None can guess, who smile
　　around me,
　How far distant is my heart, —
Far away, in a poor cottage,
　Listening to the dreary sea,
Where the treasures of my life
　　are,
　Where I fain would be !

WISHES.

ALL the fluttering wishes
　Caged within thy heart
Beat their wings against it,
　Longing to depart,

Till they shake their prison
　With their wounded cry ;
Open wide thy heart to-day,
　And let the captives fly.

Let them first fly upward
　Through the starry air,
Till you almost lose them,
　For their home is there ;
Then, with outspread pinions,
　Circling round and round,
Wing their way wherever
　Want and woe are found.

Where the weary stitcher
　Toils for daily bread ;
Where the lonely watcher
　Watches by her dead ;
Where, with thin, weak fingers,
　Toiling at the loom,
Stand the little children,
　Blighted ere they bloom ; —

Where, by darkness blinded,
　Groping for the light,
With distorted conscience,
　Men do wrong for right ;
Where, in the cold shadow,
　By smooth pleasure thrown,
Human hearts by hundreds
　Harden into stone ; —

Where on dusty highways,
　With faint heart and slow,
Cursing the glad sunlight,
　Hungry outcasts go ;
Where all mirth is silenced,
　And the hearth is chill,
For one place is empty,
　And one voice is still.

Some hearts will be lighter
   While your captives roam
For their tender singing,
   Then recall them home ;
When the sunny hours
   Into night depart,
Softly they will nestle
   In a quiet heart.

THE PEACE OF GOD.

We ask for Peace, O Lord !
   Thy children ask Thy Peace ;
Not what the world calls rest,
   That toil and care should cease,
That through bright sunny hours
   Calm Life should fleet away,
And tranquil night should fade
   In smiling day ; —
It is not for such Peace that we
   would pray.

We ask for Peace, O Lord !
   Yet not to stand secure,
Girt round with iron Pride, ·
   Contented to endure :
Crushing the gentle strings
   That human hearts should
   know,
Untouched by others' joy
   Or others' woe ; —
Thou, O dear Lord, wilt never
   teach us so.

We ask Thy Peace, O Lord !
   Through storm, and fear, and
   strife,
To light and guide us on,
   Through a long, struggling
   life :

While no success or gain
   Shall cheer the desperate fight,
Or nerve, what the world calls,
   Our wasted might : —
Yet pressing through the dark·
   ness to the light.

It is Thine own, O Lord,
   Who toil while others sleep ;
Who sow with loving care
   What other hands shall reap
They lean on Thee entranced,
   In calm and perfect rest .
Give us that Peace, O Lord,
   Divine and blest,
Thou keepest for those hearts
   who love Thee best.

LIFE IN DEATH AND DEATH IN LIFE.

I.

If the dread day that calls thee
   hence
   Through a red mist of fear
   should loom,
   (Closing in deadliest night and
   gloom
Long hours of aching, dumb sus-
   pense,)
   And leave me to my lonely
   doom, —

I think, belovéd, I could see
   In thy dear eyes the loving
   light
   Glaze into vacancy and night,

And still say, " God is good to
me,
And all that He decrees is
right."

That, watching thy slow struggling breath,
And answering each imperfect
sign,
I still could pray thy prayer
and mine,
And tell thee, dear, though this
was death,
That God was love, and love
divine.

Could hold thee in my arms,
and lay
Upon my heart thy weary
head,
And meet thy last smile ere it
fled ;
Then hear, as in a dream, one say,
" Now all is over, — she is
dead."

Could smooth thy garments with
fond care,
And cross thy hands upon thy
breast,
And kiss thine eyelids down
to rest,
And yet say no word of despair,
But, through my sobbing, " It
is best."

Could stifle down the gnawing
pain,
And say, " We still divide our
life,

She has the rest, and I the
strife,
And mine the loss, and hers the
gain :
My ill with bliss for her is
rife."

Then turn, and the old duties
take —
Alone now — yet with earnest
will
Gathering sweet, sacred traces
still
To help me on, and, for thy sake,
My heart and life and soul to
fill.

I think I could check vain, weak
tears,
And toil, — although the
world's great space
Held nothing but one vacant
place,
And see the dark and weary
years
Lit only by a vanished grace.

And sometimes, when the day
was o'er,
Call up the tender past
again :
Its painful joy, its happy pain,
And live it over yet once more,
And say, " But few more
years remain."

And then, when I had striven
my best,
And all around would smiling
say,

"See how Time makes all
 grief decay,"
Would lie down thankfully to
 rest,
And seek thee in eternal day.

II.

But if the day should ever
 rise —
 It could not and it cannot
  be —
 Yet, if the sun should ever see,
Looking upon us from his skies,
 A day that took thy heart from
  me ;

If loving thee still more and
 more,
 And still so willing to be blind,
 I should the bitter knowledge
  find,
That Time had eaten out the core
 Of love, and left the empty
  rind ;

If the poor lifeless words, at last,
 (The soul gone, that was once
  so sweet,)
 Should cease my eager heart
  to cheat,
And crumble back into the past,
 And show the whole a vain
  deceit ;

If I should see thee turn away,
 And know that prayer, and
  time, and pain,
  Could no more thy lost love
   regain,

Than bid the hours of dying day
 Gleam in their mid-day noon
  again ;

If I should loose thy hand, and
 know
 That henceforth we must
  dwell apart,
 Since I had seen thy love depart,
And only count the hours flow
 By the dull throbbing of my
  heart ;

If I should gaze and gaze in vain
 Into thine eyes so deep and
  clear,
 And read the truth of all my
  fear
Half mixed with pity for my
 pain,
 And sorrow for the vanished
  year ;

If, not to grieve thee overmuch,
 I strove to counterfeit disdain,
 And weave me a new life again,
Which thy life could not mar, or
 touch,
 And so smile down my bitter
  pain ; —

The ghost of my dead Past would
 rise
 And mock me, and I could
  not dare
 Look to a future of despair,
Or even to the eternal skies,
 For I should still be lonely
  there.

All Truth, all Honor, then would
seem
   Vain clouds, which the first
   wind blew by;
   All Trust, a folly doomed to
   die;
All Life, a useless, empty dream;
   All Love — since thine had
   failed — a lie.

But see, thy tender smile has cast
   My fear away: this thought of
   mine
   Is treason to my Love and
   thine;
For Love is Life, and Death at
   last
   Crowns it eternal and divine!

———

RECOLLECTIONS.

As strangers, you and I are
   here;
We both as aliens stand
Where once, in years gone by, I
   dwelt
   No stranger in the land.
Then while you gaze on park
   and stream,
   Let me remain apart,
And listen to the awakened
   sound
   Of voices in my heart.

Here, where upon the velvet lawn
   The cedar spreads its shade,
And by the flower-beds all around
   Bright roses bloom and fade,

Shrill merry childish laughter
   rings,
   And baby voices sweet,
And by me, on the path, I hear
   The tread of little feet.

Down the dark avenue of limes,
   Whose perfume loads the air,
Whose boughs are rustling over-
   head,
   (For the west-wind is there,)
I hear the sound of earnest talk,
   Warnings and counsels wise,
And the quick questioning that
   brought
   Such gentle, calm replies.

Still the light bridge hangs o'er
   the lake,
   Where broad-leaved lilies lie,
And the cool water shows again
   The cloud that moves on
   high; —
And one voice speaks, in tones
   I thought
   The past forever kept;
But now I know, deep in my
   heart
   Its echoes only slept.

I hear, within the shady porch,
   Once more, the measured
   sound
Of the old ballads that were read,
   While we sat listening round;
The starry passion-flower still
   Up the green trellis climbs;
The tendrils waving seem to
   keep
   The cadence of the rhymes.

I might have striven, and striven
    in vain,
  Such visions to recall,
Well known and yet forgotten ;
    now
  I see, I hear, them all !
The Present pales before the Past,
  Who comes with angel wings ;
As in a dream I stand, amidst
  Strange yet familiar things !

Enough ; so let us go, mine eyes
  Are blinded by their tears ;
A voice speaks to my soul to-day
  Of long-forgotten years.
And yet the vision in my heart,
  In a few hours more,
Will fade into the silent past,
  Silently as before.

ILLUSION.

Where the golden corn is bend-
    ing,
  And the singing reapers pass,
Where the chestnut woods are
    sending
  Leafy showers upon the grass,

The blue river onward flowing
  Mingles with its noisy strife,
The murmur of the flowers
    growing,
  And the hum of insect life.

I from that rich plain was gazing
  Towards the snowy moun-
    tains high,

Who their gleaming peaks were
    raising
  Up against the purple sky.

And the glory of their shining,
  Bathed in clouds of rosy
    light,
Set my weary spirit pining
  For a home so pure and
    bright !

So I left the plain, and weary,
  Fainting, yet with hope sus-
    tained,
Toiled through pathways long
    and dreary
  Till the mountain-top was
    gained.

Lo ! the height that I had taken,
  As so shining from below,
Was a desolate, forsaken
  Region of perpetual snow.

I am faint, my feet are bleeding,
  All my feeble strength is worn,
In the plain no soul is heeding,
  I am here alone, forlorn.

Lights are shining, bells are toll
    ing,
  In the busy vale below ;
Near me night's black clouds
    are rolling,
  Gathering o'er a waste of
    snow.

So I watch the river winding
  Through the misty fading
    plain,

Bitter are the tear-drops blind-
  ing,
  Bitter, useless toil and pain,—
Bitterest of all the finding
  That my dream was false and
  vain !

A VISION.

GLOOMY and black are the cypress-trees,
Drearily waileth the chill night
  breeze.
The long grass waveth, the tombs
  are white,
And the black clouds flit o'er the
  chill moonlight.
Silent is all save the dropping
  rain,
When slowly there cometh a
  mourning train ;
The lone churchyard is dark and
  dim,
And the mourners raise a funeral
  hymn.

" Open, dark grave, and take
  her ;
  Though we have loved her so,
Yet we must now forsake her,
Love will no more awake her :
  (O bitter woe !)
Open thine arms and take her
  To rest below !

" Vain is our mournful weeping,
  Her gentle life is o'er ;
Only the worm is creeping,

Where she will soon be sleeping
  Forevermore :
Nor joy nor love is keeping
  For her in store ! "

Gloomy and black are the cypress-trees,
And drearily wave in the chill
  night breeze.
The dark clouds part and the
  heavens are blue,
Where the trembling stars are
  shining through.

Slowly across the gleaming sky,
A crowd of white angels are pass-
  ing by.
Like a fleet of swans they float
  along,
Or the silver notes of a dying
  song.
Like a cloud of incense their
  pinions rise,
Fading away up the purple skies.
But hush ! for the silent glory is
  stirred
By a strain such as earth has
  never heard :

" Open, O Heaven ! we bear
  her,
  This gentle maiden mild,
Earth's griefs we gladly spare
  her,
From earthly joys we tear her,
  Still undefiled ;
And to thine arms we bear her,
  Thine own, thy child.

" Open, O Heaven! no morrow
   Will see this joy o'ercast,
No pain, no tears, no sorrow,
Her gentle heart will borrow ;
   Sad life is past ;
Shielded and safe from sorrow,
   At home at last."

But the vision faded and all was
   still,
On the purple valley and distant
   hill.
No sound was there save the wailing breeze,
The rain, and the rustling cypress-trees.

PICTURES IN THE FIRE.

WHAT is it you ask me, darling ?
   All my stories, child, you
   know ;
I have no strange dreams to tell
   you,
   Pictures I have none to show.

Tell you glorious scenes of travel ?
   Nay, my child, that cannot be,
I have seen no foreign countries,
   Marvels none on land or sea.

Yet strange sights in truth I
   witness,
   And I gaze until I tire ;
Wondrous pictures, changing
   ever,
   As I look into the fire.

There, last night, I saw a cavern,
   Black as pitch ; within it lay,
Coiled in many folds, a dragon,
   Glaring as if turned at bay.

And a knight in dismal armor
   On a wingéd eagle came,
To do battle with this dragon :
   And his crest was all of flame.

As I gazed the dragon faded,
   And, instead, sat Pluto
   crowned
By a lake of burning fire ;
   Spirits dark were crouching
   round.

That was gone, and lo! before
   me,
   A cathedral vast and grim ;
I could almost hear the organ
   Peal along the arches dim.

As I watched the wreathéd pil-
   lars,
   Groves of stately palms arose,
And a group of swarthy Indians
   Stealing on some sleeping foes.

Stay : a cataract glancing brightly
   Dashed and sparkled ; and be
   side
Lay a broken marble monster,
   Mouth and eyes were staring
   wide.

Then I saw a maiden wreathing
   Starry flowers in garlands
   sweet ·

Did she see the fiery serpent
  That was wrapped about her
    feet?

That fell crashing all and van-
    ished;
And I saw two armies close, —
I could almost hear the clarions,
And the shouting of the foes.
They were gone; and lo! bright
    angels,
On a barren mountain wild,
Raised appealing arms to Heaven,
  Bearing up a little child.

And I gazed, and gazed, and
    slowly
  Gathered in my eyes sad tears,
And the fiery pictures bore me
  Back through distant dreams
    of years.

Once again I tasted sorrow,
  With past joy was once more
    gay,
Till the shade had gathered
    round me —
  And the fire had died away.

THE SETTLERS.

Two stranger youths in the Far
    West,
  Beneath the ancient forest
    trees,
Pausing, amid their toil to rest,
  Spake of their home beyond
    the seas;

Spake of the hearts that beat so
    warmly,
  Of the hearts they loved so
    well,
In their chilly Northern country.
  "Would," they cried, "some
    voice could tell
Where they are, our own beloved
    ones!"
  They looked up to the evening
    sky
Half hidden by the giant branch-
    es,
  But heard no angel-voice re-
    ply.

All silent was the quiet evening;
  Silent were the ancient trees;
They only heard the murmuring
    song
  Of the summer breeze,
That gently played among
  The acacia-trees.

And did no warning spirit an-
    swer,
  Amid the silence all around:
"Before the lowly village altar
  She thou lovest may be found,
Thou, who trustest still so blind-
    ly,
  Know she stands a smiling
    bride!
Forgetting thee, she turneth
    kindly
  To the stranger at her side.
Yes, this day thou art forgotten,
  Forgotten, too, thy last fare-
    well,
All the vows that she has spoken,
  And thy heart has kept so well

Dream no more of a starry fu-
 ture,
 In thy home beyond the seas!"
But he only heard the gentle sigh
 Of the summer breeze,
 So softly passing by
 The acacia-trees.

And vainly, too, the other, looking
 Smiling up through hopeful
 tears,
Asked in his heart of hearts,
 "Where is she,
 She I love these many years?"
He heard no echo calling faintly:
 "Lo, she lieth cold and pale,
And her smile so calm and saintly
 Heeds not grieving sob or
 wail, —
Heeds not the lilies strewn upon
 her;
 Pure as she is, and as white,
 Or the solemn chanting voices,
 Or the taper's ghastly light."
But silent still was the ancient
 forest,
 Silent were the gloomy trees;
He only heard the wailing sound
 Of the summer breeze,
 That sadly played around
 The acacia-trees!

HUSH!

"I CAN scarcely hear," she murmured,
 "For my heart beats loud and
 fast,

But surely, in the far, far distance,
 I can hear a sound at last."
 "It is only the reapers singing,
 As they carry home their
 sheaves;
 And the evening breeze has
 risen,
 And rustles the dying
 leaves."

"Listen! there are voices talking."
 Calmly still she strove to
 speak,
Yet her voice grew faint and
 trembling,
 And the red flushed in her
 cheek.
 "It is only the children
 playing
 Below, now their work is
 done,
 And they laugh that their
 eyes are dazzled
 By the rays of the setting
 sun."

Fainter grew her voice, and
 weaker,
 As with anxious eyes she cried,
"Down the avenue of chestnuts,
 I can hear a horseman ride."
 "It was only the deer that
 were feeding
 In a herd on the clover
 grass,

They were startled, and fled
  to the thicket,
    As they saw the reapers
    pass."

Now the night arose in silence,
  Birds lay in their leafy nest,
And the deer couched in the
  forest,
  And the children were at rest:
    There was only a sound of
    weeping
      From watchers around a
      bed,
    But Rest to the weary spirit,
      Peace to the quiet Dead!

———

HOURS.

WHEN the bright stars came out
  last night,
  And the dew lay on the flow-
  ers,
I had a vision of delight, —
  A dream of bygone hours.

Those hours that came and fled
  so fast,
  Of pleasure or of pain,
As phantoms rose from out the
  past
  Before my eyes again.

With beating heart did I behold
  A train of joyous hours,
Lit with the radiant light of old,
  And, smiling, crowned with
  flowers.

And some were hours of childish
  sorrow,
  A mimicry of pain,
That through their tears looked
  for a morrow
  They knew must smile again.

Those hours of hope that longed
  for life,
  And wished their part begun,
And ere the summons to the
  strife
  Dreamed that the field was
  won.

I knew the echo of their voice,
  The starry crowns they wore;
The vision made my soul rejoice
  With the old thrill of yore.

I knew the perfume of their
  flowers;
  The glorious shining rays
Around these happy, smiling
  hours
  Were lit in bygone days.

O stay, I cried, — bright visions,
  stay,
  And leave me not forlorn!
But, smiling still, they passed
  away,
  Like shadows of the morn.

One spirit still remained, and
  cried,
  " Thy soul shall ne'er for-
  get!"
He standeth ever by my side, —
  The phantom called Regret!

But still the spirits rose, and there
Were weary hours of pain,
And anxious hours of fear and care
Bound by an iron chain.

Dim shadows came of lonely hours,
That shunned the light of day,
And in the opening smile of flowers
Saw only quick decay.

Calm hours that sought the starry skies
For heavenly lore were there;
With folded hands and earnest eyes,
I knew the hours of prayer.

Stern hours that darkened the sun's light,
Heralds of coming woes,
With trailing wings, before my sight
From the dim past arose.

As each dark vision passed and spoke,
I prayed it to depart:
At each some buried sorrow woke
And stirred within my heart.

Until these hours of pain and care
Lifted their tearful eyes,
Spread their dark pinions in the air,
And passed into the skies.

THE TWO INTERPRETERS.

THE clouds are fleeting by, father;
Look, in the shining west,
The great white clouds sail onward
Upon the sky's blue breast.
Look at a snowy eagle,
His wings are tinged with red,
And a giant dolphin follows him,
With a crown upon his head! "

The father spake no word, but watched
The drifting clouds roll by;
He traced a misty vision too
Upon the shining sky:
A shadowy form, with well-known grace
Of weary love and care,
Above the smiling child she held,
Shook down her floating hair.

"The clouds are changing now, father,
Mountains rise higher and higher!
And see where red and purple ships
Sail in a sea of fire! "
The father pressed the little hand
More closely in his own,
And watched a cloud-dream in the sky
That he could see alone:

Bright angels carrying far away
  A white form, cold and dead,
Two held the feet, and two bore
    up
  The flower-crowned, drooping
    head.

"See, father, see! a glory floods
  The sky, and all is bright,
And clouds of every hue and
    shade
  Burn in the golden light.
And now, above an azure lake,
  Rise battlements and towers,
Where knights and ladies climb
    the heights,
  All bearing purple flowers."

The father looked, and, with a
    pang
  Of love and strange alarm,
Drew close the little eager child
  Within his sheltering arm ;
From out the clouds the mother
    looks
  With wistful glance below,
She seems to seek the treasure
    left
  On earth so long ago ;
She holds her arms out to her
    child,
  His cradle-song she sings :
The last rays of the sunset gleam
  Upon her outspread wings.

Calm twilight veils the summer
    sky,
  The shining clouds are gone ;
In vain the merry laughing child
  Still gayly prattles on ;

In vain the bright stars, one by
    one,
  On the blue silence start,
A dreary shadow rests to-night
  Upon the father's heart.

———

COMFORT.

Hast thou o'er the clear heaven
    of thy soul
  Seen tempests roll ?
Hast thou watched all the hopes
    thou wouldst have won
  Fade, one by one ?
Wait till the clouds are past,
    then raise thine eyes
  To bluer skies.

Hast thou gone sadly through a ·
    dreary night,
  And found no light,
No guide, no star, to cheer thee
    through the plain,
  No friend, save pain ?
Wait, and thy soul shall see,
    when most forlorn,
  Rise a new morn.

Hast thou beneath another's stern
    control
  Bent thy sad soul,
And wasted sacred hopes and
    precious tears ?
  Yet calm thy fears,
For thou canst gain, even from
    the bitterest part,
  A stronger heart.

Has Fate o'erwhelmed thee with
some sudden blow?
Let thy tears flow;
But know when storms are past,
the heavens appear
More pure, more clear;
And hope, when farthest from
their shining rays,
For brighter days.

Hast thou found life a cheat, and
worn in vain
Its iron chain?
Has thy soul bent beneath earth's
heavy bond?
Look thou beyond;
If life is bitter — *there* forever
shine
Hopes more divine.

Art thou alone, and does thy
soul complain
It lives in vain?
Not vainly does he live who can
endure.
O be thou sure,
That he who hopes and suffers
here, can earn
A sure return.

Hast thou found naught within
thy troubled life
Save inward strife?
Hast thou found all she promised
thee, Deceit,
And Hope a cheat?
Endure, and there shall dawn
within thy breast
Eternal rest!

HOME AT LAST.

CHILD, do not fear;
We shall reach our home to-
night,
For the sky is clear,
And the waters bright;
And the breezes have scarcely
strength
To unfold that little cloud,
That like a shroud
Spreads out its fleecy length;
Then have no fear,
As we cleave our silver way
Through the waters clear.

Fear not, my child!
Though the waves are white and
high,
And the storm blows wild
Through the gloomy sky;
On the edge of the western sea,
See that line of golden light,
Is the haven bright
Where home is awaiting thee;
Where, this peril past,
We shall rest from our stormy
voyage
In peace at last.

Be not afraid;
But give me thy hand, and see
How the waves have made
A cradle for thee.
Night is come, dear, and we shall
rest;
So turn from the angry skies,
And close thine eyes,
And lay thy head on my breast:

Child, do not weep;
In the calm, cold, purple depths
There we shall sleep.

UNEXPRESSED.

DWELLS within the soul of every
    Artist
More than all his effort can ex-
    press;
And he knows the best remains
    unuttered;
Sighing at what *we* call his suc-
    cess.

Vainly he may strive; he dare
    not tell us
All the sacred mysteries of the
    skies;
Vainly he may strive, the deep-
    est beauty
Cannot be unveiled to mortal
    eyes.

And the more devoutly that he
    listens,
And the holier message that is
    sent,
Still the more his soul must
    struggle vainly,
Bowed beneath a noble discon-
    tent.

No great Thinker ever lived and
    taught you
All the wonder that his soul re-
    ceived;

No true Painter ever set on
    canvas
All the glorious vision he con-
    ceived.

No Musician ever held your
    spirit
Charmed and bound in his me-
    lodious chains,
But be sure he heard, and strove
    to render,
Feeble echoes of celestial strains.

No real Poet ever wove in num-
    bers
All his dream; but the diviner
    part,
Hidden from all the world, spake
    to him only
In the voiceless silence of his
    heart.

So with Love: for Love and Art
    united
Are twin mysteries; different, yet
    the same:
Poor indeed would be the love
    of any
Who could find its full and per-
    fect name.

Love may strive, but vain is the
    endeavor
All its boundless riches to un-
    fold;
Still its tenderest, truest secret
    lingers
Ever in its deepest depths un-
    told.

Things of Time have voices:
    speak and perish.
Art and Love speak; but their
    words must be
Like sighings of illimitable for-
    ests,
And waves of an unfathomable
    sea.

BECAUSE.

It is not because your heart is
    mine — mine only —
    Mine alone;
It is not because you chose me,
    weak and lonely,
    For your own;
Not because the earth is fairer,
    and the skies
    Spread above you
Are more radiant for the shining
    of your eyes —
    That I love you!

It is not because the world's per-
    plexéd meaning
    Grows more clear;
And the Parapets of Heaven,
    with angels leaning,
    Seem more near;
And Nature sings of praise with
    all her voices
    Since yours spoke,
Since within my silent heart,
    that now rejoices,
    Love awoke!

Nay, not even because your hand
    holds heart and life;
    At your will

Soothing, hushing all its discord,
    making strife
    Calm and still;
Teaching Trust to fold her wings,
    nor ever roam
    From her nest;
Teaching Love that her securest,
    safest home
    Must be Rest.

But because this human Love,
    though true and sweet —
    Yours and mine —
Has been sent by Love more ten-
    der, more complete,
    More divine;
That it leads our hearts to rest
    at last in Heaven,
    Far above you;
Do I take you as a gift that God
    has given —
    — And I love you!

REST AT EVENING.

When the weariness of Life is
    ended,
And the task of our long day is
    done,
And the props, on which our
    hearts depended,
All have failed or broken, one
    by one;
Evening and our Sorrow's shad-
    ow blended,
Telling us that peace is now be-
    gun.

How far back will seem the sun's
    first dawning,
And those early mists so cold and
    gray !
Half forgotten even the toil of
    morning,
And the heat and burden of the
    day :
Flowers that we were tending,
    and weeds scorning,
All alike withered and cast away.

Vain will seem the impatient
    heart, which waited
Toils that gathered but too quick-
    ly round ;
And the childish joy, so soon
    elated
At the path we thought none else
    had found ;
And the foolish ardor, soon
    abated
By the storm which cast us to
    the ground.

Vain those pauses on the road,
    each seeming
As our final home and resting-
    place ;
And the leaving them, while
    tears were streaming
Of eternal sorrow down our
    face ;
And the hands we held, fond
    folly dreaming
That no future could their touch
    efface.

All will then be faded : — night
    will borrow
Stars of light to crown our per-
    fect rest ;
And the dim vague memory of
    faint sorrow
Just remain to show us all was
    best,
Then melt into a divine to-mor-
    row : —
O how poor a day to be so blest!

A RETROSPECT.

FROM this fair point of present
    bliss,
    Where we together stand,
Let me look back once more,
    and trace
    That long and desert land,
Wherein till now was cast my lot,
    and I could live, and thou
    wert not.

Strange that my heart could beat,
    and know
    Alternate joy and pain,
That suns could roll from east
    to west,
    And clouds could pass in rain,
And the slow hours without thee
    fleet, nor stay their noiseless
    silver feet.

What had I then ? a Hope, that
    grew
    Each hour more bright and
    dear,

The flush upon the eastern skies
  That showed the sun was
  near : —
Now night has faded far away,
  my sun has risen, and it is
  day.

A dim Ideal of tender grace
  In my soul reigned supreme ;
Too noble and too sweet I
  thought
  To live, save in a dream ; —
Within thy heart to-day it lies,
  and looks on me from thy
  dear eyes.

Some gentle spirit — Love I
  thought —
  Built many a shrine of pain ;
Though each false Idol fell to
  dust,
  The worship was not vain,
But a faint, radiant shadow cast
  back from our Love upon
  the Past.

And Grief, too, held her vigil
  there ;
  With unrelenting sway
Breaking my cloudy visions
  ʹ down,
  Throwing my flowers away : —
I owe to her fond care alone
  that I may now be all thine
  own.

Fair Joy was there, — her fluttering wings
  At times she strove to raise ;

Watching through long and patient nights,
  Listening long eager days :
I know now that her heart and
  mine were waiting, Love, to
  welcome thine.

Thus I can read thy name
  throughout,
  And, now her task is done,
Can see that even that faded Past
  Was thine, belovéd one,
And so rejoice my Life may be all
  consecrated, dear, to thee.

———

TRUE OR FALSE.

So you think you love me, do
  you ?
  Well, it may be so ;
But there are many ways of lov-
  ing
  I have learnt to know.
Many ways, and but one true
  way,
  Which is very rare ;
And the counterfeits look bright-
  est,
  Though they will not wear.

Yet they ring, almost, quite
  truly,
  Last (with care) for long ;
But in time must break, may
  shiver
  At a touch of wrong :

Having seen what looked most
    real
  Crumble into dust;
Now I chose that test and trial
  Should precede my trust.

I have seen a love demanding
  Time and hope and tears,
Chaining all the past, exacting
  Bonds from future years;
Mind and heart, and joy and
    sorrow,
  Claiming as its fee:
That was Love of Self, and
    never,
  Never Love of me!

I have seen a love forgetting
  All above, beyond,
Linking every dream and fancy
  In a sweeter bond;
Counting every hour worthless,
  Which was cold or free:—
That, perhaps, was — Love of
    Pleasure,
  But not Love of me!

I have seen a love whose pa-
    tience
  Never turned aside,
Full of tender, fond devices;
  Constant, even when tried;
Smallest boons were held as vic-
    tories,
  Drops that swelled the sea:
That I think was — Love of
    Power,
  But not Love of me!

I have seen a love disdaining
  Ease and pride and fame,
Burning even its own white pin-
    ions
  Just to feed its flame;
Reigning thus, supreme, trium-
    phant,
  By the soul's decree;
That was — Love of Love, I
    fancy,
  But not Love of me!

I have heard — or dreamt, it
    may be —
  What Love is when true;
How to test and how to try it,
  Is the gift of few:
These few say (or did I dream
    it?)
  That true Love abides
In these very things, but always
  Has a soul besides.

Lives among the false loves,
    knowing
  Just their peace and strife;
Bears the self-same look, but al-
    ways
  Has an inner life.
Only a true heart can find it,
  True as it is true,
Only eyes as clear and tender
  Look it through and through.

If it dies, it will not perish
  By Time's slow decay,
True Love only grows (they tell
    me)
  Stronger, day by day:

Pain — has been its friend and
   comrade ;
Fate — it can defy ;
Only by its own sword, sometimes
   Love can choose to die.

And its grave shall be more
   noble
And more sacred still,
Than a throne, where one less
   worthy
Reigns and rules at will.
Tell me then, do you dare offer
   This true Love to me ? . . .
Neither you nor I can answer ;
   We will — wait and see !

GOLDEN WORDS.

SOME words are played on
   golden strings,
Which I so highly rate,
I cannot bear for meaner things
   Their sound to desecrate.

For every day they are not meet,
   Or for a careless tone ;
They are for rarest, and most
   sweet,
And noblest use alone.

One word is POET : which is
   flung
So carelessly away,
When such as you and I have
   sung,
We hear it, day by day.

Men pay it for a tender phrase
   Set in a cadenced rhyme :
I keep it as a crown of praise
   To crown the kings of time.

And LOVE : the slightest feel-
   ings, stirred
By trivial fancy, seek
Expression in that golden word
   They tarnish while they speak.

Nay, let the heart's slow, rare
   decree,
That word in reverence keep ;
Silence herself should only be
   More sacred and more deep.

FOREVER : men have grown at
   length
To use that word, to raise
Some feeble protest into strength,
   Or turn some tender phrase.

It should be said in awe and fear
   By true heart and strong will,
And burn more brightly year by
   year,
   A starry witness still.

HONOR : all trifling hearts are
   fond
Of that divine appeal,
And men, upon the slightest
   bond,
Set it as slighter seal.

That word should meet a noble foe
   Upon a noble field,
And echo — like a deadly blow
   Turned by a silver shield.

Trust me, the worth of words is
   such
They guard all noble things,
And that this rash irreverent
   touch
   Has jarred some golden
   strings.

For what the lips have lightly
   said
The heart will lightly hold,
And things on which we daily
   tread
Are lightly bought and sold.

The sun of every day will bleach
   The costliest purple hue,

And so our common daily
   speech
Discolors what was true.

But as you keep some thoughts
   apart
In sacred honored care,
If in the silence of your heart,
   Their utterance too be rare;

Then, while a thousand words
   repeat
Unmeaning clamors all,
Melodious golden echoes sweet
   Shall answer when you call.

LEGENDS AND LYRICS.

A BOOK OF VERSES.

SECOND SERIES.

LEGENDS AND LYRICS.

A LEGEND OF PROVENCE.

THE lights extinguished, by the hearth I leant,
Half weary with a listless discontent.
The flickering giant-shadows, gathering near,
Closed round me with a dim and silent fear.
All dull, all dark; save when the leaping flame,
Glancing, lit up a Picture's ancient frame.
Above the hearth it hung.   Perhaps the night,
My foolish tremors, or the gleaming light,
Lent power to that Portrait dark and quaint, —
A Portrait such as Rembrandt loved to paint, —
The likeness of a Nun.   I seemed to trace
A world of sorrow in the patient face,
In the thin hands folded across her breast: —
Its own and the room's shadow hid the rest.
I gazed and dreamed, and the dull embers stirred,
Till an old legend that I once had heard
Came back to me; linked to the mystic gloom
Of that dark Picture in the ghostly room

In the far south, where clustering vines are hung;
Where first the old chivalric lays were sung ;
Where earliest smiled that gracious child of France
Angel and knight and fairy, called Romance,
I stood one day.   The warm blue June was spread
Upon the earth ; blue summer overhead,
Without a cloud to fleck its radiant glare,
Without a breath to stir its sultry air.
All still, all silent, save the sobbing rush
Of rippling waves, that lapsed in silver hush

Upon the beach ; where, glittering towards the strand,
The purple Mediterranean kissed the land.

All still, all peaceful ; when a convent chime
Broke on the mid-day silence for a time,
Then trembling into quiet, seemed to cease,
In deeper silence and more utter peace.
So as I turned to gaze, where gleaming white,
Half hid by shadowy trees from passers' sight,
The Convent lay, one who had dwelt for long
In that fair home of ancient tale and song,
Who knew the story of each cave and hill,
And every haunting fancy lingering still
Within the land, spake thus to me, and told
The Convent's treasured Legend, quaint and old : —

Long years ago, a dense and flowering wood,
Still more concealed where the white convent stood,
Borne on its perfumed wings the title came :
" Our Lady of the Hawthorns " is its name.
Then did that bell, which still rings out to-day,
Bid all the country rise, or eat, or pray.
Before that convent shrine, the haughty knight
Passed the lone vigil of his perilous fight ;
For humbler cottage strife or village brawl,
The Abbess listened, prayed, and settled all.
Young hearts that came, weighed down by love or wrong,
Left her kind presence comforted and strong.
Each passing pilgrim, and each beggar's right
Was food, and rest, and shelter for the night.
But, more than this, the Nuns could well impart
The deepest mysteries of the healing art ;
Their store of herbs and simples was renowned,
And held in wondering faith for miles around.
Thus strife, love, sorrow, good and evil fate,
Found help and blessing at the convent gate.

Of all the nuns, no heart was half so light,
No eyelids veiling glances half as bright,
No step that glided with such noiseless feet,
No face that looked so tender or so sweet,

No voice that rose in choir so pure, so clear,
No heart to all the others half so dear,
So surely touched by others' pain or woe,
(Guessing the grief her young life could not know,)
No soul in childlike faith so undefiled,
As Sister Angela's, the "Convent Child."
For thus they loved to call her. She had known
No home, no love, no kindred, save their own.
An orphan, to their tender nursing given,
Child, plaything, pupil, now the Bride of Heaven.
And she it was who trimmed the lamp's red light
That swung before the altar, day and night;
Her hands it was whose patient skill could trace
The finest broidery, weave the costliest lace ;
But most of all, her first and dearest care,
The office she would never miss or share,
Was every day to weave fresh garlands sweet,
To place before the shrine at Mary's feet.
Nature is bounteous in that region fair,
For even winter has her blossoms there.
Thus Angela loved to count each feast the best,
By telling with what flowers the shrine was dressed.
In pomp supreme the countless Roses passed,
Battalion on battalion thronging fast,
Each with a different banner, flaming bright,
Damask, or striped, or crimson, pink, or white,
Until they bowed before a newborn queen,
And the pure virgin Lily rose serene.
Though Angela always thought the Mother blest
Must love the time of her own hawthorn best,
Each evening through the year, with equal care,
She placed her flowers ; then kneeling down in prayer,
As their faint perfume rose before the shrine,
So rose her thoughts, as pure and as divine.
She knelt until the shades grew dim without,
Till one by one the altar lights shone out,
Till one by one the Nuns, like shadows dim,
Gathered around to chant their vesper hymn ;
Her voice then led the music's wingéd flight,
And " Ave, Maris Stella " filled the night.

But wherefore linger on those days of peace?
When storms draw near, then quiet hours must cease.
War, cruel war, defaced the land, and came
So near the convent with its breath of flame,
That, seeking shelter, frightened peasants fled,
Sobbing out tales of coming fear and dread.
Till after a fierce skirmish, down the road,
One night came straggling soldiers, with their load
Of wounded, dying comrades; and the band,
Half pleading, yet as if they could command,
Summoned the trembling Sisters, craved their care,
Then rode away, and left the wounded there.
But soon compassion bade all fear depart,
And bidding every Sister do her part,
Some prepare simples, healing salves, or bands,
The Abbess chose the more experienced hands,
To dress the wounds needing most skilful care;
Yet even the youngest Novice took her share.
To Angela, who had but ready will
And tender pity, yet no special skill,
Was given the charge of a young foreign knight,
Whose wounds were painful, but whose danger slight.
Day after day she watched beside his bed,
And first in hushed repose the hours fled:
His feverish moans alone the silence stirred,
Or her soft voice, uttering some pious word.
At last the fever left him; day by day
The hours, no longer silent, passed away.
What could she speak of? First, to still his plaints,
She told him legends of the martyred Saints;
Described the pangs, which, through God's plenteous grace,
Had gained their souls so high and bright a place.
This pious artifice soon found success —
Or so she fancied — for he murmured less.
So she described the glorious pomp sublime,
In which the chapel shone at Easter time,
The Banners, Vestments, gold, and colors bright,
Counted how many tapers gave their light;
Then in minute detail went on to say,
How the High Altar looked on Christmas-day:

The kings and shepherds, all in green and red,
And a bright star of jewels overhead.
Then told the sign by which they all had seen
How even nature loved to greet her Queen,
For, when Our Lady's last procession went
Down the long garden, every head was bent,
And, rosary in hand, each Sister prayed;
As the long floating banners were displayed,
They struck the hawthorn boughs, and showers and showers
Of buds and blossoms strewed her way with flowers.
The knight unwearied listened; till at last,
He too described the glories of his past;
Tourney, and joust, and pageant bright and fair,
And all the lovely ladies who were there.
But half incredulous she heard.   Could this —
This be the world? this place of love and bliss!
Where then was hid the strange and hideous charm,
That never failed to bring the gazer harm?
She crossed herself, yet asked, and listened still,
And still the knight described with all his skill
The glorious world of joy, all joys above,
Transfigured in the golden mist of love.
Spread, spread your wings, ye angel·guardians bright,
And shield these dazzling phantoms from her sight!
But no; days passed, matins and vespers rang,
And still the quiet Nuns toiled, prayed, and sang,
And never guessed the fatal, coiling net
Which every day drew near, and nearer yet,
Around their darling; for she went and came
About her duties, outwardly the same.
The same? ah, no! even when she knelt to pray,
Some charmèd dream kept all her heart away.
So days went on, until the convent gate
Opened one night.   Who durst go forth so late?
Across the moonlit grass, with stealthy tread,
Two silent, shrouded figures passed and fled.
And all was silent, save the moaning seas,
That sobbed and pleaded, and a wailing breeze
That sighed among the perfumed hawthorn-trees.

What need to tell that dream so bright and brief,
Of joy uncheckered by a dread of grief?
What need to tell how all such dreams must fade,
Before the slow, foreboding, dreaded shade,
That floated nearer, until pomp and pride,
Pleasure and wealth, were summoned to her side,
To bid, at least, the noisy hours forget,
And clamor down the whispers of regret.
Still Angela strove to dream, and strove in vain;
Awakened once, she could not sleep again.
She saw, each day and hour, more worthless grown
The heart for which she cast away her own;
And her soul learnt, through bitterest inward strife,
The slight, frail love for which she wrecked her life,
The phantom for which all her hope was given,
The cold bleak earth for which she bartered heaven!
But all in vain; would even the tenderest heart
Now stoop to take so poor an outcast's part?

Years fled, and she grew reckless more and more,
Until the humblest peasant closed his door,
And where she passed, fair dames, in scorn and pride,
Shuddered, and drew their rustling robes aside.
At last a yearning seemed to fill her soul,
A longing that was stronger than control:
Once more, just once again, to see the place
That knew her young and innocent; to retrace
The long and weary southern path; to gaze
Upon the haven of her childish days;
Once more beneath the convent roof to lie;
Once more to look upon her home — and die!
Weary and worn — her comrades, chill remorse
And black despair, yet a strange silent force
Within her heart, that drew her more and more —
Onward she crawled, and begged from door to door.
Weighed down with weary days, her failing strength
Grew less each hour, till one day's dawn at length,
As first its rays flooded the world with light,
Showed the broad waters, glittering blue and bright,

And where, amid the leafy hawthorn wood,
Just as of old the quiet cloister stood.
Would any know her? Nay, no fear. Her face
Had lost all trace of youth, of joy, of grace,
Of the pure, happy soul they used to know —
The novice Angela — so long ago.
She rang the convent bell. The well-known sound
Smote on her heart, and bowed her to the ground.
And she, who had not wept for long, dry years,
Felt the strange rush of unaccustomed tears ;
Terror and anguish seemed to check her breath,
And stop her heart. O God! could this be death?
Crouching against the iron gate, she laid
Her weary head against the bars, and prayed :
But nearer footsteps drew, then seemed to wait ;
And then she heard the opening of the grate,
And saw the withered face, on which awoke
Pity and sorrow, as the portress spoke,
And asked the stranger's bidding: "Take me in,"
She faltered, "Sister Monica, from sin,
And sorrow, and despair, that will not cease;
O, take me in, and let me die in peace!"
With soothing words the Sister bade her wait,
Until she brought the key to unbar the gate.
The beggar tried to thank her as she lay,
And heard the echoing footsteps die away.
But what soft voice was that which sounded near,
And stirred strange trouble in her heart to hear?
She raised her head ; she saw — she seemed to know —
A face that came from long, long years ago :
Herself; yet not as when she fled away,
The young and blooming novice, fair and gay,
But a grave woman, gentle and serene :
The outcast knew it, — *what she might have been.*
But, as she gazed and gazed, a radiance bright
Filled all the place with strange and sudden light;
The Nun was there no longer, but instead,
A figure with a circle round its head,
A ring of glory ; and a face, so meek,
So soft, so tender. . . . Angela strove to speak,

And stretched her hands out, crying, " Mary mild,
Mother of mercy, help me ! — help your child ! "
And Mary answered, " From thy bitter past,
Welcome, my child !   O, welcome home at last !
I filled thy place.   Thy flight is known to none,
For all thy daily duties I have done ;
Gathered thy flowers, and prayed, and sung, and slept ;
Didst thou not know, poor child, *thy place was kept ?*
Kind hearts are here ; yet would the tenderest one
Have limits to its mercy : God has none.
And man's forgiveness may be true and sweet,
But yet he stoops to give it.   More complete
Is Love that lays forgiveness at thy feet,
And pleads with thee to raise it.   Only Heaven
Means *crowned*, not *vanquished*, when it says, ' Forgiven ! ' "
Back hurried Sister Monica ; but where
Was the poor beggar she left lying there ?
Gone ; and she searched in vain, and sought the place
For that wan woman, with the piteous face :
But only Angela at the gateway stood,
Laden with hawthorn blossoms from the wood.
And never did a day pass by again,
But the old portress, with a sigh of pain,
Would sorrow for her loitering : with a prayer
That the poor beggar, in her wild despair,
Might not have come to any ill ; and when
She ended, " God forgive her ! " humbly then
Did Angela bow her head, and say, " Amen ! "
How pitiful her heart was ! all could trace
Something that dimmed the brightness of her face
After that day, which none had seen before ;
Not trouble — but a shadow — nothing more.

Years passed away.   Then, one dark day of dread
Saw all the Sisters kneeling round a bed,
Where Angela lay dying ; every breath
Struggling beneath the heavy hand of death.
But suddenly a flush lit up her cheek,
She raised her wan right hand, and strove to speak

In sorrowing love they listened ; not a sound
Or sigh disturbed the utter silence round.
The very tapers' flames were scarcely stirred,
In such hushed awe the Sisters knelt and heard.
And through that silence Angela told her life :
Her sin, her flight ; the sorrow and the strife,
And the return ; and then clear, low, and calm,
" Praise God for me, my sisters " ; and the psalm
Rang up to heaven, far and clear and wide,
Again, and yet again, then sank and died ;
While her white face had such a smile of peace,
They saw she never heard the music cease ;
And weeping Sisters laid her in her tomb,
Crowned with a wreath of perfumed hawthorn bloom.

And thus the Legend ended.   It may be
Something is hidden in the mystery,
Besides the lesson of God's pardon shown,
Never enough believed, or asked, or known.
Have we not all, amid life's petty strife,
Some pure ideal of a noble life
That once seemed possible?   Did we not hear
The flutter of its wings, and feel it near,
And just within our reach?   It was.   And yet
We lost it in this daily jar and fret,
And now live idle in a vague regret.
But still *our place is kept*, and it will wait,
Ready for us to fill it, soon or late:
No star is ever lost we once have seen,
We always may be what we might have been.
Since Good, though only thought, has life and breath,
God's life — can always be redeemed from death ;
And evil, in its nature, is decay,
And any hour can blot it all away ;
The hopes that lost in some far distance seem,
May be the truer life, and this the dream.

ENVY.

HE was the first always: For-
tune
Shone bright in his face.
I fought for years; with no ef-
fort
He conquered the place :
We ran ; my feet were all bleed-
ing,
But he won the race.

Spite of his many successes,
Men loved him the same ;
My one pale ray of good for-
tune
Met scoffing and blame.
When we erred, they gave him
pity,
But me — only shame.

My home was still in the shadow,
His lay in the sun :
I longed in vain : what he asked
for
It straightway was done.
Once I staked all my heart's
treasure,
We played — and he won.

Yes , and just now I have seen
him,
Cold, smiling, and blest,
Laid in his coffin. God help
me !
While he is at rest,
I am cursed still to live : — even
Death loved him the best.

OVER THE MOUNTAIN.

LIKE dreary prison walls
The stern, gray mountains
rise,
Until their topmost crags
Touch the far gloomy skies :
One steep and narrow path
Winds up the mountain's
crest,
And from our valley leads
Out to the golden West.

I dwell here in content,
Thankful for tranquil days ;
And yet my eyes grow dim,
As still I gaze and gaze
Upon that mountain pass,
That leads — or so it seems —
To some far happy land,
Known in a world of dreams.

And as I watch that path
Over the distant hill,
A foolish longing comes
My heart and soul to fill,
A painful, strange desire
To break some weary bond ;
A vague unuttered wish
For what might lie beyond !

In that far world unknown,
Over that distant hill,
May dwell the loved and lost,
Lost — yet belovéd still ;
I have a yearning hope,
Half longing, and half pain,
That by that mountain pass
They may return again.

Space may keep friends apart,
　Death has a mighty thrall;
There is another gulf
　Harder to cross than all;
Yet watching that far road,
　My heart beats full and fast:
If they should come once more,
　If they should come at last!

See, down the mountain-side
　The silver vapors creep;
They hide the rocky cliffs,
　They hide the craggy steep,
They hide the narrow path
　That comes across the hill: —
O foolish longing, cease,
　O beating Heart, be stiU !

BEYOND.

WE must not doubt, or fear, or dread, that love for life is only given,
And that the calm and sainted dead will meet estranged and cold in
　　heaven : —
O, Love were poor and vain indeed, based on so harsh and stern a
　creed.

True that this earth must pass away, with all the starry worlds of
　light,
With all the glory of the day, and calmer tenderness of night;
For in that radiant home can shine alone the immortal and divine.

Earth's lower things — her pride, her fame, her science, learning,
　　wealth, and power —
Slow growths that through long ages came, or fruits of some con-
　vulsive hour,
Whose very memory must decay — Heaven is too pure for such as they.

They are complete : their work is done.　So let them sleep in end-
　less rest.
Love's life is only here begun, nor is, nor can be, fully blest;
It has no room to spread its wings, amid this crowd of meaner things.

Just for the very shadow thrown upon its sweetness here below,
The cross that it must bear alone, and bloody baptism of woe,
Crowned and completed through its pain, we know that it shall rise
　again.

So if its flame burn pure and bright, here, where our air is dark and
　　dense,
And nothing in this world of night lives with a living so intense;
When it shall reach its home at length — how bright its light! how
　　strong its strength!

And while the vain weak loves of earth (for such base counterfeits
　　abound)
Shall perish with what gave them birth — their graves are green and
　　fresh around,
No funeral song shall need to rise for the true Love that never dies.

If in my heart I now could fear that, risen again, we should not know
What was our Life of Life when here, — the hearts we loved so much
　　below, —
I would arise this very day, and cast so poor a thing away.

But Love is no such soulless clod : living, perfected it shall rise
Transfigured in the light of God, and giving glory to the skies :
And that which makes this life so sweet shall render Heaven's joy
　　complete.

———

A WARNING.

Place your hands in mine, dear,
　　With their rose-leaf touch :
If you heed my warning,
　　It will spare you much.

Ah! with just such smiling
　　Unbelieving eyes,
Years ago I heard it : —
　　You shall be more wise.

You have one great treasure,
　　Joy for all your life ;
Do not let it perish
　　In one reckless strife.

Do not venture all, child,
　　In one frail, weak heart ;
So, through any shipwreck,
　　You may save a part

Where your soul is tempted
　　Most to trust your fate,
There, with double caution,
　　Linger, fear, and wait.

Measure all you give, still
　　Counting what you take :
Love for love, so placing
　　Each an equal stake.

Treasure love; though ready
  Still to live without.
In your fondest trust, keep
  Just one thread of doubt.

Build on no to-morrow;
  Love has but to-day:
If the links seem slackening,
  Cut the bond away.

Trust no prayer nor promise;
  Words are grains of sand:
To keep your heart unbroken,
  Hold it in your hand.

That your love may finish
  Calm as it begun,
Learn this lesson better,
  Dear, than I have done.

Years hence, perhaps, this warn-
    ing
  You shall give again,
In just the self-same words, dear,
  And — just as much — in vain.

MAXIMUS.

MANY, if God should make
    them kings,
  Might not disgrace the throne
    He gave;
How few who could as well fulfil
  The holier office of a slave!

I hold him great who, for Love's
    sake,
  Can give, with generous, ear-
    nest will, —

Yet he who takes for Love's
    sweet sake,
  I think I hold more generous
    still.

I prize the instinct that can
    turn
  From vain pretence with proud
    disdain;
Yet more I prize a simple heart
  Paying credulity with pain.

I bow before the noble mind
  That freely some great wrong
    forgives;
Yet nobler is the one forgiven,
  Who bears that burden well,
    and lives.

It may be hard to gain, and still
  To keep a lowly steadfast
    heart;
Yet he who loses has to fill
  A harder and a truer part.

Glorious it is to wear the crown
  Of a deserved and pure suc-
    cess; —
He who knows how to fail has
    won
  A Crown whose lustre is not
    less.

Great may he be who can com-
    mand
  And rule with just and tender
    sway;
Yet is diviner wisdom taught
  Better by him who can obey.

Blesséd are those who die for
    God,
    And earn the Martyr's crown
        of light;
Yet he who lives for God may be
    A greater Conqueror in His
    sight.

OPTIMUS.

There is a deep and subtle snare
Whose sure temptation hardly
    fails,
Which, just because it looks so
    fair,
Only a noble heart assails.

So all the more we need be strong
Against this false and seeming
    Right;
Which none the less is deadly
    wrong,
Because it glitters clothed in
    light.

When duties unfulfilled remain,
Or noble works are left un-
    planned,
Or when great deeds cry out in
    vain
On coward heart and trembling
    hand, —

Then will a seeming Angel
    speak : —
" The hours are fleeting — great
    the need —

If thou art strong and others weak,
    Thine be the effort and the deed.

" Deaf are their ears who ought
    to hear;
Idle their hands, and dull their
    soul;
While sloth, or ignorance, or fear,
Fetters them with a blind control.

" Sort thou the tangled web
    aright;
Take thou the toil, take thou the
    pain :
For fear the hour begin its flight,
While Right and Duty plead in
    vain."

And now it is I bid thee pause,
Nor let this Tempter bend thy will;
There are diviner, truer laws
That teach a nobler lesson still.

Learn that each duty makes its
    claim
Upon one soul : not each on all.
How, if God speaks thy Brother's
    name,
Dare thou make answer to the
    call ?

The greater peril in the strife,
The less this evil should be done;
For as in battle, so in life,
Danger and honor still are one.

Arouse him then : — this is thy
    part:
Show him the claim; point out
    the need;

And nerve his arm, and cheer
  his heart ;
Then stand aside, and say, " God
  speed ! "

Smooth thou his path ere it is
  trod ;
Burnish the arms that he must
  wield ;
And pray, with all thy strength,
  that God
May crown him Victor of the
  field.

And then, I think, thy soul shall
  feel
A nobler thrill of true content,
Than if presumptuous, eager zeal
Had seized a crown for others
  meant.

And even that very deed shall
  shine
In mystic sense, divine and true,
More wholly and more purely
  thine —
Because it is another's too.

A LOST CHORD.

Seated one day at the Organ,
  I was weary and ill at ease,
And my fingers wandered idly
  Over the noisy keys.

I do not know what I was playing,
  Or what I was dreaming then ;

But I struck one chord of music,
  Like the sound of a great
  Amen.

It flooded the crimson twilight,
  Like the close of an Angel's
  Psalm,
And it lay on my fevered spirit
  With a touch of infinite calm.

It quieted pain and sorrow,
  Like love overcoming strife ;
It seemed the harmonious echo
  From our discordant life.

It linked all perplexéd meanings
  Into one perfect peace,
And trembled away into silence
  As if it were loth to cease.

I have sought, but I seek it vainly,
  That one lost chord divine,
Which came from the soul of the
  Organ,
  And entered into mine.

It may be that Death's bright
  angel
  Will speak in that chord again,
It may be that only in Heaven
  I shall hear that grand Amen.

TOO LATE.

Hush ! speak low ; tread softly;
  Draw the sheet aside ; —
Yes, she does look peaceful ;
  With that smile she died.

Yet stern want and sorrow
  Even now you trace
On the wan, worn features
  Of the still white face.

Restless, helpless, hopeless,
  Was her bitter part; —
Now — how still the Violets
  Lie upon her Heart!

She who toiled and labored
  For her daily bread;
See the velvet hangings
  Of this stately bed.

Yes, they did forgive her;
  Brought her home at last;
Strove to cover over
  Their relentless past.

Ah, they would have given
  Wealth, and home, and pride,
To see her just look happy
  Once before she died!

They strove hard to please her,
  But, when death is near,
All you know is deadened,
  Hope, and joy, and fear.

And besides, one sorrow
  Deeper still — one pain
Was beyond them: healing
  Came to-day — in vain!

If she had but lingered
  Just a few hours more;
Or had this letter reached her
  Just one day before!

I can almost pity
  Even him to-day;
Though he let this anguish
  Eat her heart away.

Yet she never blamed him; —
  One day you shall know
How this sorrow happened;
  It was long ago.

I have read the letter;
  Many a weary year,
For one word she hungered, —
  There are thousands here.

If she could but hear it,
  Could but understand;
See, — I put the letter
  In her cold white hand.

Even these words, so longed for,
  Do not stir her rest;
Well, I should not murmur,
  For God judges best.

She needs no more pity, —
  But I mourn his fate,
When he hears his letter
  Came a day too late.

THE REQUITAL.

Loud roared the Tempest,
  Fast fell the sleet;
A little Child Angel
  Passed down the street,
With trailing pinions,
  And weary feet.

The moon was hidden ;
　No stars were bright ;
So she could not shelter
　In heaven that night,
For the Angels' ladders
　Are rays of light.

She beat her wings
　At each window-pane,
And pleaded for shelter,
　But all in vain ; —
."Listen," they said,
　"To the pelting rain ! "

She sobbed, as the laughter
　And mirth grew higher,
" Give me rest and shelter
　Beside your fire,
And I will give you
　Your heart's desire."

The dreamer sat watching
　His embers gleam,
While his heart was floating
　Down hope's bright stream ;
. . . So he wove her wailing
　Into his dream.

The worker toiled on,
　For his time was brief ;
The mourner was nursing
　Her own pale grief ;
They heard not the promise
　That brought relief.

But fiercer the Tempest
　Rose than before,
When the Angel paused
　At a humble door,

And asked for shelter
　And help once more

A weary woman,
　Pale, worn, and thin,
With the brand upon her
　Of want and sin,
Heard the Child Angel
　And took her in.

Took her in gently,
　And did her best
To dry her pinions ;
　And made her rest
With tender pity
　Upon her breast.

When the eastern morning
　Grew bright and red,
Up the first sunbeam
　The Angel fled ;
Having kissed the woman
　And left her — dead.

RETURNED — " MISSING."

(FIVE YEARS AFTER.)

YES, I was sad and anxious,
　But now, dear, I am gay ;
I know that it is wisest
　To put all hope away : —
Thank God that I have done
　so,
　And can be calm to-day !

For hope deferred — you know
    it —
    Once made my heart so sick :
Now, I expect no longer;
    It is but the old trick
Of hope, that makes me tremble,
    And makes my heart beat
    quick.

All day I sit here calmly;
    Not as I did before,
Watching for one whose footstep
    Comes never, never more. . . .
Hush ! was that some one pass-
    ing,
    Who paused beside the door ?

For years I hung on chances,
    Longing for just one word;
At last I feel it : — silence
    Will never more be stirred. . .
Tell me once more that rumor
    You fancied you had heard.

Life has more things to dwell on
    Than just one useless pain,
Useless and past forever;
    But noble things remain,
And wait us all : . . . you too,
    dear,
    Do you think hope quite vain ?

All others have forgotten,
    'T is right I should forget,
Nor live on a keen longing
    Which shadows forth re-
    gret : . . .
Are not the letters coming ?
    The sun is almost set.

Now that my restless legion
    Of hopes and fears is fled,
Reading is joy and comfort . . .
    . . . This very day I read,
O, such a strange returning
    Of one whom all thought
    dead !

Not that *I* dream or fancy,
    You know all that is past;
Earth has no hope to give me,
    And yet — Time flies so fast
That all but the impossible
    Might be brought back at last.

IN THE WOOD.

In the wood where shadows are
    deepest
    From the branches overhead,
Where the wild wood-strawber-
    ries cluster,
    And the softest moss is spread,
I met to-day with a fairy,
    And I followed her where she
    led.

Some magical words she uttered,
    I alone could understand,
For the sky grew bluer and
    brighter;
    While there rose on either
    hand
The cloudy walls of a palace
    That was built in Fairy-land.

And I stood in a strange en-
chantment;
I had known it all before:
In my heart of hearts was the
magic
Of days that will come no
more,
The magic of joy departed,
That Time can never restore.

That never, ah, never, never,
Never again can be: —
Shall I tell you what powerful
fairy
Built up this palace for me?
It was only a little white Violet
I found at the root of a tree.

———

TWO WORLDS.

GOD'S world is bathed in beauty,
God's world is steeped in light;
It is the self-same glory
That makes the day so bright,
Which thrills the earth with
music,
Or hangs the stars in night.

Hid in earth's mines of silver,
Floating on clouds above, —
Ringing in Autumn's tempest,
Murmured by every dove, —
One thought fills God's creation,
His own great name of Love!

In God's world Strength is
lovely,
And so is Beauty strong,

And Light — God's glorious
shadow —
To both great gifts belong;
And they all melt into sweetness,
And fill the earth with Song.

Above God's world bends
Heaven,
With day's kiss pure and
bright,
Or folds her still more fondly
In the tender shade of night;
And she casts back Heaven's
sweetness,
In fragrant love and light.

God's world has one great echo;
Whether calm blue mists are
curled,
Or lingering dew-drops quiver,
Or red storms are unfurled;
The same deep love is throbbing
Through the great heart of
God's world.

Man's world is black and blight-
ed,
Steeped through with self and
sin;
And should his feeble purpose
Some feeble good begin,
The work is marred and tainted
By Leprosy within.

Man's world is bleak and bitter;
Wherever he has trod
He spoils the tender beauty
That blossoms on the sod,

And blasts the loving Heaven
　　Of the great, good world of
　　　God.

There Strength on coward weak-
　　ness
In cruel might will roll;
Beauty and Joy are cankers
　　That eat away the soul;
And Love — O God, avenge it —
　　The plague-spot of the whole.

Man's world is Pain and Terror;
　　He found it pure and fair,
And wove in nets of sorrow
　　The golden summer air.
Black, hideous, cold, and dreary,
　　Man's curse, not God's, is there.

And yet God's world is speaking:
　　Man will not hear it call;
But listens where the echoes
　　Of his own discords fall,
Then clamors back to Heaven
　　That God has done it all.

O God, man's heart is darkened,
　　He will not understand!
Show him Thy cloud and fire;
　　And, with Thine own right
　　　hand,
Then lead him through his desert,
　　Back to Thy Holy Land!

————

A NEW MOTHER.

I was with my lady when she
　　died:
I it was who guided her weak hand

For a blessing on each little
　　head,
Laid her baby by her on the
　　bed,
Heard the words they could not
　　understand.

And I drew them round my
　　knee that night,
Hushed their childish glee, and
　　made them say
　　They would keep her words
　　　with loving tears,
　　They would not forget her
　　　dying fears
Lest the thought of her should
　　fade away.

I, who guessed what her last
　　dread had been,
Made a promise to that still,
　　cold face,
　　That her children's hearts, at
　　　any cost,
　　Should be with the mother
　　　they had lost,
When a stranger came to take
　　her place.

And I knew so much! for I had
　　lived
With my lady since her child-
　　hood: known
　　What her young and happy
　　　days had been,
　　And the grief no other eyes
　　　had seen
I had watched and sorrowed for
　　alone.

Ah! she once had such a happy
smile!
I had known how sorely she was
tried:
  Six short years before, her eyes
  were bright
  As her little blue-eyed May's
  that night,
When she stood by her dead
mother's side.

No, I will not say he was unkind;
But she had been used to love
and praise.
  He was somewhat grave, —
  perhaps, in truth,
  Could not weave her joyous,
  smiling youth
Into all his stern and serious
ways.

She, who should have reigned a
blooming flower,
First in pride and honor, as in
grace, —
  She, whose will had once ruled
  all around,
  Queen and darling of us all, —
  she found
Change indeed in that cold,
stately place.

Yet she would not blame him,
even to me,
Though she often sat and wept
alone;
  But she could not hide it near
  her death,

  When she said with her last
  struggling breath,
"Let my babies still remain my
own!"

I it was who drew the sheet aside,
When he saw his dead wife's
face. That test
  Seemed to strike right to his
  heart. He said,
  In a strange, low whisper, to
  the dead,
"God knows, love, I did it for
the best!"

And he wept — O yes, I will be
just —
When I brought the children to
him there,
  Wondering sorrow in their
  baby eyes;
  And he soothed them with his
  fond replies,
Bidding me give double love and
care.

Ah, I loved them well for her
dear sake:
Little Arthur, with his serious air;
  May, with all her mother's
  pretty ways,
  Blushing, and at any word of
  praise
Shaking out her sunny golden
hair.

And the little one of all — poor
child!
She had cost that dear and precious life.

Once Sir Arthur spoke my
lady's name,
When the baby's gloomy chris-
tening came,
And he called her " Olga — like
my wife ! "

Save that time, he never spoke
of her :
He grew graver, sterner, every
day ;
And the children felt it, for
they dropped
Low their voices, and their
laughter stopped,
While he stood and watched them
at their play.

No, he never named their mother's name.
But I told them of her : told
them all
She had been ; so gentle, good,
and bright ;
And I always took them every
night
Where her picture hung in the
great hall.

There she stood : white daisies
in her hand,
And her red lips parted as to
speak
With a smile ; the blue and
sunny air
Seemed to stir her floating
golden hair,
And to bring a faint blush on
her cheek.

Well, so time passed on ; a year
was gone,
And Sir Arthur had been much
away.
Then the news came ! I shed
many tears
When I saw the truth of all
my fears
Rise before me on that bitter
day.

Any one but her I could have
borne !
But my lady loved her as her
friend.
Through their childhood and
their early youth,
How she used to count upon
the truth
Of this friendship that would
never end !

Older, graver than my lady was,
Whose young, gentle heart on
her relied,
She would give advice, and
praise, and blame,
And my lady leant on Mar-
garet's name,
As her dearest comfort, help, and
guide.

I had never liked her, and I
think
That my lady grew to doubt her
too,
Since her marriage ; for she
named her less,

Never saw her, and I used to
guess
At some secret wrong I never
knew.

That might be or not. But now,
to hear
She would come and reign here
in her stead,
With the pomp and splendor
of a bride :
Would no thought reproach
her in her pride
With the silent memory of the
dead ?

So, the day came, and the bells
rang out,
And I laid the children's black
aside ;
And I held each little trembling hand,
As I strove to make them understand
They must greet their father's
new-made bride.

Ah, Sir Arthur might look grave
and stern,
And his lady's eyes might well
grow dim,
When the children shrank in
fear away, —
Little Arthur hid his face, and
May
Would not raise her eyes, or
speak to him.

When Sir Arthur bade them
greet their "mother,"
I was forced to chide, yet proud
to hear
How my little loving May replied,
With her mother's pretty air
of pride, —
" Our dear mother has been dead
a year ! "

Ah, the lady's tears might well
fall fast,
As she kissed them, and then
turned away.
She might strive to smile or
to forget,
But I think some shadow of
regret
Must have risen to blight her
wedding-day.

She had some strange touch of
self-reproach ;
For she used to linger day by
day,
By the nursery door, or garden
gate,
With a sad, calm, wistful look,
and wait
Watching the three children at
their play.

But they always shrank away
from her
When she strove to comfort their
alarms,

And their grave, cold silence
    to beguile :
Even little Olga's baby-smile
Quivered into tears when in her
    arms.

I could never chide them : for I
    saw
How their mother's memory grew
    more deep
    In their hearts. Each night I
    had to tell
    Stories of her whom I loved
    so well
When a child, to send them off
    to sleep.

But Sir Arthur — O, this was
    too hard ! —
He, who had been always stern
    and sad
    In my lady's time, seemed to
    rejoice
    Each day more ; and I could
    hear his voice
Even, sounding younger and
    more glad.

He might perhaps have blamed
    them, but his wife
Never failed to take the children's
    part :
    She would stay him with her
    pleading tone,
    Saying she would strive, and
    strive alone,
Till she gained each little way-
    ward heart.

And she strove indeed, and
    seemed to be
Always waiting for their love,
    in vain ;
    Yet, when May had most her
    mother's look,
    Then the lady's calm, cold ac-
    cents shook
With some memory of reproach-
    ful pain.

Little May would never call her
    mother :
So, one day, the lady, bending
    low,
    Kissed her golden curls, and
    softly said,
    " Sweet one, call me Marga-
    ret, instead, —
Your dear mother used to call
    me so."

She was gentle, kind, and pa-
    tient too,
Yet in vain : the children held
    apart.
    Ah, their mother's gentle
    memory dwelt
    Near them, and her little or-
    phans felt
She had the first claim upon
    their heart.

So three years passed ; then the
    war broke out ;
And a rumor seemed to spread
    and rise ;

First we guessed what sorrow
  must befall,
Then all doubt fled, for we
  read it all
    In the depths of her despairing
    eyes.

Yes; Sir Arthur had been called
  away
.To that scene of slaughter, fear,
  and strife, —
    Now he seemed to know with
    double pain
    The cold, bitter gulf that must
    remain
To divide his children from his
  wife.

Nearer came the day he was to
  sail,
Deeper grew the coming woe
  and fear,
    When, one night, the children
    at my knee
    Knelt to say their evening
    prayer to me,
I looked up and saw Sir Arthur
  near.

There they knelt with folded
  hands, and said
Low, soft words in stammering
  accents sweet;
    In the firelight shone their
    golden hair
    And white robes: my darlings
    looked so fair,
With their little bare and rosy
  feet!

There he waited till their low
  " Amen!"
Stopped the rosy lips raised for
  " Good night!" —
    Drew them with a fond clasp,
    close and near,
    As he bade them stay with
    him, and hear
Something that would make his
  heart more light.

Little Olga crept into his arms;
Arthur leant upon his shoulder;
  May
    Knelt beside him, with her
    earnest eyes
    Lifted up in patient, calm sur-
    prise, —
I can almost hear his words to-
  day.

" Years ago, my children, years
  ago,
When your mother was a child,
  she came
    From her Northern home,
    and here she met
    Love for love, and comfort for
    regret,
In one early friend, — you know
  her name.

" And this friend — a few years
  older — gave
Such fond care, such love, that
  day by day
    The new home grew happy,
    joy complete,

Studies easier, and play more
  sweet,
While all childish sorrows passed
  away.

"And your mother—fragile,
  like my May—
Leant on this deep love,—nor
  leant in vain.
  For this friend (strong, generous, noble heart!)
  Gave the sweet, and took the
  bitter part,—
Brought her all the joy, and kept
  the pain.

"Years passed on, and then I
  saw them first:
It was hard to say which was
  most fair,
  Your sweet mother's bright
  and blushing face,
  Or the graver Margaret's stately grace;
Golden locks, or braided raven
  hair.

"Then it happened, by a
  strange, sad fate,
One thought entered into each
  young soul:
  Joy for one—if for the other
  pain;
  Loss for one—if for the other
  gain:
One must lose, and one possess
  the whole.

"And so this—this—what they
  cared for—came
And belonged to Margaret: was
  her own.
  But she laid the gift aside, to
  take
  Pain and sorrow for your
  mother's sake,
And none knew it but herself
  alone.

"Then she travelled far away,
  and none
The strange mystery of her ab-
  sence knew.
  Margaret's secret thought was
  never told:
  Even your mother thought
  her changed and cold,
And for many years I thought
  so too.

"She was gone; and then your
  mother took
That poor gift which Margaret
  laid aside:
  Flower, or toy, or trinket,
  matters not:
  What it was had better be
  forgot . . .
It was just then she became my
  bride.

"Now, I think May knows the
  hope I have.
Arthur, darling, can you guess
  the rest?

Even my little Olga understands
Great gifts can be given by
little hands,
Since of all gifts Love is still the
best.

" Margaret is my dear and honored wife,
And I hold her so. But she
can claim
From your hearts, dear ones,
a loving debt
I can neither pay, nor yet forget :
You can give it in your mother's
name.

" Earth spoils even Love, and
here a shade
On the purest, noblest heart may
fall :
Now your mother dwells in
perfect light,
She will bless us, I believe,
to-night, —
She is happy now, and she knows
all."

Next day was farewell, — a day
of tears ;
Yet Sir Arthur, as he rode away,
And turned back to see his
lady stand
With the children clinging to
her hand,
Looked as if it were a happy
day.

Ah, they loved her soon !   The
little one
Crept into her arms as to a nest ;
Arthur always with her now ;
and May
Growing nearer to her every
day : —
— Well, I loved my own dear
lady best.

GIVE PLACE.

STARRY Crowns of Heaven
Set in azure night !
Linger yet a little
Ere you hide your light : —
— Nay ; let Starlight fade
away,
Heralding the day !

Snow-flakes pure and spotless,
Still, O, still remain,
Binding dreary winter,
In your silver chain : —
— Nay ; but melt at once
and bring
Radiant sunny Spring !

Blossoms, gentle blossoms,
Do not wither yet ;
Still for you the sun shines,
Still the dews are wet : —
— Nay ; but fade and wither
fast,
Fruit must come at last !

Joy, so true and tender,
　Dare you not abide?
Will you spread your pinions,
　Must you leave our side?
　　— Nay; an Angel's shin-
　　ing grace
　Waits to fill your place!

———

MY WILL.

Since I have no lands or houses,
　And no hoarded golden store,
What can I leave those who love
　me
　When they see my face no
　more?
Do not smile; I am not jesting,
　Though my words sound gay
　and light,
Listen to me, dearest Alice,
　I will make my Will to-night.

First for Mabel, — who will
　never
Let the dust of future years
Dim the thought of me, but keep
　it
　Brighter still: perhaps with
　tears.
In whose eyes, whate'er I glance
　at,
　Touch, or praise, will always
　shine,
Through a strange and sacred
　radiance,
　By Love's Charter, wholly
　mine;

She will never lend to others
　Slenderest link of thought I
　claim,
I will, therefore, to her keeping
　Leave my memory and my
　name.

Bertha will do truer service
　To her· kind than I have
　done,
So I leave to her young spirit
　The long Work I have begun.
Well! the threads are tangled,
　broken,
　And the colors do not blend,
She will bend her earnest striving
　Both to finish and amend:
And, when it is all completed,
　Strong with care and rich with
　skill,
Just because my hands began
　it,
　She will love it better still.

Ruth shall have my dearest
　token,
　The one link I dread to break,
The one duty that I live for,
　She, when I am gone, will
　take.
Sacred is the trust I leave her,
　Needing patience, prayer, and
　tears;
I have striven to fulfil it,
　As she knows, these many
　years.
Sometimes hopeless, faint, and
　weary,
　Yet a blessing shall remain

With the task, and Ruth will
  prize it,
  For my many hours of pain.

What must I leave you, my
  Alice?
Nothing, Love, to do or bear,
Nothing that can dim your blue
  eyes
  With the slightest cloud of
  care.
I will leave my heart to love you,
  With the tender faith of old;
Still to comfort, warm, and light
  you,
. Should your life grow dark or
  cold.
No one else, my child, can claim
  it;
  Though you find old scars of
  pain,
They were only wounds, my dar-
  ling,
  There is not, I trust, one
  stain.

Are my gifts indeed so worthless
  Now the slender sum is told?
Well, I know not: years may
  bless them
  With a nobler price than gold.
Am I poor? ah no, most
  wealthy,
  Not in these poor gifts you
  take,
But in the true hearts that tell
  me
  You will keep them for my
  sake.

KING AND SLAVE.

IF in my soul, dear,
  An omen should dwell,
Bidding me pause, ere
  I love thee too well;
If the whole circle
  Of noble and wise,
With stern forebodings,
  Between us should rise; —

I will tell *them*, dear,
  That Love reigns — a King,
Where storms cannot reach him,
  And words cannot sting;
He counts it dishonor
  His faith to recall;
He trusts; — and forever
  He gives — and gives all!

I will tell *thee*, dear,
  That Love is — a Slave,
Who dreads thought of freedom,
  As life dreads the grave;
And if doubt or peril
  Of change there may be,
Such fear would but drive him
  Still nearer to thee!

A CHANT.

" *Benedictus qui venit in nomine Do-
mini.*"

I.

WHO is the Angel that cometh?
  Life!
Let us not question what he
  brings,
  Peace or Strife;

Under the shade of his mighty
    wings,
      One by one,
    Are his secrets told ;
      One by one,
Lit by the rays of each morning
    sun,
    Shall a new flower its petals
      unfold,
    With the mystery hid in its
      heart of gold.
We will arise and go forth to
    greet him,
    Singly, gladly, with one ac-
      cord ; —
" Blessed is he that cometh
    In the name of the Lord ! "

II.

Who is the Angel that cometh ?
    Joy !
Look at his glittering rainbow
    wings, —
    No alloy
Lies in the radiant gifts he
    brings ;
    Tender and sweet,
    He is come to-day,
    Tender and sweet :
While chains of love on his
    silver feet
Will hold him in lingering fond
    delay.
But greet him quickly, he will
    not stay,
Soon he will leave us ; but
    though for others
    All his brightest treasures are
    stored, —

" Blessed is he that cometh
    In the name of the Lord ! "

III.

Who is the Angel that cometh ?
    Pain !
Let us arise and go forth to greet
    him ;
    Not in vain
Is the summons come for us to
    meet him ;
    He will stay,
    And darken our sun ;
    He will stay
A desolate night, a weary day.
    Since in that shadow our
      work is done,
    And in that shadow our
      crowns are won,
Let us say still, while his bitter
    chalice
    Slowly into our hearts is
      poured, —
" Blessed is he that cometh
    In the name of the Lord ! "

IV.

Who is the Angel that cometh ?
    Death !
But do not shudder and do not
    fear ;
    Hold your breath,
For a kingly presence is drawing
    near,
    Cold and bright
    Is his flashing steel,
    Cold and bright

The smile that comes like a
    starry light
  To calm the terror and grief
    we feel;
  He comes to help and to save
    and heal:
Then let us, baring our hearts
    and kneeling,
  Sing, while we wait this An-
    gel's sword, —
" Blessed is he that cometh
    In the name of the Lord! "

DREAM-LIFE.

LISTEN, friend, and I will tell
    you
  Why I sometimes seem so
    glad,
Then, without a reason, chang-
    ing,
  Soon become so grave and
    sad.

Half my life I live a beggar,
  Ragged, helpless, and alone;
But the other half a monarch,
  With my courtiers round my
    throne.

Half my life is full of sorrow,
  Half of joy, still fresh and
    new;
One of these lives is a fancy,
  But the other one is true.

While I live and feast on glad-
    ness,
  Still I feel the thought remain,
This must soon end, — nearer,
    nearer,
  Comes the life of grief and
    pain.

While I live a wretched beggar,
  One bright hope my lot can
    cheer;
Soon, soon thou shalt have thy
    kingdom,
  Brighter hours are drawing
    near.

So you see my life is twofold,
  Half a pleasure, half a grief;
Thus all joy is somewhat tem-
    pered,
  And all sorrow finds relief.

Which, you ask me, is the real life,
  Which the dream, — the joy,
    or woe?
Hush, friend! it is little matter,
  And, indeed — I never know.

REST.

SPREAD, spread thy silver wings,
    O Dove!
And seek for rest by land and
    sea,
And bring the tidings back to me
For thee and me and those I
    love.

Look how my Dove soars
far away;
Go with her, heart of mine,
I pray;
Go where her fluttering silver
pinions
Follow the track of the crim-
son day.

Is rest where cloudlets slowly
creep,
And sobbing winds forget to
grieve,
And quiet waters gently heave,
As if they rocked the ship to
sleep?
Ah no! that southern vapor
white
Will bring a tempest ere the
night,
And thunder through the
quiet heaven,
Lashing the sea in its angry
might.

The battle-field lies still and cold,
While stars that watch in silent
light
Gleam here and there on weapons bright,
In weary sleepers' slackened
hold;
Nay, though they dream of no
alarm,
One bugle sound will stir that
calm,
And all the strength of two
great nations,
Eager for battle, will rise and
arm.

Pause where the Pilgrims' day is
done,
Where scrip and staff aside are
laid,
And, resting in the silent shade,
They watch the slowly sinking
sun.
Ah no! that worn and weary
band
Must journey long before they
stand,
With bleeding feet, and hearts
rejoicing,
Kissing the dust of the Holy
Land.

Then find a soul who meets at
last
A noble prize but hard to gain,
Or joy long pleaded for in vain,
Now sweeter for a bitter past.
Ah no! for Time can rob her
yet,
And even should cruel Time
forget,
Then Death will come, and,
unrelenting,
Brand her with sorrowful long
regret.

Seek farther, farther yet, O Dove!
Beyond the Land, beyond the
Sea,
There shall be rest for thee and
me,
For thee and me and those I
love.
I heard a promise gently fall,
I heard a far-off Shepherd call

The weary and the broken-
hearted,
Promising rest unto each and
all-

It is not marred by outward
strife,
It is not lost in calm repose,
It heedeth neither joys nor woes,
Is not disturbed by death or life ;
Through, and beyond them,
lies our Rest :
Then cease, O Heart, thy
longing quest!
And thou, my Dove, with sil-
ver pinions
Flutter again to thy quiet
nest!

THE TYRANT AND THE
CAPTIVE.

It was midnight when I listened,
And I heard two Voices
speak ;
One was harsh, and stern, and
cruel,
And the other soft and weak :
Yet I saw no Vision enter,
And I heard no steps depart,
Of this Tyrant and his Cap-
tive, . . .
Fate it might be and a *Heart.*

Thus the stern Voice spake in
triumph : —
" I have shut your life away

From the radiant world of na-
ture,
And the perfumed light of day.
You, who loved to steep your
spirit
In the charm of Earth's de-
light,
See no glory of the daytime,
And no sweetness of the
night."

But the soft Voice answered
calmly : —
" Nay, for when the March
winds bring
Just a whisper to my window,
I can dream the rest of Spring;
And to-day I saw a swallow
Flitting past my prison bars,
And my cell has just one corner
Whence at night I see the
stars."

But its bitter taunt repeating,
Cried the harsh Voice : —
" Where are they,
All the friends of former hours,
Who forget your name to-day ?
All the links of love are shattered,
Which you thought so strong
before ;
And your very heart is lonely,
And alone since loved no
more."

But the low Voice spoke still
lower : —
" Nay, I know the golden chain
Of my love is purer, stronger,
For the cruel fire of pain :

They remember me no longer,
But I, grieving here alone,
Bind their souls to me forever
By the love within my own."

But the Voice cried : — "Once
remember
You devoted soul and mind
To the welfare of your brethren,
And the service of your kind.
Now, what sorrow can you com-
fort ?
You, who lie in helpless pain,
With an impotent compassion
Fretting out your life in vain."

"Nay"; and then the gentle
answer
Rose more loud, and full, and
clear :
"For the sake of all my brethren
I thank God that I am here!
Poor had been my Life's best
efforts,
Now I waste no thought or
breath, —
For the prayer of those who suf-
fer
Has the strength of Love and
Death."

THE CARVER'S LESSON.

Trust me, no mere skill of subtle tracery,
No mere practice of a dexter-
ous hand,

Will suffice, without a hidden
spirit,
That we may, or may not,
understand.

And those quaint old fragments
that are left us
Have their power in this, —
the Carver brought
Earnest care, and reverent patience, only
Worthily to clothe some noble
thought.

Shut then in the petals of the
flowers,
Round the stems of all the
lilies twine,
Hide beneath each bird's or
angel's pinion,
Some wise meaning or some
thought divine.

Place in stony hands that pray
forever
Tender words of peace, and
strive to wind
Round the leafy scrolls and
fretted niches
Some true, loving message to
your kind.

Some will praise, some blame,
and, soon forgetting,
Come and go, nor even pause
to gaze ;
Only now and then a passing
stranger
Just may loiter with a word
of praise.

But I think, when years have
floated onward,
  And the stone is gray, and
dim, and old,
And the hand forgotten that
has carved it,
  And the heart that dreamt it
still and cold ;

There may come some weary
soul, o'erladen
  With perplexéd struggle in
his brain,
Or, it may be, fretted with life's
turmoil,
  Or made sore with some perpetual pain.

Then, I think those stony hands
will open,
  And the gentle lilies overflow,
With the blessing and the loving token
  That you hid there many
years ago.

And the tendrils will unroll,
and teach him
  How to solve the problem of
his pain ;
And the birds' and angels'
wings shake downward
  On his heart a sweet and
tender rain.

While he marvels at his fancy,
reading
  Meaning in that quaint and
ancient scroll,

Little guessing that the loving
Carver
  Left a message for his weary
soul.

THREE ROSES.

JUST when the red June Roses
blow
She gave me one, — a year ago.
A Rose whose crimson breath
revealed
The secret that its heart con-
cealed,
And whose half-shy, half-tender
grace
Blushed back upon the giver's
face.
  A year ago — a year ago —
  To hope was not to know.

Just when the red June Roses
blow
I plucked her one, — a month
ago :
Its half-blown crimson to eclipse,
I laid it on her smiling lips ;
The balmy fragrance of the south
Drew sweetness from her sweet-
er mouth.
  Swiftly do golden hours
creep, —
  To hold is not to keep.

The red June Roses now are
past,
This very day I broke the last, —

And now its perfumed breath is
  hid,
With her, beneath a coffin-lid;
There will its petals fall apart,
And wither on her icy heart:—
  At three red Roses' cost
  My world was gained and lost.

MY PICTURE GALLERY.

I.

You write and think of me, my
  friend, with pity;
While you are basking in the
  light of Rome,
Shut up within the heart of this
  great city,
Too busy and too poor to leave
  my home.

II.

You think my life debarred all
  rest or pleasure,
Chained all day to my ledger
  and my pen;
Too sickly even to use my little
  leisure
To bear me from the strife and
  din of men.

III.

Well, it is true; yet, now the
  days are longer,
At sunset I can lay my writing
  down,

And slowly crawl (summer has
  made me stronger)
Just to the nearest outskirt of the
  town.

IV.

There a wide Common, black-
  ened though and dreary
With factory smoke, spreads
  outward to the West;
I lie down on the parched-up
  grass, if weary,
Or lean against a broken wall
  to rest.

V.

So might a King, turning to
  Art's rich treasure,
At evening, when the cares of
  state were done,
Enter his royal gallery, drinking
  pleasure
Slowly from each great picture,
  one by one.

VI.

Towards the West I turn my
  weary spirit,
And watch my pictures: one
  each night is mine.
Earth and my soul, sick of day's
  toil, inherit
A portion of that luminous
  peace divine.

VII.

There I have seen a sunset's
  crimson glory,
Burn as if earth were one great
  Altar's blaze;

Or, like the closing of a piteous
story,
Light up the misty world with
dying rays.

VIII.

There I have seen the clouds,
in pomp and splendor,
Their gold and purple banners
all unfurl;
There I have watched colors,
more faint and tender
Than pure and delicate tints
upon a pearl.

IX.

Skies strewn with roses fading,
fading slowly,
While one star trembling watched
the daylight die;
Or deep in gloom a sunset, hidden wholly,
Save through gold rents torn in
a violet sky.

X.

Or parted clouds, as if asunder
riven
By some great angel, and beyond a space
Of far-off tranquil light; the gates
of Heaven
Will lead as grandly to as calm
a place.

XI.

Or stern dark walls of cloudy
mountain ranges
Hid all the wonders that we knew
must be ;

While, far on high, some little
white clouds' changes
Revealed the glory they alone
could see.

XII.

Or in wild wrath the affrighted
clouds lay shattered,
Like treasures of the lost Hes-
perides,
All in a wealth of ruined splendor scattered,
Save one strange light on distant
silver seas.

XIII.

What land or time can claim the
Master Painter,
Whose art could teach him half
such gorgeous dyes ?
Or skill so rare, but purer hues
and fainter
Melt every evening in my western
skies.

XIV.

So there I wait, until the shade
has lengthened,
And night's blue misty curtain
floated down ;
Then, with my heart calmed, and
my spirit strengthened,
I crawl once more back to the
sultry town.

XV.

What Monarch, then, has nobler
recreations
Than mine ? Or where the great
and classic Land

Whose wealth of Art delights the
gathered nations
That owns a Picture Gallery half
as grand ?

SENT TO HEAVEN.

I HAD a Message to send her,
  To her whom my soul loved
    best;
But I had my task to finish,
  And she was gone home to
    rest.

To rest in the far bright heaven:
  O, so far away from here,
It was vain to speak to my dar-
    ling,
  For I knew she could not
    hear !

I had a message to send her,
  So tender, and true, and
    sweet,
I longed for an Angel to bear it,
  And lay it down at her feet.

I placed it, one summer evening,
  On a Cloudlet's fleecy breast;
But it faded in golden splendor,
  And died in the crimson west.

I gave it the Lark, next morning,
  And I watched it soar and
    soar ;

But its pinions grew faint and
  weary,
  And it fluttered to earth once
    more.

To the heart of a Rose I told it ;
  And the perfume, sweet and
    rare,
Growing faint on the blue bright
  ether,
  Was lost in the balmy air.

I laid it upon a Censer,
  And I saw the incense rise ;
But its clouds of rolling silver
  Could not reach the far blue
    skies.

I cried, in my passionate long
  ing : —
  " Has the earth no Angel
    friend
Who will carry my love the mes-
    sage
  That my heart desires to
    send ? "

Then I heard a strain of music,
  So mighty, so pure, so clear,
That my very sorrow was silent,
  And my heart stood still to
    hear.

And I felt, in my soul's deep
  yearning,
  At last the sure answer stir : —
" The music will go up to
  Heaven,
  And carry my thought to her."

It rose in harmonious rushing
  Of mingled voices and strings,
And I tenderly laid my message
  On the Music's outspread
    wings.

I heard it float farther and far-
    ther,
  In sound more perfect than
    speech;
Farther than sight can follow,
  Farther than soul can reach.

And I know that at last my
    message
  Has passed through the golden
    gate:
So my heart is no longer rest-
    less,
  And I am content to wait.

NEVER AGAIN.

"Never again!" vow hearts
    when reunited,
  "Never again shall Love be
    cast aside;
Forever now the shadow has de-
    parted;
  Nor bitter sorrow, veiled in
    scornful pride,
Shall feign indifference, or affect
    disdain, —
Never, O Love, again, never
    again!"

"Never again!" so sobs, in bro-
    ken accents,
  A soul laid prostrate at a holy
    shrine, —
"Once more, once more forgive,
    O Lord, and pardon,
  My wayward life shall bend to
    love divine;
And nevermore shall sin its
    whiteness stain, —
Never, O God, again, never
    again!"

"Never again!" so speaketh
    one forsaken,
  In the blank desolate passion
    of despair, —
"Never again shall the bright
    dream I cherished
  Delude my heart, for bitter
    truth is there, —
The angel, Hope, shall still thy
    cruel pain
Never again, my heart, never
    again!"

"Never again!" so speaks the
    sudden silence,
  When round the hearth gathers
    each well-known face,
But one is missing, and no future
    presence,
  However dear, can fill that
    vacant place;
Forever shall the burning
    thought remain, —
"Never, beloved, again! never
    again!"

" Never again ! " so — but beyond
    our hearing —
    Ring out far voices fading up
    the sky ;
Never again shall earthly care
    and sorrow
    Weigh down the wings that
    bear those souls on high ;
" Listen, O earth, and hear that
    glorious strain, —
Never, never again ! never
    again ! "

LISTENING ANGELS.

BLUE against the bluer heavens
    Stood the mountain, calm and
    still,
Two white Angels, bending
    earthward,
    Leant upon the hill.

Listening leant those silent An-
    gels,
    And I also longed to hear
What sweet strain of earthly
    music
    Thus could charm their ear.

I heard the sound of many trum-
    pets
    In a warlike march draw
    nigh ;
Solemnly a mighty army
    Passed in order by.

But the clang had ceased ; the
    echoes
    Soon had faded from the hill ;
While the Angels, calm and ear-
    nest,
    Leant and listened still.

Then I heard a fainter clamor,
    Forge and wheel were clashing
    near,
And the Reapers in the meadow
    Singing loud and clear.

When the sunset came in glory,
    And the toil of day was o'er,
Still the Angels leant in silence,
    Listening as before.

Then, as daylight slowly van-
    ished,
    And the evening mists grew
    dim,
Solemnly from distant voices
    Rose a vesper hymn.

When the chant was done, and
    lingering
    Died upon the evening air,
From the hill the radiant Angels
    Still were listening there.

Silent came the gathering dark-
    ness,
    Bringing with it sleep and
    rest ;
Save a little bird was singing
    Near her leafy nest.

Through the sounds of war and
labor
She had warbled all day long,
While the Angels leant and lis-
tened
Only to her song.

But the starry night was com-
ing;
When she ceased her little lay,
From the mountain-top the An-
gels
Slowly passed away.

GOLDEN DAYS.

GOLDEN days—where are they?
Pilgrims east and west
Cry; if we could find them
We would pause and rest:
We would pause and rest a little
From our long and weary
ways:—
Where are they, then, where are
they—
Golden days?

Golden days—where are they?
Ask of childhood's years,
Still untouched by sorrow,
Still undimmed by tears:
Ah, they seek a phantom Future,
Crowned with brighter, starry
rays;—
Where are they, then, where are
they—
Golden days?

Golden days—where are they?
Has Love learnt the spell
That will charm them hither,
Near our hearth to dwell?
Insecure are all her treasures,
Restless is her anxious
gaze:—
Where are they, then, where are
they—
Golden Days?

Golden days—where are they?
Farther up the hill
I can hear the echo
Faintly calling still:
Faintly calling, faintly dying,
In a far-off misty haze:—
Where are they, then, where are
they—
Golden days?

PHILIP AND MILDRED.

Lingering fade the rays of daylight, and the listening air is chilly;
  Voice of bird and forest murmur, insect hum and quivering spray,
Stir not in that quiet hour : through the valley, calm and stilly,
  All in hushed and loving silence watch the slow departing Day.

Till the last faint western cloudlet, faint and rosy, ceases blushing,
  And the blue grows deep and deeper where one trembling planet
    shines,
And the day has gone forever — then, like some great ocean rushing,
  The sad night wind wails lamenting, sobbing through the moan-
    ing pines.

Such, of all day's changing hours, is the fittest and the meetest
  For a farewell hour — and parting looks less bitter and more blest;
Earth seems like a shrine for sorrow, Nature's mother voice is
    sweetest,
  And her hand seems laid in chiding on the unquiet throbbing
    breast.

Words are lower, for the twilight seems rebuking sad repining,
  And wild murmur and rebellion, as all childish and in vain;
Breaking through dark future hours clustering starry hopes seem
    shining,
  Then the calm and tender midnight folds her shadow round the
    pain.

So they paced the shady lime-walk in that twilight dim and holy,
  Still the last farewell deferring, she could hear or he should say;
Every word, weighed down by sorrow, fell more tenderly and
    slowly —
  This, which now beheld their parting, should have been their
    wedding-day.

Should have been : her dreams of childhood, never straying, never
    faltering,
Still had needed Philip's image to make future life complete ;
Philip's young hopes of ambition, ever changing, ever altering,
    Needed Mildred's gentle presence even to make successes sweet.

This day should have seen their marriage ; the calm crowning and
    assurance
Of two hearts, fulfilling rather, and not changing, either life :
Now they must be rent asunder, and her heart must learn endurance,
    For he leaves their home, and enters on a world of work and strife

But her gentle spirit long had learnt, unquestioning, submitting,
    To revere his youthful longings, and to marvel at the fate
That gave such a humble office, all unworthy and unfitting,
    To the genius of the village, who was born for something great.

When the learnéd Traveller came there who had gained renown at
    college,
    Whose abstruse research had won him even European fame,
Questioned Philip, praised his genius, marvelled at his self-taught
    knowledge,
    Could she murmur if he called him up to London and to fame ?

Could she waver when he bade her take the burden of decision,
    Since his troth to her was plighted, and his life was now her own ?
Could she doom him to inaction ? could she, when a new-born vision
    Rose in glory for his future, check it for her sake alone ?

So her little trembling fingers, that had toiled with such fond pleasure,
    Paused, and laid aside, and folded the unfinished wedding gown ;
Faltering earnestly assurance, that she too could, in her measure,
    Prize for him the present honor, and the future's sure renown.

Now they pace the shady lime-walk, now the last words must be
    spoken,
    Words of trust, for neither dreaded more than waiting and delay;

Was not love still called eternal, — could a plighted vow be
    broken ? —
See the crimson light of sunset fades in purple mist away.

" Yes, my Mildred," Philip told her, " one calm thought of joy and
    blessing,
Like a guardian spirit by me, through the world's tumultuous stir,
Still will spread its wings above me, and now urging, now repressing,
    With my Mildred's voice will murmur thoughts of home, and love,
    and her.

" It will charm my peaceful leisure, sanctify my daily toiling,
    With a right none else possesses, touching my heart's inmost string ;
And to keep its pure wings spotless I shall fly the world's touch,
    soiling
    .Even in thought this Angel Guardian of my Mildred's Wedding
    Ring.

" Take it, dear ; this little circlet is the first link, strong and holy,
    Of a life-long chain, and holds me from all other love apart ;
Till the day when you may wear it as my wife — my own — mine
    wholly —
    Let me know it rests forever near the beating of your heart."

Dawn of day saw Philip speeding on his road to the Great City,
    Thinking how the stars gazed downward just with Mildred's patient
    eyes ;
Dreams of work, and fame, and honor struggling with a tender pity,
    Till the loving Past receding saw the conquering Future rise.

Daybreak still found Mildred watching, with the wonder of first
    sorrow,
How the outward world unaltered shone the same this very day ;
How unpitying and relentless busy life met this new morrow,
    Earth, and sky, and man unheeding that her joy had passed away.

Then the round of weary duties, cold and formal, came to meet her,
    With the life within departed that had given them each a soul ;
And her sick heart even slighted gentle words that came to greet her ;
    For Grief spread its shadowy pinions, like a blight upon the whole.

Jar one chord, the harp is silent ; move one stone, the arch is shattered ;
  One small clarion-cry of sorrow bids an arméd host awake ;
One dark cloud can hide the sunlight ; loose one string, the pearls
    are scattered ;
  Think one thought, a soul may perish ; say one word, a heart
    may break !

Life went on, he two lives running side by side ; the outward seeming,
  And the truer and diviner hidden in the heart and brain ;
Dreams grow holy, put in action ; work grows fair through starry
    dreaming ;
  But where each flows on unmingling, both are fruitless and in vain.

Such was Mildred's life ; her dreaming lay in some far-distant region,
  All the fairer, all the brighter, that its glories were but guessed ;
And the daily round of duties seemed an unreal, airy legion, —
  Nothing true save Philip's letters and the ring upon her breast.

Letters telling how he struggled, for some plan or vision aiming,
  And at last how he just grasped it as a fresh one spread its wings ;
How the honor or the learning, once the climax, now were claiming,
  Only more and more, becoming merely steps to higher things.

Telling her of foreign countries : little store had she of learning,
  So her earnest, simple spirit answered as he touched the string ;
Day by day, to these bright fancies all her silent thoughts were turning,
  Seeing every radiant picture framed within her golden Ring.

O poor heart ! love, if thou willest ; but, thine own soul still possessing,
  Live thy life : not a reflection or a shadow of his own :
Lean as fondly, as completely, as thou willest, — but confessing
  That thy strength is God's, and therefore can, if need be, stand
    alone.

Little means were there around her to make farther, wider ranges,
  Where her loving gentle spirit could try any stronger flight ;
And she turned aside, half fearing that fresh thoughts were fickle
    changes, —
  That she *must* stay as he left her on that farewell summer night.

Love should still be guide and leader, like a herald should have risen,
    Lighting up the long dark vistas, conquering all opposing fates;
But new claims, new thoughts, new duties found her heart a silent
    prison,
    And found Love, with folded pinions, like a jailer by the gates.

Yet why blame her? it had needed greater strength than she was given
    To have gone against the current that so calmly flowed along;
Nothing fresh came near the village save the rain and dew of heaven,
    And her nature was too passive, and her love perhaps too strong.

The great world of thought, that rushes down the years, and on-
    ward sweeping
Bears upon its mighty billows in its progress each and all,
Flowed so far away, its murmur did not rouse them from their
    sleeping;
    Life and Time and Truth were speaking, but they did not hear
    their call.

Years flowed on; and every morning heard her prayer grow lower,
    deeper,
    As she called all blessings on him, and bade every ill depart,
And each night when the cold moonlight shone upon that quiet sleeper,
    It would show her ring that glittered with each throbbing of her
    heart.

Years passed on. Fame came for Philip in a full, o'erflowing
    measure;
    He was spoken of and honored through the breadth of many lands,
And he wrote it all to Mildred, as if praise were only pleasure,
    As if fame were only honor, when he laid them in her hands.

Mildred heard it without wonder, as a sure result expected,
    For how could it fail, since merit and renown go side by side?
And the neighbors, who first fancied genius ought to be suspected,
    Might at last give up their caution, and could own him now with
    pride.

Years flowed on. These empty honors led to others they called better,
    He had saved some slender fortune, and might claim his bride at last

Mildred, grown so used to waiting, felt half startled by the letter
   That now made her future certain, and would consecrate her past.

And he came : grown sterner, older — changed indeed : a grave
      reliance
Had replaced his eager manner, and the quick short speech of old :
He had gone forth with a spirit half of hope and half defiance ;
   He returned with proud assurance half disdainful and half cold.

Yet his old self seemed returning while he stood sometimes, and lis-
      tened
To her calm, soft voice, relating all the thoughts of these long years ;
And if Mildred's heart was heavy, and at times her blue eyes glistened,
   Still in thought she would not whisper aught of sorrow or of fears.

Autumn with its golden cornfields, autumn with its storms and showers,
   Had been there to greet his coming with its forests gold and brown ;
And the last leaves still were falling, fading still the year's last flowers,
   When he left the quiet village, and took back his bride to town.

Home, — the home that she had pictured many a time in twilight,
      dwelling
On that tender, gentle fancy, folded round with loving care ;
Here was home, — the end, the haven ; and what spirit voice
      seemed telling,
   That she only held the casket, with the gem no longer there ?

Sad it may be to be longing, with a patience faint and weary,
   For a hope deferred, — and sadder still to see it fade and fall ;
Yet to grasp the thing we long for, and, with sorrow sick and dreary,
   Then to find how it can fail us, is the saddest pain of all.

What was wanting ? He was gentle, kind, and generous still,
      deferring
To her wishes always ; nothing seemed to mar their tranquil life :
There are skies so calm and leaden that we long for storm-winds
      stirring,
   There is peace so cold and bitter, that we almost welcome strife.

Darker grew the clouds above her, and the slow conviction clearer
   That he gave her home and pity, but that heart and soul and mind

Were beyond her now; he loved her, and in youth he had been near her,
But he now had gone far onward, and had left her there behind.

Yes, beyond her: yes, quick-hearted, her Love helped her in revealing
It was worthless, while so mighty; was too weak, although so strong;
There were courts she could not enter, depths she could not sound;
yet feeling
It was vain to strive or struggle, vainer still to mourn or long.

He would give her words of kindness, he would talk of home, but
seeming
With an absent look, forgetting if he held or dropped her hand;
And then turn with eager pleasure to his writing, reading, dreaming,
Or to speak of things with others that she could not understand.

He had paid, and paid most nobly, all he owed; no need of blaming;
It had cost him something, maybe, that no future could restore:
In her heart of hearts she knew it; Love and Sorrow, not complaining,
Only suffered all the deeper, only loved him all the more.

Sometimes then a stronger anguish, and more cruel, weighed upon
her,
That, through all those years of waiting, he had slowly learnt the
truth;
He had known himself mistaken, but that, bound to her in honor,
He renounced his life, to pay her for the patience of her youth.

But a star was slowly rising from that mist of grief, and brighter
Grew her eyes, for each slow hour surer comfort seemed to bring;
And she watched with strange sad smiling how her trembling hands
grew slighter,
And how thin her slender finger, and how large her wedding-ring.

And the tears dropped slowly on it, as she kissed that golden token
With a deeper love, it may be, than was in the far-off past;
And remembering Philip's fancy, that so long ago was spoken,
Thought her Ring's bright angel guardian had stayed near her to
the last.

Grieving sorely, grieving truly, with a tender care and sorrow,
  Philip watched the slow, sure fading of his gentle, patient wife;
Could he guess with what a yearning she was longing for the morrow,
  Could he guess the bitter knowledge that had wearied her of life?

Now with violets strewn upon her, Mildred lies in peaceful sleeping;
  All unbound her long, bright tresses, and her throbbing heart at rest,
And the cold, blue rays of moonlight, through the open casement
    creeping,
  Show the ring upon her finger, and her hands crossed on her breast.

Peace at last. Of peace eternal is her calm, sweet smile a token.
  Has some angel lingering near her let a radiant promise fall?
Has he told her Heaven unites again the links that Earth has broken?
  For on Earth so much is needed, but in Heaven Love is all!

BORROWED THOUGHTS.

I. FROM "LAVATER."

Trust him little who doth raise
  To one height both great and
    small,
And sets the sacred crown of
    praise,
  Smiling, on the head of all.

Trust him less who looks
    around
  To censure all with scornful
    eyes,
And in everything has found
  Something that he dare de-
    spise.

But for one who stands apart,
  Stirred by naught that can
    befall,

With a cold, indifferent heart, —
  Trust him least and last of
    all.

II. FROM "PHANTASTES."

I have a bitter Thought, a
    Snake
  That used to sting my life to
    pain.
I strove to cast it far away,
But every night and every day
  It crawled back to my heart
    again!

It was in vain to live or strive,
  To think or sleep, to work or
    pray;
At last I bade this thing accursed

Gnaw at my heart, and do its
worst,
  And so I let it have its way.

Thus said I, " I shall never fall
  Into a false and dreaming
  peace,
And then awake, with sudden
start,
To feel it biting at my heart,
  For now the pain can never
  cease."

But I gained more; for I have
found
  That such a snake's enven-
  omed charm
Must always, always find a part,
Deep in the centre of my heart,
  Which it can never wound or
  harm.   •

It is coiled round my heart to-
day.
  It sleeps at times, this cruel
  snake,   .
And while it sleeps it never
stings : —
Hush ! let us talk of other things,
  Lest it should hear me and
  awake.

———

III. FROM "LOST ALICE."

  Yes, dear, our Love is slain;
In the cold grave forevermore it
  lies,
  Never to wake again,

Or light our sorrow with its
starry eyes :
  And so — regret is vain.

One hour of pain and dread,
We killed our Love, we took its
  life away
  With the false words we
  said ;
And so we watch it, since that
cruel day,
  Silent, and cold, and dead.

We should have seen it
shine
Long years beside us. Time and
Death might try
  To touch that life divine,
Whose strength could every other
stroke defy
  Save only thine and mine.

No longing can restore
Our dead again. Vain are the
tears we weep,
  And vainly we deplore
Our buried Love : its grave lies
dark and deep
  Between us evermore.

———

IV. FROM * * *

Within the kingdom of my
Soul
I bid you enter, Love, to-day ;
Submit my life to your control,
And give my Heart up to your
sway.

My Past, whose light and life is
flown,
Shall live through memory for
you still;
Take all my Present for your
own,
And mould my Future to your
will.

One only thought remains apart,
And will forever so remain ;
There is one Chamber in my
• heart
Where even you might knock in
vain.

A haunted Chamber : — long ago
I closed it, and I cast the key
Where deep and bitter waters
flow,
Into a vast and silent sea.

Dear, it is haunted. All the
rest
Is yours; but I have shut that
door
Forever now. 'T is even best
That I should enter it no more.

No more. It is not well to stay
With ghosts; their very look
would scare
Your joyous, loving smile
away ; —
So never try to enter there.

Check, if you love me, all regret
That this one thought remains
apart : —

Now let us smile, dear, and for-
get
The haunted Chamber in my
Heart.

LIGHT AND SHADE.

THOU hast done well to kneel
and say,
" Since He who gave can take
away,
And bid me suffer, I obey."

And also well to tell thy heart,
That good lies in the bitterest
part,
And thou wilt profit by her smart.

But bitter hours come to all :
When even truths like these will
pall,
Sick hearts for humbler comfort
call.

Then I would have thee strive to
see
That good and evil come to thee,
As one of a great family.

And as material life is planned,
That even the loneliest one must
stand
Dependent on his brother's
hand ;

So links more subtle and more fine
Bind every other soul to thine
In one great brotherhood divine.

Nor with thy share of work be
vexed ;
Though incomplete, and even
perplext,
It fits exactly to the next.

What seems so dark to thy dim
sight
May be a shadow, seen aright,
Making some brightness doubly
bright.

The flash that struck thy tree —
no more
To shelter thee — lets Heaven's
blue floor
Shine where it never shone before.

Thy life that has been dropped
aside
Into Time's stream, may stir the
tide
In rippled circles spreading wide.

The cry wrung from thy spirit's
pain
May echo on some far-off plain,
And guide a wanderer home
again.

Fail — yet rejoice ; because no
less
The failure that makes thy distress
May teach another full success.

It may be that in some great
need
Thy life's poor fragments are
decreed
To help build up a lofty deed.

Thy heart should throb in vast
content,
Thus knowing that it was but
meant
As chord in one great instru-
ment ;

That even the discord in thy
soul
May make completer music roll
From out the great harmonious
whole.

It may be, that when all is light,
Deep set within that deep delight
Will be to know *why* all was
right ;

To hear life's perfect music rise,
And, while it floods the happy
skies,
Thy feeble voice to recognize.

Then strive more gladly to fulfil
Thy little part. This darkness
still
Is light to every loving will.

And trust, as if already plain
How just thy share of loss and
pain
Is for another fuller gain.

I dare not limit time or place
Touched by thy life : nor dare I
    trace
Its far vibrations into space.

One only knows. Yet if the fret
Of thy weak heart, in weak re-
    gret
Needs a more tender comfort yet :

Then thou mayst take thy lone-
    liest fears,
The bitterest drops of all thy
    tears,
The dreariest hours of all thy
    years ;

And through thy anguish there
    outspread,
May ask that God's great love
    would shed
Blessings on one belovéd head.

And thus thy soul shall learn to
    draw
Sweetness from out that loving
    law
That sees no failure and no flaw,

Where all is good. And life is
    good,
Were the one lesson understood
Of its most sacred brotherhood.

A CHANGELING.

A LITTLE changeling spirit
    Crept to my arms one day :

I had no heart or courage
    To drive the child away.

So all day long I soothed her,
    And hushed her on my breast;
And all night long her wailing
    Would never let me rest.

I dug a grave to hold her,
    A grave both dark and deep ;
I covered her with violets,
    And laid her there to sleep.

I used to go and watch there,
    Both night and morning
    too : —
It was my tears, I fancy,
    That kept the violets blue.

I took her up: and once more
    I felt the clinging hold,
And heard the ceaseless wailing
    That wearied me of old.

I wandered, and I wandered,
    With my burden on my breast,
Till I saw a church-door open,
    And entered in to rest.

In the dim, dying daylight,
    Set in a flowery shrine,
I saw the Virgin Mother
    Holding her Child divine.

I knelt down there in silence,
    And on the altar-stone
I laid my wailing burden,
    And came away — alone.

And now that little spirit,
   That sobbed so all day long,
Is grown a shining Angel,
   With wings both wide and
     strong.

She watches me from Heaven
   With loving, tender care,
And one day she has promised
   That I shall find her there.

DISCOURAGED.

WHERE the little babbling
   streamlet
   First brings forth to light,
Trickling through soft velvet
   mosses,
   Almost hid from sight;
   Vowed I with delight, —
" River, I will follow thee,
Through thy wanderings to the
   Sea ! "

Gleaming 'mid the purple heather,
   Downward then it sped,
Glancing through the mountain
   gorges,
   Like a silver thread,
   As it quicker fled,
Louder music in its flow,
Dashing to the vale below.

Then its voice grew lower, gentler,
   And its pace less fleet,

Just as though it loved to linger
   Round the rushes' feet,
   As they stooped to meet
Their clear images below,
Broken by the ripples' flow.

Purple Willow-herb bent over
   To her shadow fair ;
Meadow-sweet, in feathery clus-
   ters,
   Perfumed all the air ;
   Silver-weed was there,
And in one calm, grassy spot,
Starry, blue Forget-me-not.

Tangled weeds, below the waters,
   Still seemed drawn away ;
Yet the current, floating onward,
   Was less strong than they ; —
   Sunbeams watched their play,
With a flickering light and shade,
Through the screen the Alders
   made.

Broader grew the flowing River ;
   To its grassy brink
Slowly, in the slanting sun-rays,
   Cattle trooped to drink ;
   The blue sky, I think,
Was no bluer than that stream,
Slipping onward, like a dream.

Quicker, deeper then it hurried,
   Rushing fierce and free ;
But I said, " It should grow
   calmer
   Ere it meets the Sea,
   The wide purple Sea,

Which I weary for in vain,
Wasting all my toil and pain."

But it rushed still quicker, fiercer,
   In its rocky bed,
Hard and stony was the pathway
   To my tired tread ;
   " I despair," I said,
" Of that wide and glorious Sea
That was promised unto me."

So I turned aside, and wandered
   Through green meadows near,
Far away, among the daisies,
   Far away, for fear
   Lest I still should hear
The loud murmur of its song,
As the River flowed along.

Now I hear it not : — I loiter
   Gayly as before ;
Yet I sometimes think, — and
   thinking
   Makes my heart so sore, —
   Just a few steps more,
And there might have shone for
   me,
Blue and infinite, the Sea.

IF THOU COULDST KNOW.

I think if thou couldst know,
   O soul that will complain,
What lies concealed below
   Our burden and our pain ;

How just our anguish brings
Nearer those longed-for things
We seek for now in vain, —
I think thou wouldst rejoice, and
   not complain.

I think if thou couldst see,
   With thy dim mortal sight·
How meanings, dark to thee,
   Are shadows hiding light ;
Truth's efforts crossed and
   vexed,
Life's purpose all perplexed, —
If thou couldst see them right,
I think that they would seem all
   clear, and wise, and bright.

And yet thou canst not know,
   And yet thou canst not see ;
Wisdom and sight are slow
   In poor humanity.
If thou couldst *trust*, poor soul,
In Him who rules the whole,
Thou wouldst find peace and
   rest :
Wisdom and sight are well, but
   Trust is best.

THE WARRIOR TO HIS DEAD BRIDE.

If in the fight my arm was strong,
   And forced my foes to yield, —
If conquering and unhurt I came
   Back from the battle-field, —
It is because thy prayers have
   been
My safeguard and my shield.

My comrades smile to see my arm
  Spare or protect a foe,
They think thy gentle pleading
    voice
Was silenced long ago ;
But pity and compassion, love,
  Were taught me first by woe.

Thy heart, my own, still beats
    in Heaven
With the same love divine
That made thee stoop to such a
    soul,
So hard, so stern as mine, —
My eyes have learnt to weep, be-
    loved,
  Since last they looked on thine

I hear thee murmur words of
    peace
  Through the dim midnight air,
And a calm falls from the angel
    stars
    And soothes my great de-
      spair, —
The heavens themselves look
    brighter, love,
  Since thy sweet soul is there.

And if my heart is once more
    calm,
  My step is once more free,
It is because each hour I feel
  Thou prayest still for me ;
Because no fate or change can
    come
  Between my soul and thee.

It is because my heart is stilled,
  Not broken by despair,

Because I see the grave is bright,
  And death itself is fair : —
I dread no more the wrath of
    Heaven, —
  I have an angel there !

————

A LETTER.

DEAR, I tried to write you such
    a letter
As would tell you all my heart
    to-day.
Written Love is poor ; one word
    were better ;
Easier, too, a thousand times, to
    say.

I can tell you all : fears, doubts
    unheeding,
While I can be near you, hold
    your hand,
Looking right into your eyes,
    and reading
Reassurance that you understand.

Yet I wrote it through, then
    lingered, thinking
Of its reaching you, — what hour,
    what day ;
Till I felt my heart and courage
    sinking
With a strange, new, wondering
    dismay.

" Will my letter fall," I wondered
    sadly,
" On her mood like some dis-
    cordant tone,

Or be welcomed tenderly and
gladly?
Will she be with others, or alone?

" It may find her too absorbed to
read it,
Save with hurried glance and
careless air :
Sad and weary, she may scarcely
heed it ;
Gay and happy, she may hardly
care.

" Shall I — dare I — risk the
chances?" slowly
Something — was it shyness,
love, or pride? —
Chilled my heart, and checked
my courage wholly ;
So I laid it wistfully aside.

Then I leant against the casement, turning
Tearful eyes towards the far-off
west,
Where the golden evening light
was burning,
Till my heart throbbed back
again to rest.

And I thought : " Love's soul is
not in fetters,
Neither space nor time keeps
souls apart ;
Since I cannot — dare not —
send my letters,
Through the silence I will send
my heart.

" If, perhaps now, while my
tears are falling,
She is dreaming quietly alone,
She will hear my Love's far echo
calling,
Feel my spirit drawing near her
own.

" She will hear, while twilight
shades enfold her,
All the gathered Love she knows
so well, —
Deepest Love my words have
ever told her,
Deeper still — all I could never
tell.

" Wondering at the strange,
mysterious power
That has touched her heart, then
she will say :
'Some one whom I love, this
very hour,
Thinks of me, and loves me, far
away.'

" If, as well may be, to-night
has found her
Full of other thoughts, with
others by,
Through the words and claims
that gather round her
She will hear just one half-
smothered sigh ;

" Or will marvel why, without
her seeking,
Suddenly the thought of me re-
curs ;

Or, while listening to another
    speaking,
Fancy that my hand is holding
    hers."

So I dreamed, and watched the
    stars' far splendor
Glimmering on the azure dark-
    ness, start, —
While the star of trust rose bright
    and tender,
Through the twilight shadows of
    my heart.

A COMFORTER.

I.

"WILL she come to me, little
    Effie,
Will she come in my arms to
    rest,
And nestle her head on my
    shoulder,
While the sun goes down in
    the west?

II.

"I and Effie will sit together,
    All alone, in this great arm-
    chair : —
Is it silly to mind it, darling,
    When Life is so hard to bear?

III.

"No one comforts me like my
    Effie,
Just I think that she does not
    try, —

Only looks with a wistful won-
    der
Why grown people should
    ever cry;

IV.

"While her little soft arms close
    tighter
Round my neck in their cling-
    ing hold : —
Well, I must not cry on your
    hair, dear,
For my tears might tarnish
    the gold.

V.

"I am tired of trying to read,
    dear;
It is worse to talk and seem
    gay:
There are some kinds of sorrow,
    Effie,
It is useless to thrust away.

VI.

"Ah, advice may be wise, my
    darling,
But one always knows it be-
    fore;
And the reasoning down one's
    sorrow
Seems to make one suffer the
    more.

VII.

"But my Effie won't reason,
    will she?
Or endeavor to understand :

Only holds up her mouth to kiss
  me,
  As she strokes my face with
    her hand.

VIII.

"If you break your plaything
  yourself, dear,
  Don't you cry for it all the
    same?
I don't think it is such a com-
  fort,
  One has only one's self to
    blame.

IX.

" People say things cannot be
  helped, dear,
  But then that is the reason
    why;
For if things could be helped or
  altered,
  One would never sit down to
    cry:

X.

" They say, too, that tears are
  quite useless
  To undo, amend, or restore,—
When I think *how* useless, my
  Effie,
  Then my tears only fall the
    more.

XI.

• All to-day I struggled against
  it ;
  But that does not make sor-
    row cease ;

And now, dear, it is such a
  comfort
  To be able to cry in peace.

XII.

" Though wise people would call
  that folly,
And remonstrate with grave surprise ;
We won't mind what they say,
  my Effie ; —
  We never professed to be wise.

XIII.

" But my comforter knows a
  lesson
  Wiser, truer than all the
    rest : —
That to help and to heal a sor-
  row,
  Love and silence are always
    best.

XIV.

" Well, who is my comforter, —
  tell me ?
  Effie smiles, but she will not
    speak :
Or look up through the long
  curled lashes
  That are shading her rosy
    cheek.

XV.

" Is she thinking of talking fishes,
  The bluebird, or magical tree ?

Perhaps I am thinking, my dar-
      ling,
  Of something that never can be.

XVI.

" You long — don't you, dear ?
      — for the Genii,
  Who were slaves of lamps and
      of rings ;
And, I — I am sometimes afraid,
      dear,
  I want as impossible things.

XVII.

" But hark ! there is Nurse call-
      ing Effie !
  It is bedtime, so run away ;
And I must go back, or the
      others
  Will be wondering why I stay.

XVIII.

" So good night to my darling
      Effie ;
  Keep happy, sweetheart, and
      grow wise : —
There 's one kiss for her golden
      tresses,
  And two for her sleepy eyes."

UNSEEN.

There are more things in
  Heaven and Earth than we
Can dream of, or than nature
  understands ;

We learn not through our poor
  philosophy
What hidden chords are touched
  by unseen hands.

The present hour repeats upon
  its strings
Echoes of some vague dream we
  have forgot ;
Dim voices whisper half-remem-
  bered things,
And when we pause to listen —
  answer not.

Forebodings come : we know not
  how, or whence,
Shadowing a nameless fear upon
  the soul,
And stir within our hearts a
  subtler sense
Than light may read, or wisdom
  may control.

And who can tell what secret
  links of thought
Bind heart to heart ? Unspoken
  things are heard,
As if within our deepest selves
  was brought
The soul, perhaps, of some unuttered word.

But, though a veil of shadow
  hangs between
That hidden life and what we see
  and hear,
Let us revere the power of the
  Unseen,
And know a world of mystery is
  near.

A REMEMBRANCE OF AUTUMN.

NOTHING stirs the sunny silence, —
　Save the drowsy humming of
　　the bees
　　Round the rich ripe peaches
　　on the wall,
　And the south-wind sighing
　　in the trees,
　　And the dead leaves rustling
　　as they fall :
While the swallows, one by
　one, are gathering,
　All impatient to be on the
　　wing,
　And to wander from us, seek-
　　ing
　　　Their belovéd Spring !

Cloudless rise the azure heavens !
　Only vaporous wreaths of
　　snowy white
　　Nestle in the gray hill's
　　rugged side ;
　And the golden woods are
　　bathed in light,
　　Dying, if they must, with
　　kingly pride :
While the swallows, in the
　blue air wheeling,
　Circle now an eager, flutter-
　　ing band,
　Ready to depart and leave us
　　　For a brighter land !

But a voice is sounding sadly,
　Telling of a glory that has
　　been ;

Of a day that faded all too
　fast : —
See afar through the blue air
　serene,
　Where the swallows wing
　　their way at last,
　And our hearts perchance as
　　sadly wandering,
　　Vainly seeking for a long-
　　lost day,
While we watch the far-off
　swallows,
　　　Flee with them away !

THREE EVENINGS IN A LIFE.

I.

YES, it looked dark and dreary,
　That long and narrow street :
Only the sound of the rain,
　And the tramp of passing feet,
The duller glow of the fire,
　And gathering mists of night,
To mark how slow and weary
　The long day's cheerless
　　flight !

II.

Watching the sullen fire,
　Hearing the dismal rain,
Drop after drop, run down
　On the darkening window
　　pane :
Chill was the heart of Alice,
　Chill as that winter day, —

For the star of her life had risen
   Only to fade away.

III.

The voice that had been so
   strong
   To bid the snare depart,
The true and earnest will,
   The calm and steadfast heart,
Were now weighed down by sor-
   row,
   Were quivering now with
   pain;
The clear path now seemed
   clouded,
   And all her grief in vain.

IV.

Duty, Right, Truth, who prom-
   ised
   To help and save their own,
Seemed spreading wide their pin-
   ions
   To leave her there alone.
So, turning from the Present
   To well-known days of yore,
She called on them to strengthen
   And guard her soul once
   more.

V.

She thought how in her girlhood
   Her life was given away,
The solemn promise spoken
   She kept so well to-day;
How to her brother Herbert
   She had been help and guide,
And how his artist nature
   On her calm strength relied.

VI.

How through life's fret and tur-
   moil
   The passion and fire of art
In him was soothed and quick-
   ened
   By her true sister heart;
How future hopes had always
   Been for his sake alone;
And now — what strange new
   feeling
   Possessed her as its own?

VII.

Her home — each flower that
   breathed there,
   The wind's sigh, soft and low,
Each trembling spray of ivy,
   The river's murmuring flow,
The shadow of the forest,
   Sunset, or twilight dim, —
Dear as they were, were dearer
   By leaving them for him.

VIII.

And each year as it found her
   In the dull, feverish town,
Saw self still more forgotten,
   And selfish care kept down
By the calm joy of evening
   That brought him to her side,
To warn him with wise counsel,
   Or praise with tender pride.

IX.

Her heart, her life, her future,
   Her genius, only meant
Another thing to give him,
   And be therewith content.

To-day, what words had stirred
  her,
    Her soul could not forget?
What dream had filled her spirit
  With strange and wild regret?

X.

To leave him for another, —
  Could it indeed be so?
Could it have cost such anguish
  To bid this vision go?
Was this her faith?   Was Her-
  bert
The second in her heart?
Did it need all this struggle
  To bid a dream depart?

XI.

And yet, within her spirit
  A far-off land was seen,
A home, which might have held
  her,
    A love, which might have
    been.
And Life — not the mere being
  Of daily ebb and flow,
But Life itself — had claimed her,
  And she had let it go!

XII.

Within her heart there echoed
  Again the well-known tone
That promised this bright future,
  And asked her for her own:
Then words of sorrow, broken
  By half-reproachful pain:
And then a farewell, spoken
  In words of cold disdain.

XIII.

Where now was the stern pur-
  pose
    That nerved her soul so long?
Whence came the words she
  uttered,
    So hard, so cold, so strong?
What right had she to banish
  A hope that God had given?
Why must she choose earth's
  portion,
    And turn aside from Heaven?

XIV.

To-day!   Was it this morning?
  If this long, fearful strife
Was but the work of hours,
  What would be years of life?
Why did a cruel Heaven
  For such great suffering call?
And why — O still more cruel! —
  Must her own words do all?

XV.

Did she repent?   O Sorrow!
  Why do we linger still
To take thy loving message,
  And do thy gentle will?
See, her tears fall more slowly,
  The passionate murmurs cease,
And back upon her spirit
  Flow strength, and love, and
  peace.

XVI.

The fire burns more brightly,
  The rain has passed away,
Herbert will see no shadow
  Upon his home to-day:

Only that Alice greets him
  With doubly tender care,
Kissing a fonder blessing
  Down on his golden hair.

II.

I.

THE Studio is deserted,
  Palette and brush laid by,
The sketch rests on the easel,
  The paint is scarcely dry;
And Silence — who seems always
  Within her depths to bear
The next sound that will utter —
  Now holds a dumb despair.

II.

So Alice feels it : listening
  With breathless, stony fear,
Waiting the dreadful summons
  Each minute brings more
    near :
When the young life, now ebb-
    ing,
  Shall fail, and pass away
Into that mighty shadow
  Who shrouds the house to-day.

III.

But why — when the sick-cham-
    ber
  Is on the upper floor —
Why dares not Alice enter
  Within the close-shut door?
If he — her all — her Brother,
  Lies dying in that gloom,

What strange mysterious power
  Has sent her from the room?

IV.

It is not one week's anguish
  That can have changed her so;
Joy has not died here lately,
  Struck down by one quick
    blow;
But cruel months have needed
  Their long relentless chain,
To teach that shrinking manner
  Of helpless, hopeless pain.

V.

The struggle was scarce over
  Last Christmas eve had
    brought;
The fibres still were quivering
  Of the one wounded thought,
When Herbert — who, uncon-
    scious,
  Had guessed no inward strife—
Bade her, in pride and pleasure,
  Welcome his fair young wife.

VI.

Bade her rejoice, and smiling,
  Although his eyes were dim,
Thanked God he thus could pay
    her
  The care she gave to him.
This fresh bright life would bring
    her
  A new and joyous fate —
O Alice, check the murmur
  That cries, "Too late! too
    late!"

VII.

Too late! Could she have
known it
A few short weeks before,
That his life was completed,
And needing hers no more,
She might — O sad repining!
What "might have been " for-
get;
"It was not " should suffice us
To stifle vain regret.

VIII.

He needed her no longer,
Each day it grew more plain;
First with a startled wonder,
Then with a wondering pain.
Love : why, his wife best gave it;
Comfort : durst Alice speak
Or counsel, when resentment
Flushed on the young wife's
cheek ?

IX.

No more long talks by firelight
Of childish times long past,
And dreams of future greatness
Which he must reach at last ;
Dreams, where her purer instinct
With truth unerring told,
Where was the worthless gilding,
And where refinéd gold.

X.

Slowly, but surely ever,
Dora's poor jealous pride,
Which she called love for Her-
bert,
Drove Alice from his side ;

And, spite of nervous effort
To share their altered life,
She felt a check to Herbert,
A burden to his wife.

XI.

This was the least ; for Alice
Feared, dreaded, *knew* at length
How much his nature owed her
Of truth, and power, and
strength ;
And watched the daily failing
Of all his nobler part :
Low aims, weak purpose, telling
In lower, weaker art.

XII.

And now, when he is dying,
The last words she could hear
Must not be hers, but given
The bride of one short year.
The last care is another's ;
The last prayer must not be
The one they learnt together
Beside their mother's knee.

XIII.

Summoned at last : she kisses
The clay-cold stiffening hand .
And, reading pleading efforts
To make her understand,
Answers, with solemn promise,
In clear but trembling tone,
To Dora's life henceforward
She will devote her own.

XIV.

Now all is over. Alice
Dares not remain to weep,

But soothes the frightened Dora
  Into a sobbing sleep.
The poor weak child will need
    her : . . .
  O, who can dare complain,
When God sends a new Duty
  To comfort each new Pain !

III.

I.

The House is all deserted
  In the dim evening gloom,
Only one figure passes
  Slowly from room to room ;
And, pausing at each doorway,
  Seems gathering up again
Within her heart the relics
  Of bygone joy and pain.

II.

There is an earnest longing
  In those who onward gaze,
Looking with weary patience
  Towards the coming days.
There is a deeper longing,
  More sad, more strong, more
    keen :
Those know it who look back-
    ward,
  And yearn for what has been.

III.

At every hearth she pauses,
  Touches each well-known
    chair ;
Gazes from every window,
  Lingers on every stair.

What have these months brought
    Alice
  Now one more year is past ?
This Christmas eve shall tell us,
  The third one and the last.

IV.

The wilful, wayward Dora,
  In those first weeks of grief,
Could seek and find in Alice
  Strength, soothing, and relief.
And Alice — last sad comfort
  True woman-heart can take —
Had something still to suffer
  And bear for Herbert's sake.

V.

Spring, with her western breezes,
  From Indian islands bore
To Alice news that Leonard
  Would seek his home once
    more.
What was it, — joy, or sorrow ?
  What were they, — hopes, or
    fears ?
That flushed her cheeks with
    crimson,
  And filled her eyes with tears ?

VI.

He came.   And who so kindly
  Could ask and hear her tell
Herbert's last hours ; for Leon-
    ard
  Had known and loved him
    well.
Daily he came ; and Alice,
  Poor weary heart, at length,

Weighed down by others' weak-
　　ness,
　Could lean upon his strength.

VII.

Yet not the voice of Leonard
　Could her true care beguile,
That turned to watch, rejoicing,
　Dora's reviving smile.
So, from that little household
　The worst gloom passed away,
The one bright hour of evening
　Lit up the livelong day.

VIII.

Days passed.　The golden sum-
　　mer
In sudden heat bore down
Its blue, bright, glowing sweet-
　　ness
Upon the scorching town.
And sights and sounds of country
　Came in the warm soft tune
Sung by the honeyed breezes
　Borne on the wings of June.

IX.

One twilight hour, but earlier
　Than usual, Alice thought
She knew the fresh sweet fra-
　　grance
　Of flowers that Leonard
　　brought;
Through opened doors and win-
　　dows
　It stole up through the gloom,
And with appealing sweetness
　Drew Alice from her room.

X.

Yes, he was there; and, pausing
　Just near the opened door,
To check her heart's quick beat-
　　ing,
　She heard — and paused still
　　more —
His　low　voice — Dora's　an-
　　swers —
　His pleading — Yes, she knew
The tone — the words — the ac-
　　cents;
　She once had heard them too.

XI.

" Would　Alice　blame　her ? "
　　Leonard's
　Low, tender answer came :
" Alice was far too noble
　To think or dream of blame."
" And　was　he　sure　he　loved
　　her ? "
　" Yes, with the one love given
Once in a lifetime only,
　With one soul and one heav-
　　en ! "

XII.

Then came　a plaintive mur-
　　mur, —
　" Dora had once been told
That he and Alice — " " Dear-
　　est,
　Alice is far too cold
To love ; and I, my Dora,
　If once I fancied so,
It was a brief delusion,
　And over — long ago."

XIII.

Between the Past and Present,
  On that bleak moment's height,
She stood. As some lost trav-
  eller,
By a quick flash of light
Seeing a gulf before him,
  With dizzy, sick despair,
Reels backward, but to find it
  A deeper chasm there.

XIV.

The twilight grew still darker,
  The fragrant flowers more
    sweet,
The stars shone out in heaven,
  The lamps gleamed down the
    street ;
And hours passed in dreaming
  Over their new-found fate,
Ere they could think of wonder-
    ing
  Why Alice was so late.

XV.

She came, and calmly listened ;
  In vain they strove to trace
If Herbert's memory shadowed
  In grief upon her face.
No blame, no wonder showed
    there,
  No feeling could be told ;
Her voice was not less steady,
  Her manner not more cold.

XVI.

They could not hear the anguish
  That broke in words of pain

Through the calm summer mid-
    night, —
  "My Herbert — mine again !"
Yes, they have once been parted,
  But this day shall restore
The long-lost one : she claims
    him ;
  "My Herbert — mine once
    more ! "

XVII.

Now Christmas eve returning
  Saw Alice stand beside
The altar, greeting Dora,
  Again a smiling bride ;
And now the gloomy evening
  Sees Alice pale and worn,
Leaving the house forever,
  To wander out forlorn.

XVIII.

Forlorn — nay, not so. Anguish
  Shall do its work at length ;
Her soul, passed through the fire,
  Shall gain still purer strength.
Somewhere there waits for Alice
  An earnest, noble part ;
And meanwhile God is with
    her, —
  God, and her own true heart!

THE WIND.

THE wind went forth o'er land
    and sea,
  Loud and free ;

Foaming waves leapt up to
    meet it,
Stately pines bowed down to
    greet it ;
While the wailing sea
And the forest's murmured sigh
    Joined the cry
Of the wind that swept o'er land
    and sea.

The wind that blew upon the sea
    Fierce and free,
Cast the bark upon the shore,
Whence it sailed the night be-
    fore
Full of hope and glee ;
And the cry of pain and death
    Was but a breath,
Through the wind that roared
    upon the sea.

The wind was whispering on the
    lea
    Tenderly ;
But the white rose felt it pass,
And the fragile stalks of grass
    Shook with fear to see
All her trembling petals shed,
    As it fled
So gently by, — the wind upon
    the lea.

Blow, thou wind, upon the sea
    Fierce and free,
And a gentler message send,
Where frail flowers and grasses
    bend,
    On the sunny lea ·

For thy bidding still is one,
    Be it done
In tenderness or wrath, on land
    or sea !

EXPECTATION.

THE ·King's three daughters
    stood on the terrace,
The hanging terrace, so broad
    and green,
Which keeps the sea from the
    marble Palace :
There was Princess May, and
    Princess Alice,
And the youngest Princess,
    Gwendoline.

Sighed Princess May, " Will it
    last much longer,
Time throbs so slow and my
    Heart so quick ;
And O, how long is the day in
    dying !
Weary am I of waiting and
    sighing,
For Hope deferred makes the
    spirit sick."

But Princess Gwendoline smiled
    and kissed her : —
" Am I not sadder than you, my
    Sister ?
Expecting joy is a happy pain.
The Future's fathomless mine of
    treasures,

All countless hordes of possible
pleasures,
Might bring their store to my
feet in vain."

Sighed Princess Alice as night
grew nearer : —
" So soon, so soon, is the daylight fled !
And O, how fast comes the dark
to-morrow,
Who hides, perhaps, in her veil
of sorrow
The terrible hour I wait and
dread ! "

But Princess Gwendoline kissed
her, sighing : —
" It is only Life that can fear
dying ;
Possible loss means possible gain.
Those who still dread are not
quite forsaken ;
But not to fear, because all is
taken,
Is the loneliest depth of human
pain."

.

———

AN IDEAL.

While the gray mists of early
dawn
Were lingering round the hill,
And the dew was still upon the
flowers,
And the earth lay calm and
still,

A wingéd Spirit came to me,
Noble, and radiant, and free.

Folding his blue and shining
wings,
He laid his hand on mine.
I know not if I felt, or heard
The mystic word divine,
Which woke the trembling air
to sighs,
And shone from out his starry
eyes.

The word he spoke within my
heart
Stirred life unknown before,
And cast a spell upon my soul
To chain it evermore ;
Making the cold, dull earth look
bright,
And skies flame out in sapphire
light.

When noon ruled from the heav-
ens, and man
Through busy day toiled on,
My Spirit drooped his shining
wings ;
His radiant smile was gone ;
His voice had ceased, his grace
had flown,
His hand grew cold within my
own.

Bitter, O bitter tears I wept,
Yet still I held his hand,
Hoping with vague unreasoning
hope :
I would not understand

That this pale Spirit nevermore
Could be what he had been before.

Could it be so ? My heart stood
    still.
Yet he was by my side.
I strove ; but my despair was
    vain ;
Vain too was love and pride.
Could he have changed to me
    so soon ?
My day was only at its noon.

Now stars are rising one by one,
    Through the dim evening air ;
Near me a household Spirit waits,
    With tender loving care ;
He speaks and smiles, but never
    sings,
Long since he lost his shining
    wings.

With thankful, true content, I
    know
This is the better way ;
Is not a faithful spirit mine —
    Mine still — at close of
    day ? . . .
Yet will my foolish heart repine
For that bright morning dream
    of mine.

OUR DEAD.

NOTHING is our own : we hold
    our pleasures
Just a little while, ere they are
    fled :

One by one life robs us of our
    treasures ;
Nothing is our own except our
    Dead.

They are ours, and hold in faith-
    ful keeping,
Safe forever, all they took away.
Cruel life can never stir that
    sleeping,
Cruel time can never seize that
    prey.

Justice pales ; truth fades ; stars
    fall from heaven ;
Human are the great whom we
    revere :
No true crown of honor can be
    given,
Till we place it on a funeral bier.

How the Children leave us : and
    no traces
Linger of that smiling angel
    band ;
Gone, forever gone ; and in their
    their places
Weary men and anxious women
    stand.

Yet we have some little ones,
    still ours ;
They have kept the baby smile
    we know,
Which we kissed one day, and
    hid with flowers,
On their dead white faces, long
    ago.

When our Joy is lost — and life
   will take it —
Then no memory of the past
   remains ;
Save with some strange, cruel
   sting, to make it
Bitterness beyond all present
   pains.

Death, more tender - hearted,
   leaves to sorrow
Still the radiant shadow, fond
   regret :
We shall find, in some far, bright
   to-morrow,
Joy that he has taken, living yet.

Is Love ours, and do we dream
   we know it,
Bound with all our heart-strings,
   all our own ?
Any cold and cruel dawn may
   show it,
Shattered, desecrated, over-
   thrown.

Only the dead Hearts forsake us
   never ;
Death's last kiss has been the
   mystic sign
Consecrating Love our own forever,
Crowning it eternal and divine.

So when Fate would fain besiege
   our city,
Dim our gold, or make our
   flowers fall,

Death, the Angel, comes in love
   and pity,
And, to save our treasures, claims
   them all.

A WOMAN'S ANSWER.

I WILL not let you say a Woman's part
   Must be to give exclusive love
   alone ;
Dearest, although I love you so,
   my heart
   Answers a thousand claims
   besides your own.

I love — what do I not love ?
   earth and air
   Find space within my heart,
   and myriad things
You would not deign to heed are
   cherished there,
   And vibrate on its very inmost strings.

I love the Summer with her ebb
   and flow
   Of light, and warmth, and
   music, that have nurst
Her tender buds to blossoms . . .
   and you know
   It was in summer that I saw
   you first.

I love the Winter dearly, too, . . .
  but then
  I owe it so much ; on a win-
    ter's day,
Bleak, cold, and stormy, you re-
    turned again,
  When you had been those
    weary months away.

I love the Stars like friends ; so
  many nights
  I gazed at them, when you
    were far from me,
Till I grew blind with tears . . . .
    those far-off lights
  Could watch you, whom I
    longed in vain to see.

I love the Flowers ; happy hours
    lie
  Shut up within their petals
    close and fast :
You have forgotten, dear ; but
    they and I
  Keep every fragment of the
    golden Past.

I love, too, to be loved ; all lov-
    ing praise
  Seems like a crown upon my
    Life, — to make
It better worth the giving, and
    to raise
  Still nearer to your own the
    heart you take.

I love all good and noble souls ;
  — I heard
  One speak of you but lately,
    and for days,

Only to think of it, my soul was
    stirred
  In tender memory of such
    generous praise.

I love all those who love you ;
    all who owe
  Comfort to you : and I can
    find regret
Even for those poorer hearts
    who once could know
  And once could love you, and
    can now forget.

Well, is my heart so narrow, —
    I, who spare
  Love for all these ?   Do I not
    even hold
My favorite books in special ten-
    der care,
  And prize them as a miser
    does his gold ?

The Poets that you used to read
    to me
  While summer twilights faded
    in the sky ;
But most of all I think Aurora
    Leigh,
  Because — because — do you
    remember why ?

Will you be jealous ?   Did you
    guess before
  I loved so many things ? —
    Still you the best : —
Dearest, remember that I love
    you more,
  O, more a thousand times,
    than all the rest !

THE STORY OF THE FAITHFUL SOUL.

FOUNDED ON AN OLD FRENCH
LEGEND.

THE fettered Spirits linger
  In purgatorial pain,
With penal fires effacing
  Their last faint earthly stain,
Which Life's imperfect sorrow
  Had tried to cleanse in vain.

Yet, on each feast of Mary
  Their sorrow finds release,
For the Great Archangel Mi-
  chael
Comes down and bids it cease;
And the name of these brief
  respites
Is called " Our Lady's Peace."

Yet once — so runs the Legend —
  When the Archangel came,
And all these holy spirits
  Rejoiced at Mary's name,
One voice alone was wailing,
  Still wailing on the same.

And though a great Te Deum
  The happy echoes woke,
This one discordant wailing
  Through the sweet voices
  broke :
So when St. Michael questioned,
  Thus the poor spirit spoke : —

" I am not cold or thankless,
  Although I still complain;
I prize our Lady's blessing,
  Although it comes in vain

To still my bitter anguish,
  Or quench my ceaseless pain.

" On earth a heart that loved me
  Still lives and mourns me
  there,
And the shadow of his anguish
  Is more than I can bear;
All the torment that I suffer
  Is the thought of his despair.

" The evening of my bridal
  Death took my Life away;
Not all Love's passionate plead-
  ing
  Could gain an hour's delay.
And he I left has suffered
  A whole year since that day.

" If I could only see him, —
  If I could only go
And speak one word of comfort
  And solace, — then I know
He would endure with patience,
  And strive against his woe."

Thus the Archangel answered : —
  " Your time of pain is brief,
And soon the peace of Heaven
  Will give you full relief;
Yet if his earthly comfort
  So much outweighs your grief,

" Then through a special mercy
  I offer you this grace, —
You may seek him who mourns
  you,
  And look upon his face,
And speak to him of comfort
  For one short minute's space

" But when that time is ended,
 Return here, and remain
A thousand years in torment,
 A thousand years in pain :
Thus dearly must you purchase
 The comfort he will gain."

*　　*　　*　　*

The Lime-trees' shade at evening
 Is spreading broad and wide ;
Beneath their fragrant arches,
 Pace slowly, side by side,
In low and tender converse,
 A Bridegroom and his Bride.

The night is calm and stilly,
 No other sound is there
Except their happy voices :
 What is that cold bleak air
That passes through the Lime-
 trees,
 And stirs the Bridegroom's
 hair ?

While one low cry of anguish,
 Like the last dying wail
Of some dumb, hunted creature,
 Is borne upon the gale : —
Why does the Bridegroom shud-
 der
And turn so deathly pale ?

*　　*　　*　　*

Near Purgatory's entrance
・ The radiant Angels wait ;
It was the great St. Michael
 Who closed that gloomy gate,
When the poor wandering spirit
 Came back to meet her fate.

" Pass on," thus spoke the An-
 gel :
 " Heaven's joy is deep and
 vast ;
Pass on, pass on, poor Spirit,
 For Heaven is yours at last ;
In that one minute's anguish
 Your thousand years have
 passed."

————

A CONTRAST.

CAN you open that ebony Cas-
 ket ?
 Look, this is the key : but stay,
Those are only a few old letters
 Which I keep, — to burn some
 day.

Yes, that Locket is quaint and
 ancient ;
 But leave it, dear, with the ring,
And give me the little Portrait
 Which hangs by a crimson
 string.

I have never opened that Casket
 Since, many long years ago,
It was sent me back in anger
 By one whom I used to know.

But I want you to see the Por-
 trait :
 I wonder if you can trace
A look of that smiling creature
 Left now in my faded face.

It was like me once; but remember
The weary, relentless years,
And Life, with its fierce brief
tempests,
And its long, long rain. of
tears.

Is it strange to call it my Por-
trait?
' Nay, smile, dear, for well you
may,
To think of that radiant Vision
And of what I am to-day.

With restless, yet confident longing,
How those blue eyes seem to
gaze
Into deep and exhaustless treasures,
All hid in the coming days.

With that trust which leans on
the Future,
And counts on her promised
store,
Until she has taught us to
tremble
And hope, — but to trust no
more.

How that young, light heart
would have pitied
Me now — if her dreams had
shown
A quiet and weary woman
With all her illusions flown.

Yet I — who shall soon be resting,
And have passed the hardest
part —
Can look back with a deeper
pity
On that young, unconscious
heart.

It is strange; but Life's currents
drift us
So surely and swiftly on,
That we scarcely notice the
changes,
And how many things are
gone:

And forget, while to-day absorbs
us,
How old mysteries are un-
sealed;
How the old, old ties are loosened,
And the old, old wounds are
healed.

And we say that our Life is fleeting
Like a story that Time has
told;
But we fancy that we — we
only —
Are just what we were of old.

So now and then it is wisdom
To gaze, as I do to-day,
At a half-forgotten relic
Of a Time that is passed away.

The very look of that Portrait,
　The perfume that seems to
　　cling
To those fragile and faded let-
　ters,
　And the Locket, and the Ring,

If they only stirred in my spirit
　Forgotten pleasure and pain, —
Why, memory is often bitter,
　And almost always in vain ;

But the contrast of bygone hours
　Comes to rend a veil away, —
And I marvel to see the stranger
　Who is living in me to-day.

THE BRIDE'S DREAM.

THE stars are gleaming ;
　The maiden sleeps, —
What is she dreaming ?
　For see — she weeps.
By her side is an Angel
　With folded wings ;
While the Maiden slumbers,
　The Angel sings :
He sings of a Bridal,
　Of Love, of Pain,
Of a heart to be given, —
　And all in vain ;
(See, her cheek is flushing,
　As if with pain ;)
He telleth of sorrow,
　Regrets and fears,
And the few vain pleasures
　We buy with tears ;

And the bitter lesson
　We learn from years.

The stars are gleaming
　Upon her brow :
What is she dreaming
　So calmly now ?
By her side is the Angel
　With folded wings ;
She smiles in her slumber
　The while he sings.
He sings of a Bridal,
　Of Love divine ;
Of a heart to be laid
　On a sacred shrine ;
Of a crown of glory,
　Where seraphs shine ;
Of the deep, long rapture
　The chosen know
Who forsake for Heaven
　Vain joys below,
Who desire no pleasure,
　And fear no woe.

The Bells are ringing,
　The sun shines clear,
The Choir is singing,
　The guests are here.
Before the High Altar
　Behold the Bride ;
And a mournful Angel
　Is by her side.
She smiles, all content
　With her chosen lot, —
(Is her last night's dreaming
　So soon forgot ?)
And oh, may the Angel
　Forsake her not !
For on her small hand
　There glitters plain

The first sad link
Of a life-long chain ; —
And she needs his guiding
Through paths of pain.

THE ANGEL'S BIDDING.

Not a sound is heard in the
Convent ;
The Vesper Chant is sung,
The sick have all been tended,
The poor nun's toils are ended
Till the Matin bell has rung.
All is still, save the Clock, that
is ticking
So loud in the frosty air,
And the soft snow, falling as
gently
As an answer to a prayer.
But an Angel whispers,
" O Sister,
You must rise from your
bed to pray ;
In the silent, deserted chapel,
You must kneel till the
dawn of day ;
For, far on the desolate
moorland,
So dreary, and bleak, and
white,
There is one, all alone and
helpless,
In peril of death to-night.

" No sound on the moorland to
guide him,
No star in the murky air ;

And he thinks of his home and
his loved ones
With the tenderness of de-
spair ;
He has wandered for hours in
the snow-drift,
And he strives to stand in
vain,
And so lies down to dream of
his children,
And never to rise again.
Then kneel in the silent
chapel
Till the dawn of to-mor-
row's sun,
And ask of the Lord you
worship
For the life of that desolate
one ;
And the smiling eyes of his
children
Will gladden his heart
again,
And the grateful tears of
God's poor ones
Will fall on your soul like
rain !

" Yet, leave him alone to perish,
And the grace of your God
implore,
With all the strength of your
spirit,
For one who needs it more.
Far away, in the gleaming city,
Amid perfume, and song, and
light,
A soul that Jesus has ransomed
Is in peril of sin to-night.

" The Tempter is close beside him,
And his danger is all forgot,
And the far-off voices of child-
hood
Call aloud, but he hears them
not;
He sayeth no prayer, and his
mother —
He thinks not of her to-day,
And he will not look up to
heaven,
And his Angel is turning
away.

" Then pray for a soul in peril,
A soul for which Jesus died;
Ask, by the cross that bore Him,
And by her who stood beside;
And the Angels of God will
thank you,
And bend from their thrones
of light,
To tell you that Heaven rejoices
At the deed you have done to-
night."

SPRING.

Hark! the hours are softly call-
ing,
Bidding Spring arise,
To listen to the rain-drops falling
From the cloudy skies,
To listen to Earth's weary
voices,
Louder every day,

Bidding her no longer linger
On her charméd way;
But hasten to her task of beauty
Scarcely yet begun;
By the first bright day of Summer
It should all be done.
She has yet to loose the fountain
From its iron chain;
And to make the barren moun-
tain
Green and bright again;
She must clear the snow that
lingers
Round the stalks away,
And let the snow-drop's trem-
bling whiteness
See the light of day.
She must watch, and warm, and
cherish
Every blade of green,
Till the tender grass appearing
From the earth is seen;
She must bring the golden crocus
From her hidden store;
She must spread broad showers
of daisies
Each day more and more.
In each hedge-row she must
hasten
Cowslips sweet to set;
Primroses in rich profusion,
With bright dew-drops wet,
And under every leaf, in shadow
Hide a violet!
Every tree within the forest
Must be decked anew;
And the tender buds of promise
Should be peeping through,
Folded deep, and almost hidden,
Leaf by leaf beside,

What will make the Summer's
glory,
And the Autumn's pride.
She must weave the loveliest car-
pets,
Checkered sun and shade,
Every wood must have such path-
ways,
Laid in every glade ;
She must hang laburnum
branches
On each archéd bough ; —
And the white and purple lilac
Should be waving now ;
She must breathe, and cold winds
vanish
At her breath away ;
And then load the air around her
With the scent of May !
Listen then, O Spring ! nor
linger
On thy charméd way ;
Have pity on thy prisoned flowers
Wearying for the day.
Listen to the rain-drops falling
From the cloudy skies ;
Listen to the hours calling,
Bidding thee arise.

EVENING HYMN.

The shadows of the evening
hours
Fall from the darkening sky ;
Upon the fragrance of the flowers
· The dews of evening lie ;

Before thy throne, O Lord of
heaven,
We kneel at close of day ;
Look on thy children from on
high,
And hear us while we pray.

The sorrows of thy servants,
Lord,
O do not thou despise ;
But let the incense of our prayers
Before thy mercy rise ;
The brightness of the coming
night
Upon the darkness rolls :
With hopes of future glory chase
The shadows on our souls.

Slowly the rays of daylight fade ;
So fade within our heart
The hopes in earthly love and joy,
That one by one depart :
Slowly the bright stars, one by
one,
Within the heavens shine ; —
Give us, O Lord, fresh hopes in
Heaven,
And trust in things divine.

Let peace, O Lord, thy peace, O
God,
Upon our souls descend ;
From midnight fears and perils,
thou
Our trembling hearts defend ;
Give us a respite from our toil,
Calm and subdue our woes ;
Through the long day we suffer,
Lord,
O give us now repose !

THE INNER CHAMBER.

In the outer Court I was singing,
  Was singing the whole day
    long ;
From the inner chamber were
    ringing
  Echoes repeating my song.

And I sang till it grew immortal ;
  For that very song of mine,
When re-echoed behind the Por-
    tal,
  Was filled with a life divine.

Was the Chamber a silver round
  Of arches, whose magical art
Drew in coils of musical sound,
  And cast them back on my
    heart ?

Was there hidden within a lyre
  Which, as air breathed over
    its strings,
Filled my song with a soul of
    fire,
  And sent back my words with
    wings ?

Was some seraph imprisoned
    there,
  Whose Voice made my song
    complete,
And whose lingering, soft de-
    spair
Made the echo so faint and sweet ?

Long I trembled and paused, —
    then parted
  The curtains with heavy fringe ;

And, half fearing, yet eager-
    hearted,
  Turned the door on its golden
    hinge.

Now I sing in the court once
    more,
  I sing and I weep all day,
As I kneel by the close-shut
    door,
  For I know what the echoes say.

Yet I sing not the song of old,
  Ere I knew whence the echo
    came,
Ere I opened the door of gold ;
  But the music sounds just the
    same.

Then take warning, and turn
    away ;
  Do not ask of that hidden
    thing,
Do not guess what the echoes say,
  Or the meaning of what I sing.

HEARTS.

I.

A trinket made like a Heart,
    dear,
  Of red gold, bright and fine,
Was given to me for a keepsake,
  Given to me for mine.

And another heart, warm and
    tender,
  As true as a heart could be ;
And every throb that stirred it
  Was always and all for me.

Sailing over the waters,
  Watching the far blue land,
I dropped my golden heart, dear,
  Dropped it out of my hand !

It lies in the cold, blue waters,
  Fathoms and fathoms deep,
The golden heart which I prom-
    ised,
  Promised to prize and keep.

Gazing at Life's bright visions,
  So false, and fair, and new,
I forgot the other heart, dear,
  Forgot it and lost it too !

I might seek that heart forever,
  I might seek and seek in
    vain ; —
And for one short, careless hour,
  I pay with a life of pain.

———

II.

The Heart ? — Yes, I wore it
  As sign and as token
Of a love that once gave it,
  A vow that was spoken ;

But a love, and a vow, and a
  heart
  Can be broken.

The Love ? — Life and Death
  Are crushed into a day,
So what wonder that Love
  Should as soon pass away, —
What wonder I saw it
  Fade, fail, and decay ?

The Vow ? — why what was it ?
  It snapped like a thread ;
Who cares for the corpse
  When the spirit is fled ?
Then I said, " Let the Dead rise
  And bury its dead,

" While the true, living future
  Grows pure, wise, and strong."
So I cast the gold heart
  I had worn for so long
In the Lake, and bound on it
  A Stone — and a Wrong !

———

III.

Look, this little golden Heart
  Was a true-love shrine
For a tress of hair ; I held them,
  Heart and tress, as mine,
Like the Love which gave the
  token : —
See, to-day the Heart is broken !

Broken is the golden heart,
  Lost the tress of hair ;
Ah, the shrine is empty, vacant,
  Desolate and bare !
So the token should depart,
When Love dies within the heart.

Fast and deep the river floweth,
  Floweth to the west ;
I will cast the golden trinket
  In its cold dark breast : —
Flow, O river, deep and fast,
Over all the buried past !

———

TWO LOVES.

DEEP within my heart of hearts,
  dear,
  Bound with all its strings,
Two Loves are together reigning,
  Both are crowned like Kings ;
While my life, still uncomplain-
  ing,
  Rests beneath their wings.

So they both will rule my heart,
  dear,
  Till it cease to beat ;
No sway can be deeper, stronger,
  Truer, more complete ;
Growing, as it lasts the longer,
  Sweeter, and more sweet.

•

One all life and time transfigures ;
  Piercing through and through

Meaner things with magic splen-
  dor,
  Old, yet ever new :
This — so strong and yet so
  tender —
  Is . . . my Love for you.

Should it fail, — forgive my
  doubting
  In this world of pain, —
Yet my other Love would ever
  Steadfastly remain ;
And I know that I could never
  Turn to that in vain.

Though its radiance may be
  fainter,
  Yet its task is wide ;
For it lives to comfort sorrows,
  Strengthen, calm, and guide,
And from Trust and Honor bor-
  rows
  All its peace and pride.

Will you blame my dreaming,
  even
  If the first were flown ?
Ah, I would not live without it,
  It is all your own :
And the other — can you doubt
  it ? —
  Yours, and yours alone.

———

A WOMAN'S LAST WORD.

WELL — the links are broken,
  All is past ;

This farewell, when spoken,
    Is the last.
I have tried and striven
    All in vain ;
Such bonds must be riven,
    Spite of pain,
And never, never, never
    Knit again.

So I tell you plainly,
    It must be :
I shall try, not vainly,
    To be free ;
Truer, happier chances
    Wait me yet,
While you, through fresh fancies,
    Can forget ; —
And life has nobler uses
    Than Regret.

All past words retracing,
    One by one,
Does not help effacing
    What is done.
Let it be.   O, stronger
    Links can break !
Had we dreamed still longer
    We could wake, —
Yet let us part in kindness
    For Love's sake.

Bitterness and sorrow
    Will at last,
In some bright to-morrow,
    Heal their past ;
But future hearts will never
    Be as true

As mine was — is ever,
    Dear, for you . . . .
· · Then must we part, when
        loving
    As we do ?

————

PAST AND PRESENT.

"Linger," I cried, " O radiant
        Time ! thy power
Has nothing more to give ; life
    is complete :
Let but the perfect Present, hour
    by hour,
Itself remember and itself repeat.

" And Love, — the future can
    but mar its splendor,
Change can but dim the glory of
    its youth ;
Time has no star more faithful
    or more tender
To crown its constancy or light
    its truth."

But Time passed on in spite of
    prayer or pleading,
Through storm and peril ; but
    that life might gain
A Peace through strife all other
    peace exceeding,
Fresh joy from sorrow, and new
    hope from pain.

And since Love lived when all
    save Love was dying,
And, passed through fire, grew
    stronger than before : —
Dear, you know why, in double
    faith relying,
I prize the Past much, but the
    Present more.

FOR THE FUTURE.

I WONDER did you ever count
    The value of one human fate ;
Or sum the infinite amount
    Of one heart's treasures, and
      the weight
Of Life's one venture, and the
    whole concentrate purpose
    of a soul.

    And if you ever paused to
      think
    That all this in your hands I
      laid
    Without a fear : — did you
      not shrink
    From such a burden ? half
      afraid,
Half wishing that you could di-
    vide the risk, or cast it all
    aside.

    While Love has daily perils,
      such
    As none foresee and none con-
      trol ;

And hearts are strung so that
    one touch,
    Careless or rough, may jar the
      whole,
You well might feel afraid to
    reign with absolute power
    of joy and pain.

    You well might fear — if
      Love's sole claim
    Were to be happy : but true Love
    Takes joy as solace, not as aim,
    And looks beyond, and looks
      above ;
And sometimes through the bit-
    terest strife first learns to
    live her highest life.

    Earth forges joy into a chain
    Till fettered Love forgets its
      strength,
    Its purpose, and its end ; —
      but Pain
    Restores its heritage at length,
And bids Love rise again and be
    eternal, mighty, pure, and
    free.

    If then your future life should
      need
    A strength my Love can only
      gain
    Through suffering, or my heart
      be freed
    Only by sorrow from some
      stain,
Then you shall give, and I will
    take, this Crown of fire for
    Love's dear sake.

September 8, 1860.

A CHAPLET OF VERSES.

PUBLISHED FOR THE BENEFIT OF

THE PROVIDENCE ROW NIGHT REFUGE

FOR

HOMELESS WOMEN AND CHILDREN.

INTRODUCTION.

THERE is scarcely any charitable institution which should excite such universal, such unhesitating sympathy, as a Night Refuge for the Homeless Poor.

A shelter through the bleak winter nights, leave to rest in some poor shed instead of wandering through the pitiless streets, is a boon we could hardly deny to a starving dog. And yet we have all known that in this country, in this town, many of our miserable fellow-creatures were pacing the streets through the long weary nights, without a roof to shelter them, without food to eat, with their poor rags soaked in rain, and only the bitter winds of Heaven for companions; women and children utterly forlorn and helpless, either wandering about all night, or crouching under a miserable archway, or, worst of all, seeking in death or sin the refuge denied them elsewhere. It is a marvel that we could sleep in peace in our warm, comfortable homes with this horror at our very door.

But at last some efforts were made to efface this stain upon our country, public sympathy was appealed to, and a few "Refuges" were opened, to shelter our homeless poor through the winter nights.

In the autumn of 1860 there was no Catholic Refuge in the kingdom; and excellent as were the Protestant Refuges, their resources were quite inadequate to meet the claims upon them.

In this country, as we all know, the very poorest and most destitute are in many cases Catholics; and doubtless our Priests, to whom no form of sin or sorrow is strange, must see in a special manner, and in innumerable results, the sufferings, dangers, and temptations of the homeless. The Rev. Dr. Gilbert therefore resolved to open a Catholic Night Refuge in his parish, and to his zealous charity and unwearied efforts are due the foundation and success of the PROVIDENCE ROW NIGHT REFUGE FOR HOMELESS WOMEN AND CHILDREN; the first Catholic Refuge in England or Ireland, and still the only one in England.

The Sisters of Mercy had long been aiding their pastors in the schools of the parish, and when this new opening for their charity was suggested to them, they unhesitatingly accepted a task, worthy indeed of the holy name they bear. They were seeking for some house more suitable for a Convent than the one they had hitherto occupied in Broad Street; and when Dr. Gilbert saw the large stable at the back of 14 Finsbury Square, he felt that here was a suitable place for his long-cherished plan of a Night Refuge. It was separated from the house by a yard, and opened on a narrow street at the back, already called, with a happy appropriateness, Providence Row. To Finsbury Square therefore the community removed, and it was not long before the stable was fitted up with wooden beds and benches, the few preparations were completed, and on the 7th of October, 1860, the Refuge was opened. At first there were but fourteen beds, but contributions flowed in from Protestants as well as Catholics, and in February, 1861, thirty-

one more beds were added, making in all forty-five. But as many of the poor women have children with them, rarely less than sixty persons are each night admitted. Up to the present time, fourteen thousand seven hundred and eighty-five nights' lodgings have been given, with the same number of suppers and breakfasts.

From six to eight are the hours of admission; but this is indeed a needless rule, for a crowd of ragged women, with pale, weary children clinging to them, are waiting patiently long before the doors are opened, and the place is filled at once.

Means for washing are given them, they rest themselves in warmth, light, and peace, and at eight o'clock each person receives half a pound of bread and a large basin of excellent gruel. Night prayers are said by one of the Sisters, and then the poor wanderers lie down in their rude but clean and comfortable beds. They have the same meal in the morning.

Those who come on Saturday evening remain till Monday, receiving on Sunday, besides the usual breakfast and supper, an extra half-pound of bread, and a good supply of meat soup. There is no distinction of creed; Protestants and Catholics are alike admitted. There are but two conditions of admittance, — that the applicants be homeless and of good character. This is the only Refuge which makes character a condition ; and it is found that, in spite of all precautions, much harm arises in the other Refuges to the young and innocent, from the bad language and evil example of the degraded class with whom they are brought in contact.

Each evening (and on Sundays more fully) simple instructions on the Catechism are given by one of the Sisters ; but this the Protestants do not attend ; they frequently ask leave to be present, but it is not permitted, (without the special permission of one of the clergy,) as the instructions on the practice of our faith would be to them comparatively useless and unmeaning.

The temporary shelter and food which is given in Providence Row is not the only, perhaps often not the greatest, benefit bestowed upon the poor forlorn inmates. They find advice, sympathy, and help from the kind Sisters ; and the very telling their troubles to one who is there to serve and tend them, not for any earthly reward, but from Christian love and pity, must be a rest to their weary hearts, a comfort in their sore want and distress. It is touching to see their eager desire to

be allowed to help the Sister in the cleaning, cooking, etc., and the half-ashamed thankfulness with which they watch her busied in their service.

One of the Nuns sleeps every night in the Refuge, and no unruly sound, no whisper of murmur or disrespect, ever rises against her gentle sway. Nay, even more, when she has the sad task of selecting among the waiting crowd the number who may enter, choosing generally those with children and those who have not applied before, the rest submit without a murmur. Though the little ones are hardly counted, but creep in by their mothers' sides, there are still many — sometimes thirty or forty nightly — turned away for want of space. They have had a glimpse of warmth and light, and then it is the cruel office of the kind Nun to bar the door against them ; but no angry word, no remonstrance, meets her sorrowful refusal ; they turn once more to their weary wanderings in the dark, bleak streets. And so will many have to do, night after night, until the Refuge is enlarged. The present space will hold no more beds, but to build an additional dormitory is the earnest desire and intention of Dr. Gilbert.

No salaries are received by any who have charge of the Refuge.

Among the many causes for gratitude we have to our good Religious, surely it is not one of the least, that what we can spare in the cause of charity goes solely and directly to its object; the more difficult and more perfect share of the good work being taken by them out of love to God and his poor.

The Refuge is open from the month of October to April.

It is placed under the special patronage of Our Blessed Lady, and Blessed Benedict Labré.

May the Mother who wandered homeless through inhospitable Bethlehem, and the Saint who was a beggar and an outcast upon the face of the earth, watch over this Refuge for the poor and desolate, and obtain from the charity of the faithful the aid which it so sorely needs.

I may add, that donations for the Refuge will be thankfully received by the Rev. Dr. Gilbert, 22 Finsbury Circus, or by the Rev. Mother, at the Convent, 14 Finsbury Square, E. C.

We all meditate long and often on the many kinds of sufferings borne for us by our Blessed Redeemer; but perhaps, if we consider a moment, we shall most of us confess, that the one we think of least often, the one we compassionate least of all, is the only one of which he deigned to tell us himself, and for which he himself appealed to our pity in the Divine complaint, "The foxes have holes, and the birds of the air have nests, but the Son of Man *has not where to lay his head.*"

A. A. P.

May, 1862.

A CHAPLET OF VERSES.

THE ARMY OF THE LORD.

I.

To fight the battle of the Cross, Christ's chosen ones are sent, —
Good soldiers and great victors, — a noble armament.
They use no earthly weapon, they know not spear or sword,
Yet right and true and valiant is the army of the Lord.

II.

Fear them, ye mighty ones of earth ; fear them, ye demon foes ;
Slay them and think to conquer, but the ranks will always close :
In vain do Earth and Hell unite their power and skill to try,
They fight better for their wounds, and they conquer when they die.

III.

The soul of every sinner is the victory they would gain ;
They would bind each rebel heart in their Master's golden chain :
Faith is the shield they carry, and the two-edged sword they bear
Is God's strongest, mightiest weapon, and they call it Love and
        Prayer.

IV.

Where the savage hordes are dwelling by the Ganges' sacred tide,
Through the trackless Indian forests, St. Francis is their guide ;
Where crime and sin are raging, to conquer they are gone ; —
They do conquer as they go, for St. Philip leads them on.

v.

They are come where all are kneeling at the shrines of wealth and
pride,
And an old and martyred Bishop is their comrade and their guide:
To tell the toil-worn negro of freedom and repose,
O'er the vast Atlantic's bosom they are called by sweet St. Rose.

VI.

They are gone where Love is frozen, and Faith grown calm and cold,
Where the world is all triumphant, and the sheep have left the fold,
Where His children scorn His blessings, and His sacred Shrines
despise, —
And the beacon of the warriors is the light in Mary's eyes.

VII.

The bugle for their battle is the matin bell for prayer;
And for their noble standard Christ's holy Cross they bear;
His sacred name their war-cry, 't is in vain what ye can do,
They *must* conquer, for your Angels are leaguing with them too.

VIII.

Would you know, O World, these warriors?   Go where the poor,
the old,
Ask for pardon and for heaven, and you offer food and gold;
With healing and with comfort, with words of peace and prayer,
Bearing His greatest gift to man, — Christ's chosen priests are there.

IX.

Where sin and crime are dwelling, hid from the light of day,
And life and hope are fading at Death's cold touch away,
Where dying eyes in horror see the long-forgotten past,
Christ's servants claim the sinner, and gain his soul at last.

X.

Where the rich and proud and mighty God's message would defy,
In warning and reproof His anointed ones stand by:
Bright are the crowns of glory God keepeth for His own,
Their life one sigh for heaven, and their aim His will alone.

XI.

And see sweet Mercy's sister, where the poor and wretched dwell,
In gentle accents telling of Him she loves so well;
Training young hearts to serve their Lord, and place their hope in
   Heaven,
Bidding her erring sisters love much and be forgiven.

XII.

And where in cloistered silence dim the Brides of Jesus dwell,
Where purest incense rises up from every lowly cell,
They plead not vainly, — they have chosen and gained the better part,
And given their gentle life away to Him who has their heart.

XIII.

And some there are among us — the path which they have trod
Of sin and pain and anguish has led at last to God :
They plead, and Christ will hear them, that the poor slaves who pine
In the bleak dungeon they have left, may see His truth divine.

XIV.

O, who can tell how many hearts are altars to His praise,
From which the silent prayer ascends through patient nights and
   days :
The sacrifice is offered still in secret and alone,
O World, ye do not know them, but He can help His own.

XV.

They are with us, His true soldiers, they come in power and might;
Glorious the crown which they shall gain after the heavenly fight;
And you, perchance, who scoff, may yet their rest and glory share,
As the rich spoil of their battle and the captives of their prayer.

XVI.

O, who shall tell the wonder of that great day of rest,
When even in this place of strife His soldiers are so blest :
O World, O Earth, why strive ye ? join the low chant they sing, —
" O Grave, where is thy victory !   O Death, where is thy sting ! "

THE STAR OF THE SEA.

How many a mighty ship
  The stormy waves o'erwhelm ;
Yet our frail bark floats on,
  Our Angel holds the helm :
Dark storms are gathering round,
  And dangerous winds arise,
Yet see ! one trembling star
  Is shining in the skies ; —
And we are safe who trust in
    thee,
    Star of the Sea !

A long and weary voyage
  Have we to reach our home,
And dark and sunken rocks
  Are hid in silver foam ;
Each moment we may sink,
  But steadily we sail,
Our wingèd Pilot smiles,
  And says we shall not fail : —
And so we kneel and call on
    thee,
    Star of the Sea !

Yes, for those shining rays
  Shall beam upon the main,
Shall guide us safely on,
  Through fear and doubt and
    pain :
And see — the stormy wind
  Our little sail has caught,
The tempest others fear
  Shall drive us into port : —
Through Life's dark voyage we
    trust in thee,
    Star of the Sea !

The shore now looms in sight,
  The far-off golden strand,
Yet many a freight is wrecked
  And lost in sight of land ;
Then guide us safely home,
  Through that last hour of
    strife,
And welcome us to land,
  From the long voyage of
    life : —
In death and life we call on thee,
  Star of the Sea !

THE SACRED HEART.

WHAT wouldst thou have, O
    soul,
  Thou weary soul !
Lo ! I have sought for rest
On the Earth's heaving breast,
  From pole to pole.
Sleep — I have been with her,
  But she gave dreams ;
Death — nay, the rest he gives
  Rest only seems.
Fair nature knows it not —
  The grass is growing ;
The blue air knows it not —
  The winds are blowing :
Not in the changing sky,
  The stormy sea,
Yet somewhere in God's wide
    world
  Rest there must be.
Within thy Saviour's Heart
  Place all thy care,

And learn, O weary soul,
  Thy Rest is there.

What wouldst thou, trembling
    soul ?
Strength for the strife, —
Strength for this fiery war
  That we call Life.
Fears·gather thickly round ;
  Shadowy foes,
Like unto arméd men,
  Around me close. ·
What am I, frail and poor,
  When griefs arise ? .
No help from the weak earth,
  Or the cold skies.
Lo ! I can find no guards,
  No weapons borrow ;
Shrinking, alone I stand,
  With mighty sorrow.
Courage, thou trembling soul,
  Grief thou must bear,
Yet thou canst find a strength
  Will match despair ;
Within thy Saviour's Heart —
  Seek for it there.

What wouldst thou have, sad
    soul,
  Oppressed with grief? —
Comfort : I seek in vain,
  Nor find relief.
Nature, all pitiless,
  Smiles on my pain ;
I ask my fellow-men,
  They give disdain.
I asked the babbling streams,
  But they flowed on ;

I asked the wise and good,
  But they gave none.
Though I have asked the stars,
  Coldly they shine.
They are too bright to know
  Grief such as mine.
I asked for comfort still,
  And I found tears,
And I have sought in vain
  Long, weary years.
Listen, thou mournful soul,
  Thy pain shall cease ;
Deep in His sacred Heart
  Dwells joy and peace.

Yes, in that Heart divine
  The Angels bright
Find, through eternal years,
  Still new delight.
From thence his constancy
  The martyr drew,
And there the virgin band
  Their refuge knew.
There, racked by pain without,
  And dread within,
How many souls have found
  Heaven's bliss begin.
Then leave thy vain attempts
  To seek for peace ;
The world can never give
  One soul release :
But in thy Saviour's Heart
  Securely dwell,
No pain can harm thee, hid
  In that sweet cell.
Then fly, O coward soul,
  Delay no more :
What words can speak the joy
  For thee in store ?

What smiles of earth can tell
Of peace like thine?
Silence and tears are best
For things divine.

THE NAMES OF OUR LADY.

THROUGH the wide world thy
children raise
Their prayers, and still we see
Calm are the nights and bright
the days
Of those who trust in thee.

Around thy starry crown are
wreathed
So many names divine :
Which is the dearest to my heart,
And the most worthy thine ?

Star of the Sea : we kneel and
pray
When tempests raise their
voice ;
Star of the Sea ! the haven
reached,
We call thee and rejoice.

Help of the Christian : in our need
Thy mighty aid we claim ;
If we are faint and weary, then
We trust in that dear name.

Our Lady of the Rosary :
What name can be so sweet

As what we call thee when we
place
Our chaplets at thy feet.

Bright Queen of Heaven : when
we are sad,
Best solace of our pains ; —
It tells us, though on earth we
toil,
Our Mother lives and reigns.

Our Lady of Mount Carmel : thus
Sometimes thy name is known ;
It tells us of the badge we wear,
To live or die thine own.

Our Lady dear of Victories :
We see our faith oppressed,
And, praying for our erring land,
We love that name the best.

Refuge of Sinners : many a soul,
By guilt cast down, and sin,
Has learned through this dear
name of thine
Pardon and peace to win.

Health of the Sick : when anxious
hearts
Watch by the sufferer's bed,
On this sweet name of thine they
lean,
Consoled and comforted.

Mother of Sorrows : many a heart
Half broken by despair
Has laid its burden by the cross,
And found a mother there.

Queen of all Saints: the Church
    appeals
For her loved dead to thee ;
She knows they wait in patient
    pain
A bright eternity.

Fair Queen of Virgins : thy pure
    band,
The lilies round thy throne,
Love the dear title which they
    bear
Most that it is thine own.

True Queen of Martyrs : if we
    shrink
From want, or pain, or woe,
We think of the sharp sword
    that pierced
Thy heart, and call thee so.

Mary : the dearest name of all,
The holiest and the best ;
The first low word that Jesus
    lisped
Laid on His mother's breast.

Mary, the name that Gabriel
    spoke,
The name that conquers hell :
Mary, the name that through
    high heaven
The angels love so well.

Mary, — our comfort and our
    hope, —
O may that word be given
To be the last we sigh on earth, —
The first we breathe in heaven

A CHAPLET OF FLOW-
ERS.

DEAR, set the casement open,
    The evening breezes blow
Sweet perfumes from the flowers
    I cannot see below.

I can but catch the waving
    Of chestnut boughs that pass,
Their shadow must have covered
    The sun-dial on the grass.

So go and bring the flowers
    I love best to my room,
My failing strength no longer
    Can bear me where they bloom.

You know I used to love them,
    But ah ! they come too late, —
For see, my hands are trembling
    Beneath their dewy weight.

So I will watch you weaving
    A chaplet for me, dear,
Of all my favorite flowers,
    As I could do last year.

First, take those crimson roses, —
    How red their petals glow !
Red as the blood of Jesus,
    Which heals our sin and woe.

See in each heart of crimson
    A deeper crimson shine :
So in the foldings of our hearts
    Should glow a love divine.

Next place those tender violets,
  Look how they still regret
The cell where they were hid-
    den, —
  The tears are on them yet.

How many souls — His loved
  ones —
Dwell lonely and apart,
Hiding from all but One above
  The fragrance of their heart.

Then take that virgin lily,
  How holily she stands !
You know the gentle angels
  Bear lilies in their hands.

Yet crowned with purer radiance
  A deeper love they claim,
Because their queen-like white-
    ness
  Is linked with Mary's name.

And now this spray of ivy :
  You know its gradual clasp
Uproots strong trees, and towers
  Fall crumbling in its grasp.

So God's dear grace around us
  With secret patience clings,
And slow, sure power, that
    loosens
  Strong holds on human things.

Then heliotrope, that turneth
  Towards her lord the sun, —
Would that our thoughts as
    fondly
  Sought our belovéd One.

Nay, if that branch be fading,
  Cast not one blossom by,
Its little task is ended
  And it does well to die.

And let some field flowers even
  Be wreathed among the rest,
I think the infant Jesus
  Would love such ones the best.

These flowers are all too bril-
    liant,
  So place calm heart's-ease
    there,
God's last and sacred treasure
  For all who wait and bear.

Then lemon-leaves, whose sweet-
    ness
  Grows sweeter than before
When bruised, and crushed, and
    broken,
  — Hearts need that lesson
    more.

Yet stay, — one crowning glory,
  All His, and yet all ours ;
The dearest, tenderest thought of
    all,
  Is still the Passion-flower's.

So take it now, — nay, heed not
  My tears that on it fall ;
I thank Him for the flowers,
  As I can do for all.

And place it on the altar,
  Where oft, in days long flown,
I knelt by His dear Mother,
  And knew she was my own.

The bells ring out her praises,
  The evening shades grow
    dim;
Go there and say a prayer for me,
  And sing Our Lady's hymn.

While I lie here, and ask her
    help
  In that last, longed-for day —
When the Belovéd of my heart
  Will call my soul away.

KYRIE ELEISON.

In joy, in pain, in sorrow,
  Father, Thy hand we see;
But some among Thy children
  Deny this faith and Thee.
They will not ask Thy mercy,
  But we kneel for them in
    prayer;
Are they not still Thy children?
  Pity, O God! and spare.
Thy peace, O Lord, has never
  On their desolate pathway
    shone,
Darkness is all around them:
  Kyrie Eleison!

For them the starry heavens
  No hymn of worship raise;
For them, earth's innocent flow-
    ers
  Breathe not Thy silent praise;
In heaven they know no Saviour,
  No Father, and no Friend,

And life is all they hope for,
  And Death they call the end;
Their eyes, O Lord! are blinded
  To the glories of the sun,
To the shining of the sea-star —
  Kyrie Eleison!

By the love Thy saints have
    shown Thee,
  And the sorrows they have
    borne,
Leave not these erring creatures
  To wander thus forlorn.
By Thy tender name of Sa-
    viour, —
  The name they have denied;
By Thy bitter death and passion,
  And the Cross which they de-
    ride;
By the anguish Thou hast suf-
    fered,
  And the glory Thou hast won;
By Thy love and by Thy pity —
  Christe Eleison!

Pray for them, glorious seraphs,
  And ye, bright angel band,
Who chant His praises ever,
  And in His presence stand;
And thou, O gentle Mother,
  Queen of the starry sky;
Ye Saints whose toils are over,
  Join your voices to our cry, —
In Thy terror or Thy mercy,
  Call them ere life is done,
For His sake who died to save
    them,
  Kyrie Eleison!

THE ANNUNCIATION.

How pure, and frail, and white,
  The snowdrops shine!
Gather a garland bright
  For Mary's shrine.

For, born of winter snows,
  These fragile flowers
Are gifts to our fair Queen
  From Spring's first hours.

For on this blesséd day
  She knelt at prayer;
When, lo! before her shone
  An Angel fair.

"Hail, Mary!" thus he cried,
  With reverent fear:
She, with sweet wondering eyes,
  Marvelled to hear.

Be still, ye clouds of Heaven!
  Be silent, Earth!
And hear an Angel tell
  Of Jesus' birth,

While she, whom Gabriel hails
  As full of grace,
Listens with humble faith
  In her sweet face.

Be still, Pride, War, and Pomp,
  Vain Hopes, vain Fears,
For now an Angel speaks,
  And Mary hears.

"Hail, Mary!" lo, it rings
  Through ages on;
"Hail, Mary!" it shall sound,
  Till Time is done.

"Hail, Mary!" infant lips
  Lisp it to-day;
"Hail, Mary!" with faint smile
  The dying say.

"Hail, Mary!" many a heart
  Broken with grief,
In that angelic prayer
  Has found relief.

And many a half-lost soul,
  When turned at bay,
With those triumphant words
  Has won the day.

"Hail, Mary, Queen of Heaven!"
  Let us repeat,
And place our snowdrop wreath
  Here at her feet.

AN APPEAL.

"THE IRISH CHURCH MISSION
FOR CONVERTING THE CATH-
OLICS."

SPARE her, O cruel England!
  Thy Sister lieth low;
Chained and oppressed she lieth,
  Spare her that cruel blow.

We ask not for the freedom
  Heaven has vouchsafed to thee,
Nor bid thee share with Ireland
  The empire of the sea ;
Her children ask no shelter, —
  Leave them the stormy sky ;
They ask not for thy harvests,
  For they know how to die :
Deny them, if it please thee,
  A grave beneath the sod : —
But we do cry, O England,
  Leave them their faith in God !

Take, if thou wilt, the earnings
  Of the poor peasant's toil,
Take all the scanty produce
  That grows on Irish soil,
To pay the alien preachers
  Whom Ireland will not hear,
To pay the scoffers at a Creed
  Which Irish hearts hold dear:
But leave them, cruel England,
  The gift their God has given,
Leave them their ancient worship,
  Leave them their faith in
  Heaven.

You come and offer Learning, —
  A mighty gift, 't is true ;
Perchance the greatest blessing
  That now is known to you.
But not to see the wonders
  Sages of old beheld
Can they peril a priceless treas-
  ure,
  The Faith their Fathers held ;
For in learning and in science
  They may forget to pray, —
God will not ask for knowledge
  On the great judgment day.

When, in their wretched cabins,
  Racked by the fever pain,
And the weak cries of their chil-
  dren
  Who ask for food in vain ;
When starving, naked, helpless,
  From the shed that keeps them
  warm
Man has driven them forth to
  perish,
  In a less cruel storm ; —
Then, then, we plead for mercy,
  Then, Sister, hear our cry !
For all we ask, O England,
  Is — leave them there to die !
Cursed is the food and raiment
  For which a soul is sold ;
Tempt not another Judas
  To barter God for gold.
You offer food and shelter
  If they their faith deny : —
What do you gain, O England,
  By such a shallow lie ? . . . .
We will not judge the tempted, —
  May God blot out their
  shame, —
He sees the misery round them,
  He knows man's feeble frame ;
His pity still may save them,
  In His strength they must trust
Who calls us all His children,
  Yet knows we are but dust.

Then leave them the kind tending
  Which helped their childish
  years ;
Leave them the gracious comfort
  Which dries the mourner's
  tears ;

Leave them to that great mother
    In whose bosom they were
        born ;
Leave them the holy mysteries
    That comfort the forlorn :
And, amid all their trials,
    Let the Great Gift abide,
Which you, O prosperous Eng-
        land,
    Have dared to cast aside.
Leave them the pitying Angels
    And Mary's gentle aid,
For which earth's dearest treas-
    ures
    Were not too dearly paid.
Take back your bribes, then,
        England,
    Your gold is black and dim,
And if God sends plague and
        famine,
    They can die and go to Him.

———

THE JUBILEE OF 1850.

[The titles of the " Island of Saints "
and the " Dower of our Lady," though
more frequently applied to Ireland,
were often given to England in former
times.]

Bless God, ye happy Lands,
    For your more favored lot :
Our England dwells apart,
    Yet O forget her not.
While, with united joy,
    This day you all adore,

Remember what she was,
    Though her voice is heard no
        more.
    Pray for our desolate land,
    Left in her pride and pow
        er : —
    She was the Isle of Saints,
    She was Our Lady's Dower.

Look on her ruined Altars ;
    He dwelleth there no more :
Think what her empty churches
    Have been in times of yore ;
She knows the names no longer
    Of her own sainted dead,
Denies the faith they held,
    And the cause for which they
        bled.
    Then pray for our desolate
        land,
    Left in her pride and pow-
        er : —
    She was the Isle of Saints,
    She was Our Lady's Dower !

Pray that her vast Cathedrals,
    Deserted, empty, bare,
May once more echo accents
    Of Love, and Faith, and
        Prayer ;
That the holy sign may bless us,
    On wood, and field, and plain,
And Jesus, Mary, Joseph,
    May dwell with us again.
    Pray, ye more faithful na-
        tions,
    In this most happy hour : —
    She was the Isle of Saints,
    She was Our Lady's Dower

Beg of our Lord to give her
　The gift she cast aside,
And in His mercy pardon
　Her faithlessness and pride :
Pray to her Saints, who worship
　Before God's mercy Throne ;
Look where our Queen is dwell-
　　ing,
　Ask her to claim her own,
　　To give her the proud titles
　　Lost in an evil hour : —
　　She was the Isle of Saints,
　　She was Our Lady's Dower.

CHRISTMAS FLOWERS.

THE Earth is so bleak and de-
　　serted,
　So cold the winds blow,
That no bud or no blossom will
　　venture
　To peep from below ;
But, longing for springtime,
　　they nestle
　Deep under the snow.

O, in May how we honored Our
　　Lady,
　Her own month of flowers !
How happy we were with our
　　garlands
　Through all the spring hours !
All her shrines, in the church or
　　the wayside,
　Were made into bowers.

And in August — her glorious
　　Assumption ;
　What feast was so bright !
What clusters of virginal lilies,
　So pure and so white !
Why, the incense could scarce
　　overpower
　Their perfume that night.

And through her dear feasts of
　　October
　The roses bloomed still ;
Our baskets were laden with
　　flowers,
　Her vases to fill :
Oleanders, geraniums, and myr-
　　tles,
　We chose at our will.

And we know when the Purifi-
　　cation,
　Her first feast, comes round,
The early spring flowers, to greet
　　it,
　Just opening are found ;
And pure, white, and spotless,
　　the snowdrop
　Will pierce the dark ground.

And now, in this dreary Decem-
　　ber,
　Our glad hearts are fain
To see if Earth comes not to help
　　us ;
　We seek all in vain :
Not the tiniest blossom is coming
　Till Spring breathes again.

And the bright feast of Christmas
  is dawning,
  And Mary is blest;
For now she will give us her
  Jesus,
  Our dearest, our best,
And see where she stands, the
  Maid-Mother,
  Her Babe on her breast!

And not one poor garland to give
  her,
  And yet now, behold,
How the Kings bring their gifts,
  — myrrh, and incense,
  And bars of pure gold:
And the Shepherds have brought
  for the Baby
  Some lambs from their folds.

He stretches His tiny hands to-
  wards us,
  He brings us all grace;
And look at His Mother who
  holds Him, —
  The smile on her face
Says they welcome the humblest
  gifts
  In the manger we place.

Where love takes, let love give;
  and so doubt not:
  Love counts but the will,
And the heart has its flowers of
  devotion
  No Winter can chill;
They who cared for " good-will "
  that first Christmas
  Will care for it still.

In the Chaplet on Jesus and
  Mary,
  From our hearts let us call,
At each Ave Maria we whisper
  A rosebud shall fall,
And at each Gloria Patri a lily,
  The crown of them all!

A DESIRE.

O, TO have dwelt in Bethlehem
  When the star of the Lord
  shone bright!
To have sheltered the holy wan-
  derers
  On that blessèd Christmas
  night;
To have kissed the tender way-
  worn feet
  Of the Mother undefiled,
And, with reverent wonder and
  deep delight,
  To have tended the Holy
  Child!

Hush! such a glory was not for
  thee;
  But that care may still be
  thine;
For are there not little ones still
  to aid
  For the sake of the Child divine?
Are there no wandering Pilgrims
  now,
  To thy heart and thy home to
  take?

And are there no mothers whose
   weary hearts
  You can comfort for Mary's
   sake?

O to have knelt at Jesus' feet,
  And to have learnt His heav-
   enly lore!
To have listened the gentle les-
   sons He taught
  On mountain, and sea, and
   shore!
While the rich and the mighty
   knew Him not,
  To have meekly done His
   will: —
Hush! for the worldly reject Him
   yet,
  You can serve and love Him
   still.
Time cannot silence His mighty
   words,
  And though ages have fled
   away,
His gentle accents of love divine
Speak to your soul to-day.

O to have solaced that weeping
   one
  Whom the righteous dared
   despise!
To have tenderly bound up her
   scattered hair,
  And have dried her tearful
   eyes!
Hush! there are broken hearts
   to soothe,
  And penitent tears to dry,

While Magdalen prays for you
   and them,
  From her home in the starry
   sky.

O to have followed the mournful
   way
  Of those faithful few forlorn!
And grace, beyond even an an-
   gel's hope,
  The Cross for our Lord have
   borne!
To have shared in His tender
   mother's grief,
  To have wept at Mary's side,
To have lived as a child in her
   home, and then
  In her loving care have died!

Hush! and with reverent sorrow
   still,
  Mary's great anguish share;
And learn, for the sake of her
   Son divine,
  Thy cross, like His, to bear.
The sorrows that weigh on thy
   soul unite
  With those which thy Lord
   has borne,
And Mary will comfort thy dy-
   ing hour,
  Nor leave thy soul forlorn.

O to have seen what we now
   adore,
  And, though veiled to faithless
   sight,
To have known, in the form that
   Jesus wore,
  The Lord of Life and Light!

Hush! for He dwells among us
    still,
And a grace can yet be thine,
Which the scoffer and doubter
    can never know, —
The Presence of the Divine.
Jesus is with His children yet,
    For His word can never de-
    ceive ;
Go where His lowly Altars rise,
    And worship, and believe.

OUR DAILY BREAD.

GIVE us our daily Bread,
    O God, the bread of strength !
For we have learnt to know
    How weak we are at length.
As children we are weak,
    As children must be fed ; —
Give us Thy Grace, O Lord,
    To be our daily Bread.

Give us our daily Bread, —
    The bitter bread of grief.
We sought earth's poisoned feasts
    For pleasure and relief ;
We sought her deadly fruits,
    But now, O God, instead,
We ask Thy healing grief
    To be our daily Bread.

Give us our daily Bread
    To cheer our fainting soul ;
The feast of comfort, Lord,
    And peace, to make us whole :

For we are sick of tears,
    The useless tears we shed ; —
Now give us comfort, Lord,
    To be our daily Bread.

Give us our daily Bread,
    The Bread of Angels, Lord,
By us, so many times,
    Broken, betrayed, adored :
His Body and His Blood ; —
    The feast that Jesus spread :
Give Him — our life, our all —
    To be our daily Bread !

THREEFOLD.

MOTHER of grace and mercy,
    Behold how burdens three
Weigh down my weary spirit,
    And drive me here — to Thee.
Three gifts I place forever
    Before thy shrine :
The threefold offering of my love,
    Mary, to thine !

The Past : with all its memories,
    Of pain — that stings me yet ;
Of sin — that brought repent-
    ance ;
Of joy — that brought regret.
That which has been : — forever
    So bitter-sweet —
I lay in humblest offering
    Before thy feet.

The Present : that dark shadow
  Through which we toil to-day ;
The slow drops of the chalice
  That must not pass away.
Mother ! I dare not struggle,
  Still less despair :
I place my Present in thy hands,
  And leave it there.

The Future : holding all things
  Which I can hope or fear,
Brings sin and pain, it may be,
  Nearer and yet more near.
Mother ! this doubt and shrink-
    ing
Will not depart,
Unless I trust my Future
  To thy dear Heart.

Making the Past my lesson,
  Guiding the Present right,
Ruling the misty Future, —
  Bless them and me to-night.
What may be, and what must be,
  And what has been,
In thy dear care forever
  I leave, my Queen !

————

CONFIDO ET CONQUI-ESCO.

" *Seit ; potest ; vult : quid est quod
timeamus ?* " — S. Ignatius.

Fret not, poor soul : while doubt
   and fear
  Disturb thy breast,

The pitying angels, who can see
How vain thy wild regret must be,
  Say, Trust and Rest.

Plan not, nor scheme, — but
   calmly wait ;
  His choice is best.
While blind and erring is thy
   sight,
His wisdom sees and judges right,
  So Trust and Rest.

Strive not, nor struggle : thy
   poor might
  Can never wrest
The meanest thing to serve thy
   will ;
All power is His alone : Be still,
  And Trust and Rest.

Desire not : self-love is strong
   Within thy breast ;
And yet He loves thee better still,
So let Him do His loving will,
  And Trust and Rest.

What dost thou fear ? His wis-
   dom reigns
  Supreme confessed ;
His power is infinite ; his love
Thy deepest, fondest dreams
   above ; —
  So Trust and Rest.

————

ORA PRO ME.

Ave Maria ! bright and pure,
  Hear, O hear me when I pray !

Pains and pleasures try the pilgrim
  On his long and weary way;
Fears and perils are around
  me, —
      Ora pro me.

Mary, see my heart is burdened,
  Take, O take the weight away,
Or help me, that I may not mur-
  mur
If it is a cross you lay
On my weak and trembling heart,
  — but
      Ora pro me.

Mary, Mary, Queen of Heaven!
  Teach, O teach me to obey:
Lead me on, though fierce temp-
  tations
Stand and meet me in the way;
When I fail and faint, my mother,
      Ora pro me.

Then shall I — if thou, O Mary,
  Art my strong support and
  stay —
Fear nor feel the threefold danger
  Standing forth in dread array;
Now and ever shield and guard me,
      Ora pro me.

When my eyes are slowly closing,
  And I fade from earth away,
And when Death, the stern de-
  stroyer,
  Claims my body as his prey, —
Claim my soul, and then, sweet
  Mary,
      Ora pro me.

THE CHURCH IN 1849.

O MIGHTY Mother, hearken! for
  thy foes
  Gather around thee, and ex-
  ulting cry
  That thine old strength is gone
  and thou must die,
Pointing with fierce rejoicing to
  thy woes.
And is it so? The raging whirl-
  wind blows
  No stronger now than it has
  done of yore:
  Rebellion, strife, and sin have
  been before;
The same companions whom thy
  Master chose.
We too rejoice: we know thy
  might is more
  When to the world thy glory
  seemeth dim;
Nor can Hell's gates prevail to
  conquer Thee,
  Who hearest over all the voice
  of Him
Who chose thy first and great-
  est Prince should be
A fisher on the Lake of Galilee.

FISHERS OF MEN.

THE boats are out, and the storm
  is high;
  We kneel on the shore and
  pray.

The Star of the Sea shines still in
　　the sky,
　　And God is our help and stay.

The fishers are weak, and the
　　tide is strong,
　　And their boat seems slight
　　　and frail ;
But St. Peter has steered it for
　　them so long,
　　It would weather a rougher
　　　gale.

St. John the Belovéd sails with
　　them too,
　　And his loving words they
　　　hear ;
So with tender trust the boat's
　　brave crew
　　Neither doubt, or pause, or fear.

He who sent them fishing is with
　　them still,
　　And He bids them cast their
　　　net ;
And He has the power their boat
　　to fill,
　　So we know He will do it yet.

They have cast their nets again
　　and again,
　　And now call to us on shore ;
If our feeble prayers seem only
　　in vain,
　　We will pray and pray the
　　　more.

Though the storm is loud, and
　　our voice is drowned
　　By the roar of the wind and
　　　sea,
We know that more terrible
　　tempests found
　　Their Ruler, O Lord, in Thee!

See, they do not pause, they are
　　toiling on,
　　Yet they cast a loving glance
On the star above, and ever anon
　　Look up through the blue ex-
　　　panse.

O Mary, listen ! for danger is
　　nigh,
　　And we know thou art near
　　　us then ;
For thy Son's dear servants to
　　thee we cry,
　　Sent out as fishers of men.

O, watch, — as of old thou didst
　　watch the boat
　　On the Galilean lake, —
And grant that the fishers may
　　keep afloat
　　Till the nets, o'ercharged, shall
　　　break.

———

THE OLD YEAR'S BLESS-
ING.

I AM fading from you,
　　But one draweth near,
Called the Angel-guardian
　　Of the coming year.

If my gifts and graces
　Coldly you forget,
Let the New-Year's Angel
　Bless and crown them yet.

For we work together ;
　He and I are one :
Let him end and perfect
　All I leave undone.

I brought Good Desires,
　Though as yet but seeds ;
Let the New-Year make them
　Blossom into Deeds.

I brought Joy to brighten
　Many happy days ;
Let the New-Year's Angel
　Turn it into Praise.

If I gave you Sickness,
　If I brought you Care,
Let him make one Patience,
　And the other Prayer.

Where I brought you Sorrow,
　Through his care, at length,
It may rise triumphant
　Into future Strength.

If I brought you Plenty,
　All wealth's bounteous charms,
Shall not the New Angel
　Turn them into Alms ?

I gave Health and Leisure,
　Skill to dream and plan ;

Let him make them nobler ; —
　Work for God and Man.

If I broke your Idols,
　Showed you they were dust,
Let him turn the Knowledge
　Into heavenly Trust.

If I brought Temptation,
　Let sin die away
Into boundless Pity
　For all hearts that stray.

If your list of Errors
　Dark and long appears,
Let this new-born Monarch
　Melt them into Tears.

May you hold this Angel
　Dearer than the last, —
So I bless his Future,
　While he crowns my Past.

———

EVENING CHANT.

STREW before our Lady's Picture
　Roses, — flushing like the sky
Where the lingering western
　　cloudlets
　Watch the daylight die.

Violets steeped in dreamy odors,
　Humble as the Mother mild,
Blue as were her eyes when
　　watching
　O'er her sleeping Child.

Strew white Lilies, pure and spot-
  less,
  Bending on their stalks of
    green,
Bending down with tender pity,—
  Like our Holy Queen.

Let the flowers spend their fra-
    grance
  On our Lady's own dear
    shrine,
While we claim her gracious
    helping
  Near her Son divine.

Strew before our Lady's picture
  Gentle flowers, fair and sweet;
Hope, and Fear, and Joy, and
    Sorrow,
  Place, too, at her feet.

Hark! the Angelus is ringing, —
  Ringing through the fading
    light,
In the heart of every Blossom
  Leave a prayer to-night.

All night long will Mary listen,
  While our pleadings fond and
    deep
On their scented breath are rising
  For us — while we sleep.

Scarcely through the starry si-
    lence
  Shall one trembling petal stir,
While they breathe their own
    sweet fragrance
  And our prayers — to Her.

Peace to every heart that loves
  her !
  All her children shall be blest :
While She prays and watches for
  us,
  We will trust and rest.

A CHRISTMAS CAROL.

THE moon that now is shining
  In skies so blue and bright,
Shone ages since on Shepherds
  Who watched their flocks by
    night.
There was no sound upon the
  earth,
  The azure air was still,
The sheep in quiet clusters lay
  Upon the grassy hill.

When lo ! a white-winged Angel
  The watchers stood before,
And told how Christ was born
  on earth,
  For mortals to adore ;
He bade the trembling Shepherds
  Listen, nor be afraid,
And told how in a manger
  The glorious Child was laid.

When suddenly in the Heavens
  Appeared an Angel band,
(The while in reverent wonder
  The Syrian Shepherds stand.)

And all the bright host chanted
　Words that shall never cease, —
Glory to God in the highest,
　On earth good-will and peace !

The vision in the heavens
　Faded, and all was still,
And the wondering shepherds
　left their flocks,
To feed upon the hill :
Towards the blessed city
　Quickly their course they held,
And in a lowly stable
　Virgin and Child beheld.

Beside a humble manger
　Was the Maiden Mother mild.
And in her arms her Son divine,
　A new-born Infant, smiled.
No shade of future sorrow
　From Calvary then was cast ;
Only the glory was revealed,
　The suffering was not passed.

The Eastern kings before him
　knelt,
　And rarest offerings brought ;
The shepherds worshipped and
　adored
　The wonders God had
　wrought :
They saw the crown for Israel's
　King,
　The future's glorious part : —
But all these things the Mother
　kept
　And pondered in her heart.

Now we that Maiden Mother
　The Queen of Heaven call ;

And the Child we call our Jesus,
　Saviour and Judge of all.
But the star that shone in Beth-
　lehem
　Shines still, and shall not
　cease,
And we listen still to the tidings,
　Of Glory and of Peace.

OUR TITLES.

ARE we not Nobles ? we who
　trace
　Our pedigree so high
That God for us and for our race
　Created Earth and Sky,
And Light and Air and Time
　and Space,
　To serve us and then die.

Are we not Princes ? we who
　stand
　As heirs beside the Throne ;
We who can call the promised
　Land
　Our Heritage, our own ;
And answer to no less command
　Than God's and His alone.

Are we not Kings ? both night
　and day,
　From early until late,
About our bed, about our way,
　A guard of Angels wait ;
And so we watch and work and
　pray
　In more than royal state.

Are we not holy ?   Do not start:
  It is God's sacred will
To call us Temples set apart
  His Holy Ghost may fill :
Our very food . . . . O hush, my
    Heart,
  Adore IT and be still !

Are we not more ? our Life shall
    be
  Immortal and divine.
The nature Mary gave to Thee,
  Dear Jesus, still is Thine ;
Adoring in Thy Heart, I see
  Such blood as beats in mine.

O God, that we can dare to fail,
  And dare to say we must !
O God, that we can ever trail
  Such banners in the dust,
Can let such starry honors pale,
  And such a Blazon rust !

Shall we upon such Titles bring
  The taint of sin and shame ?
Shall we, the children of the
    King
  Who hold so grand a claim,
Tarnish by any meaner thing
  The glory of our name ?

MINISTERING ANGELS.

Angels of light, spread your
    bright wings and keep
  Near me at morn :

Nor in the starry eve, nor mid-
    night deep,
  Leave me forlorn.

From all dark spirits of unholy
    power
  Guard my weak heart,
Circle around me in each peril-
    ous hour,
  And take my part.

From all foreboding thoughts
    and dangerous fears,
  Keep me secure ;
Teach me to hope, and through
    the bitterest tears
  Still to endure.

If lonely in the road so fair and
    wide
  My feet should stray,
Then through a rougher, safer
    pathway guide
  Me day by day.

Should my heart faint at its un-
    equal strife,
  O still be near !
Shadow the perilous sweetness
    of this life
  With holy fear.

Then leave me not alone in this
    bleak world,
  Where'er I roam,
And at the end, with your bright
    wings unfurled,
  O take me home !

THE SHRINES OF MARY.

THERE are many shrines of Our
  Lady,
  In different lands and climes,
Where I can remember kneeling
  In old and beloved times.

They arise now like stars before
  me,
  Through the long, long night
    of years ;
Some are bright with a heavenly
  radiance,
  And others shine out through
    tears.

They arise too like mystical flow-
  ers,
  All different, and all the
    same, —
As they lie in my heart like a gar-
  land
  That is wreathed round Mary's
    name.

Thus each shrine has two conse-
  crations ;
  One all the faithful can trace,
But one is for me and me only,
  Holding my soul with its grace.

I.

A shrine in a quaint old Chapel
  Defaced and broken with years,
Where the pavement is worn
  with kneeling,
  And the step with kisses and
    tears.

She is there in the dawn of morn-
  ing,
  When the day is blue and
    bright,
In the shadowy evening twilighti
  And the silent, starry night.

Through the dim old painted win-
  dow
  The Hours look down, and
    shed
A different glory upon her,
  Violet, purple, and red.

And there — in that quaint old
  Chapel
  As I stood one day alone —
Came a royal message from Mary.
  That claimed. my life as her
    own.

II.

I remember a vast Cathedral
  Which holds the struggle and
    strife
Of a grand and powerful city,
  As the heart holds the throb of
    a life.

Where the ebb and the flow of
  passion,
  And sin in its rushing tide,
Have dashed on that worn stone
  chapel,
  Dashed, and broken, and died.

And above the voices of sorrow
  And the tempter's clamorous
    din,

The voice of Mary has spoken
  And conquered the pain and
    the sin:

For long ages and generations
  Have come there to strive and
    to pray;
She watched and guided them
    living,
  And does not forget them to-
    day.

And once, in that strange, vast
    City
  I stood in its great stone square,
Alone in the crowd and the turmoil
  Of the pitiless Southern glare;

And a grief was upon my spirit,
  Which I could not cast away,
It weighed on my heart all the
    night-time,
  And it fretted my life all day.

So then to that calm, cool refuge
  I turned from the noisy street,
And I carried my burden of sor-
    row —
  And left it at Mary's feet.

III.

I remember a lonely chapel
  With a tender claim upon me;
It was built for the sailors only,
  And they call it the Star of the
    Sea.

And the murmuring chant of the
    Vespers
  Seems caught up by the wail-
    ing breeze,
And the throb of the organ is
    echoed
  By the rush of the silver seas.

And the votive hearts and the
    anchors
  Tell of danger and peril past;
Of the hope deferred and the wait-
    ing,
  And the comfort that came at
    last.

I too had a perilous venture
  On a stormy and treacherous
    main,
And I too was pleading to Mary
  From the depths of a heart in
    pain.

It was not a life in peril, —
  O God, it was far, far more!
And the whirlpool of Hell's
    temptations
  Lay between the wreck and the
    shore.

Thick mists hid the light of the
    beacon,
  And the voices of warning
    were dumb;
So I knelt by the Altar of Mary,
  And told her Her hour was
    come.

For she waits till Earth's aid forsakes us,
    Till we know our own efforts
    are vain ;
And we wait, in our faithless
  blindness,
    Till no chance but her prayers
    remain.

And now in that seaside chapel
  By that humble village shrine
Hangs a heart of silver, that tells
  her
    Of the love and the gladness
    of mine.

IV.

There is one far shrine I remember
    In the years that are fled away,
Where the grand old mountains
  are guarding
    The glories of night and day.

Where the earth in her rich, glad
  beauty
    Seems made for our Lady's
    throne,
And the stars in their radiant
  clusters
    Seem fit for her crown alone.

Where the balmy breezes of summer
    On their odorous pinions bear

The fragrance of orange-blos-
  soms,
    And the chimes of the Convent
    prayer.

There I used to ask for Her blessing
    As each summer twilight was
    gray ;
There I used to kneel at her Altar
  At each blue, calm dawn of
  day.

There in silence was Victory
  granted,
    And the terrible strife begun,
That only with Her protection
    Could be dared, or suffered, or
    won.

If I love the name of that Altar,
  And the thought of those days
  gone by,
It is only the Heart of Mary
  And my own that remember
  why.

V.

Where long ages of toil and of
  sorrow,
  And Poverty's weary doom,
Have clustered together so closely
  That life seems shadowed with
  gloom,

Where crime that lurks in the
  darkness
  And vice that glares at the day

Make the spirit of hope grow
weary,
And the spirit of love decay,

Where the feet of the wretched
and sinful
Have closest and oftenest trod,
Is a house, as humble as any,
Yet we call it the House of
God.

It is one of our Lady's Chapels ;
And though poorer than all
the rest,
Just because of the sin and the
sorrow,
I think she loves it the best.

There are no rich gifts on the
Altar,
The shrine is humble and bare,
Yet the poor and the sick and the
tempted
Think their home and their
heaven is there.

And before that humble Altar
Where Our Lady of Sorrow
stands,
I knelt with a weary longing,
And I laid a vow in her hands.

And I know, when I enter softly
And pause at that shrine to
pray,
That the fret and the strife and
the burden
Will be softened and laid away.

And the Prayer and the Vow that
sealed it
Have bound my soul to that
shrine,
For the Mother of Sorrows re-
members
Her promise, and waits for
mine.

It is one long chaplet of memo-
ries
Tender and true and sweet,
That gleam in the Past and the
Distance
Like lamps that burn at her
feet.

Like stars that will shine forever,
For time cannot touch or stir
The graces that Mary has given,
Or the trust that we give to
her.

Past griefs are perished and over,
Past joys have vanished and
died,
Past loves are fled and forgotten,
Past hopes have been laid aside.

Past fears have faded in daylight,
Past sins have melted in
tears ; —
One Love and Remembrance
only
Seems alive in those dead old
old years.

So wherever I look in the distance,
    And whenever I turn to the Past,
There is always a shrine of Mary
    Each brighter still than the last.

I will ask for one grace, O Mother!
    And will leave the rest to thy will:
From one shrine of thine to another,
    Let my Life be a Pilgrimage still!

At each one, O Mother of Mercy!
    Let still more of thy love be given,
Till I kneel at the last and brightest, —
    The Throne of the Queen of Heaven.

THE HOMELESS POOR.

CALM the city lay in midnight silence,
    Deep on streets and roofs the snow lay white;
Then I saw an Angel spread his pinions
    Rising up to Heaven to meet the night.

In his hands he bore two crowns of lilies,
    Sweet with sweetness not of earthly flowers,
But a coronal of prayers for Heaven
    He had gathered through the evening hours; —

He had gathered in that mighty city
    Through whose streets and pathways he had trod,
Till he wove into a winter garland
    Prayers that faithful hearts had sent to God.

Through the azure midnight he was rising;
    As I watched, I saw his upward flight
Checked by a mighty Angel, whose stern challenge,
    Like a silver blast, rang through the night.

Then strange words upon the silence broke,
And I listened as the Angels spoke.

"I have come from wandering through the city,
    I have been to seek a garland meet

To be placed before His throne
in Heaven,
　To be laid at His dear Moth-
　　er's feet.

" I have been to one of England's
Havens, —
　To a HOME for peace and
　　honor planned,
Where the kindly lights of joy
and duty
　Meet and make the glory of
　　the land.

" There I heard the ring of
children's laughter
Hushed to eager silence ; I
could see
How the father stroked their
golden tresses
　As they clustered closer round
　　his knee.

" And I heard him tell, with lov-
ing honor,
　How the wanderers to Bethle-
　　hem came,
And I saw each head in rever-
ence bowing
　When he named the Holy
　　Child's dear name.

" Then he told how houseless,
homeless, friendless,
　They had wandered wearily
　　and long, —
Of the manger where our Lord
was cradled,
　Of the Shepherds listening to
　　our song.

" As he spoke, I heard his accents
falter,
　And I saw each childish heart
　　was stirred
With a loving throb of tender
pity
　At the sorrowful, sweet tale
　　they heard.

" As the children sang their
Christmas carol
　I could see the mother's eyes
　　grow dim,
And she held her baby closer, —
feeling
　Most for Mary through her
　　love for him.

" So I gathered from that home,
as flowers,
　All the tender, loving words I
　　heard
Given this night to Jesus and to
Mary, —
　Look at them, and say if I
　　have erred."

THE ANGEL OF DEEDS.

" In that very street, at that same
hour,
　In the bitter air and drifting
　　sleet,
Crouching in a doorway was a
mother,
　With her children shuddering
　　at her feet.

"She was silent; — who would
    hear her pleading?
Men and beasts were housed;
    but she must stay
Houseless in the great and piti-
    less city,
Till the dawning of the winter
    day.

"Homeless — while her fellow-
    men are resting
Calm and blest: their very
    dogs are fed,
Warm and sheltered, and their
    sleeping children
Safely nestled in each little bed.

"She can only draw her poor
    rags closer
Round her wailing baby, —
    closer hold
One, the least and sickliest, —
    while the others
Creep together, tired, hungry,
    cold.

"What are these poor flowers
    thou hast gathered?
Cast such fragile, worthless
    tokens by:
Will He prize mere words of love
    and honor
    While His Homeless Poor are
    left to die?

"He has said — His truths are all
    eternal —
What He said both has been
    and shall be, —

*What ye have not done to these my
    poor ones,
Lo! ye have not done it unto
    Me.*"

Then I saw the Angel with the
    flowers
Bow his head and answer, "It
    is well,"
As he cast a wreath of lilies
    earthward,
And I saw them wither as they
    fell.

Once again the Angel raised his
    head,
Smiled and showed the other
    wreath and said: —

THE ANGEL OF PRAYERS.

"I have been where, kneeling at
    the Altar,
Hushed in reverent awe, a
    faithful throng
Have this night adored the Holy
    Presence,
Worshipping with incense,
    prayer, and song.

"Every head was bowed in lov-
    ing honor,
Every heart with loving awe
    was thrilled;
Earth and things of earth seemed
    all forgotten;
He was there — and meaner
    thoughts were stilled.

" There on many souls in strait
and peril
Did that gracious Benediction
fall,
With the strength or peace or
joy or warning
He could give, who loved and
knew them all.

" There was silence, but all
hearts were speaking :
When the deepest hush of
silence fell,
On the fragrant air and breathless longing
Came the echo of one silver bell.

" On each spirit such a flood of
sweetness
Broke — as we who dwell in
Heaven feel,
Then the *Adoremus in eternum*,
Jubilant and strong, rolled
peal on peal.

" They had given holy adoration,
Tender words of love and
praise ; all bright
With the dew of contrite tears —
such blossoms
I am bearing to His throne to-
night."

THE ANGEL OF DEEDS.

" Pause again : these flowers are
fair and lovely,
Radiant in their perfume and
their bloom ;

But not far from where you
plucked this garland
Is a squalid place in ghastly
gloom.

" There black waters in their
luring silence
Under loathsome arches crawl
and creep,
There the rats and vermin herd
together . . . .
*There God's poor ones sometimes
come to sleep.*

" There the weary come, who
through the daylight
Pace the town, and crave for
work in vain ;
There they crouch in cold and
rain and hunger,
Waiting for another day of
pain.

" In slow darkness creeps the
dismal river ;
From its depths looks up a
sinful rest ;
Many a weary, baffled, hopeless
wanderer
Has it drawn into its treacherous breast.

" There is near *another River* flowing,
Black with guilt, and deep as
hell and sin ;
On its brink even sinners stand
and shudder, —
Cold and hunger goad the
homeless in.

" Yet these poor ones to His
      heart are dearer
    For their grief and peril : dear
      indeed
Would have been the love that
      sought and fed them,
    Gave them warmth and shelter
      in their need.

" For His sake those tears and
      prayers are offered
    Which you bear as flowers to
      His throne ;
Better still would be the food and
      shelter,
    Given for Him and given to
      His own.

" Praise with loving deeds is dear
      and holy,
    Words of praise will never
      serve instead :
Lo ! you offer music, hymn, and
      incense —
    When *He has not where to lay
      His head.*"

Then once more the Angel with
      the Flowers
    Bowed his head, and answered,
      " It is well,"
As he cast a wreath of lilies
      earthwards,
    And I saw them wither as they
      fell.

So the Vision faded, and the
      Angels
    Melted far into the starry sky ;

By the light upon the eastern
      Heaven
    I could see another day was
      nigh.

Was it quite a dream ? O God !
      we love Him ;
    All our love, though weak, is
      given to Him ; —
Why is it our hearts have been
      so hardened ?
    Why is it our eyes have been
      so dim ?

Still as for Himself the Infant
      Jesus
    In His little ones asks food
      and rest, —
Still as for His Mother He is
      pleading
    Just as when He lay upon her
      breast.

Jesus, then, and Mary still are
      with us, —
    Night will find the Child and
      Mother near,
Waiting for the shelter we deny
      them,
    While we tell them that we
      hold them dear.

Help us, Lord ! not these Thy
      poor ones only,
    They are with us always, and
      shall be ; —
Help the blindness of our hearts
      and teach us
    In Thy homeless ones to suc-
      cor Thee.

MILLY'S EXPIATION.

THE PRIEST'S STORY.

I.

THERE are times when all these
    terrors
  Seem to fade, and fade away,
Like a nightmare's ghastly pres-
    ence
  In the truthful dawn of day.
There are times, too, when be-
    fore me
  They arise, and seem to hold
In their grasp my very being
  With the deadly strength of
    old,
Till my spirit quails within me,
  And my very heart grows cold.

II.

For I watched when Cold and
    Hunger,
  Like wild beasts that sought
    for prey,
With a savage glare crept on-
    ward
  Until men were turned at
    bay.
You have never seen those hunt-
    ers,
  Who have never known that
    fear,
When life costs a crust, and
    costing
  Even that is still too dear:
But, you know, I lived in Ire-
    land
  In the fatal famine year.

III.

Yes, those days are now forgot-
    ten;
  God be thanked! men can
    forget;
Time's great gift can heal the
    fevers
  Called Remembrance and Re-
    gret.
Man despises such forgetting;
  But I think the Angels know,
Since each hour brings new bur-
    dens,
  We must let the old ones
    go, —
Very weak or very noble
  Are the few who cling to woe.

IV.

As a child, I lived in Connaught,
  And from dawn till set of sun
Played with all the peasant-
    children,
  So I knew them every one.
There was not a cabin near us,
  But I had my welcome there;
Though of money-help in those
    days
  We had none ourselves to
    spare,
Yet the neighbors had no trouble
  That I did not know and
    share.

V.

O that great estate! the Land-
    lord
  Was abroad, a good man too;

And the agent was not cruel,
  But he had hard things to do.
As a child I saw great suffering
  Which I could not under-
    stand,
So I went back as a man there
  With redress and helping
    planned;
But I found, on reaching Con-
  naught,
  There was famine in the land.

VI.

Well, I worked, I toiled, I la-
  bored;
  So, thank God, did many
    more;
But I had a special pity
  For the place I knew before.
It was changed; the old were
  vanished;
  Those who had been workers
    there
Were grown old now; and the
  children,
  With their sunny eyes and
    hair,
Were a ragged army, fighting
  Hand to hand with black de-
    spair.

VII.

There were some I sought out,
  longing
  For the old familiar face,
For the hearty Irish welcome
  To the well-known corner
    place;

So I saw them, and I found it.
  But of all whom I had known,
I cared most to see the Connors.
  Their poor cabin stood alone
In the deep heart of the valley,
  By the old gray fairy stone.

VIII.

They were decent people, hold-
  ing,
  Though no richer than the
    rest,
Still a place beyond their neigh-
  bors,
  With a tacit, unconfessed
Pride — it may have been —
  that held them
  From complaint when things
    went ill:
I might guess when work was
  slacker,
  But no shadow seemed to chill
The warm welcome which they
  offered;
  It was warm and cheerful still.

IX.

Yet their home was changed: the
  father
  And the mother were no more;
And the brothers, Phil and Pat-
  rick,
  Kept starvation from the door
There were many little faces
  Gathered round the old hearth-
    stone;

But the children I had played
  with
    Were the men and women
    grown ;
Phil and Patrick, Kate and Milly,
  Were the ones whom I had
  known.

X.

Kate was grown, but little al-
  tered,
  Just the sunburnt, rosy face,
With its merry smile, whose shin-
  ing
    Seemed to light the darkest
    place.
But all, young and old, held
  Milly
  As their dearest and their best,
From the baby orphan-sisters
  Whom she hushed upon her
  breast, —
She it was who bore the burdens,
  Love and sorrow, for the rest.

XI.

Yes, I knew the tall slight figure,
  And the face so pale and fair,
Crowned with long, long plaited
  tresses
  Of her shining yellow hair ;
She was very calm and tender,
  Warm and brave, yet just and
  wise,
Meeting grief with tender pity,
  Sin with sorrowful surprise :
I have fancied Angels watch us
  With such sad and loving eyes.

XII.

Well, I questioned past and fut-
  ure,
  Heard of plans and hopes and
  fears ;
How all prospects grew still
  darker
  With the shade of coming
  years.
Milly still deferred her marriage ;
  But the brothers urged of late
She would leave them and old
  Ireland,
  And at least secure her fate ;
Michael pleaded too, — but vain-
  ly ;
Milly chose to wait and wait.

XIII.

Though all liked her cousin Mi-
  chael, —
  He was steady, a good son, —
Yet we wondered at the treasure
  Which his careless heart had
  won.
Ah, he was not worth her ! Milly
  Must have guessed our thought
  in part,
For she feigned such special def-
  erence
  For his judgment and his
  heart :
The defiance and the answer
  Of instinctive woman's art.

XIV.

But my duties would not let me
  Stay in one place ; I must go

Where the want and need were
  greatest ;
So I travelled to and fro.
And I could not give the bounty
  Which was meant for all to
    share,
Save in scanty portions, counting
  What each hamlet had to
    bear ;
So my old home and old com-
    rades
  Had to struggle with despair.

XV.

I could note at every visit
  How all suffered more and
    more ;
How the rich were growing
    poorer,
  The poor, poorer than before.
And each time that I returned
    there,
  I could see the famine spread ;
Till I heard of each fresh horror,
  Each new tale of fear and dread,
With more pity for the living,
  More rejoicing for the dead.

XVI.

Yet through all the bitter trials
  Of that long and fearful time,
Still the suffering came untended
  By its hideous sister, Crime.
Earthly things seemed grown less
    potent,
  Fellow-sufferers grown more
    dear,
Murmurs even hushed in silence,
  Just as if, in listening fear,

While God spoke so loud in sor-
    row,
  They all felt He must be near.

XVII.

But one day — I well remember
  How the warm soft autumn
    breeze,
And the gladness of the sunshine,
  And the calmness of the seas,
Seemed in strange unnatural con-
    trast
  To the tale of woe and dread
Which I heard with painful won-
    der, —
  That the agent — I have said
That he was not harsh or cruel —
  Had been shot at, and was
    dead.

XVIII.

For I felt in that small hamlet
  More or less I knew them all,
And on some I cared for, surely,
  Must this bitter vengeance fall ;
But I little dreamed how bitter,
  And the grief how great and
    wide,
Till I heard that Michael Connor
  Was accused, and would be
    tried
For this base and bloody murder ;
  Then I cried out that they lied !

XIX.

He, who might be weak and reck-
    less,
  Yet was gentle and humane ;

He who scarcely had the courage
  To inflict a needful pain, —
Why, it could not be! And
  Milly,
With her honest, noble pride,
And her faith and love, God help
  her!
It were better she had died.
So I thought, and thought, and
  pondered,
  Till I knew they must have
  lied.

XX.

There was want and death and
  hunger
  Near me then; but this great
  crime
Seemed to haunt me with its ter-
  ror,
  And grow worse and worse
  with time,
Till I could not bear it longer,
  And I turned my steps once
  more
To the hamlet; did not slacken
  Till I reached the cabin-door:
Then I paused; I never dreaded
  The kind welcome there be-
  fore.

XXI.

So I entered. Kate was sitting
  By the empty hearth; around
Were the children, ragged, hun-
  gry,
  Crouching silent on the
  ground.

But a wail of grief and sorrow
  Rose, and Katie hid her face,
Sobbing out she had no welcome,
  For a curse was on the place,
And their honest name was cov-
  ered
  With another's black disgrace.

XXII.

Then I soothed her; asked for
  Milly;
  And was told she was away;
Gone as witness to the trial,
  And the trial was that day.
But all knew, so Katie told me,
  Hope or comfort there was
  none;
They were sure to find him guilty,
  And before to-morrow's sun
He must die. I dared not loiter,
  For the trial had begun.

XXIII.

Yet I asked how Milly bore it;
  And Kate told me some strange
  gleam
Of wild hope seemed living in
  her,
  But all knew it was a dream.
Then I mounted; rode on faster
  Faster still; the way was
  long;
Hope and anger, fear and pity,
  Each by turns were loud and
  strong,
And above all, infinite pity
  For the sorrow and the wrong.

XXIV.

So I rode and rode, and entered
  On the crowded market-place.
There was wonder, too, and pity
  Upon many a hungry face;
But I pushed on quicker, quicker,
  Every moment held a fate.
As the great town-clock struck
    mid-day,
  I alighted at the gate:
No, the trial was not over;
  I was not, thank God, too late,

XXV.

For I hoped — the chance was
    meagre —
  That my true and earnest
    word
Might avail him, if the question
  Of his former life was stirred;
So the crowd believed: they
    parted,
  Let me take a foremost place,
Till I saw a shaking figure
  And a terror-stricken face:
Was it guilt, or only terror?
  Fear of death, or of disgrace?

XXVI.

But a sudden breathless silence
  Hushed the lowest whisper
    there,
And I saw a slight young fig-
    ure
  Crowned with yellow plaited
    hair,

Rise, and answer as they called
    her;
  Rise before them all, and stand
With no quiver in her accent,
  And no trembling in her hand,
Just a flush upon her forehead
  Like a burning crimson brand.

XXVII.

Slowly, steadily, and calmly,
  Then the awful words were
    said,
Calling God in Heaven to wit·
    ness
  To the truth of what she said.
As the oath in solemn order
  On the reverent silence broke,
Some strange terror and misgiv·
    ing
  With a sudden start awoke:
What fear was it seized upon
    me
  As I heard the words she
    spoke?

XXVIII.

As she stood there, looking on·
    ward,
  Onward, neither left nor right,
Did she see some deadly purpose
  Buried, hidden out of sight?
Did she see a blighting shadow
  From the cloudy future cast?
Or reluctant fading from her
  Right and honor, — fading
    fast

All her youth's remembered les-
sons,
All the honest, noble past?

XXIX.

But her accents never faltered,
    As she swore the day and
    time,
At the hour of the murder,
    At the moment of the crime,
She had spoken with the prison-
    er . . . .
Then a gasping joyful sigh
Ran through all the court; they
    knew it, —
    Now the prisoner would not
    die . . . .
And I knew that God in Heaven
Had been witness to a lie!

XXX.

Then I turned and looked at
    Michael;
    Saw a rush of wonder stir
Through his soul; perplexed, be-
    wildered,
    He looked strangely up at her.
Would he speak? could he have
    courage?
Where she fell, could he be
    strong?
Where she sinned, and sinned to
    save him,
    Could he thrust away the
    wrong?
That one moment's strange re-
    vulsion
Seemed to me an hour long.

XXXI.

And I saw the sudden shrinking
    In her brothers; wondering
    scorn
In the glance they cast upon her
    Showed they knew she was
    forsworn.
They were stern, by want made
    sterner;
    But the spot where Milly
    came
In their hearts was soft and ten-
    der
    For her dear and honored
    name:
Now the very love was hardened,
    And the honor turned to
    shame.

XXXII.

So I left the place, nor lingered
    To see Michael, or to feign
Joy where joy was mixed so
    strangely
    Both with pity and with pain.
Many weeks I toiled and labored
    Far from there, but night and
    day
One sad memory dwelt beside me,
    On my heart one shadow
    lay; —
Light was faded, glory tarnished,
    And a soul was cast away.

*   *   *   *

XXXIII.

It was evening; and the sunset
    Glowed and glittered on the
    seas,

When a great ship heaved its an-
    chor,
  Loosed its sails to meet the
    breeze,
Sailing, sailing to the westward.
  Eyes were wet and hearts
    were sore;
Many a heart that left its coun-
    try,
  Many a heart upon the shore,
Knew that parting was forever,
  Said farewell forevermore.

XXXIV.

In that sad and silent evening,
  On the sunny, quiet beach,
Lingered little groups of watch-
    ers,
  But with hearts too full for
    speech.
As I passed, I knew so many,
  That my heart ached too that
    night,
For the yearning love, that, gaz-
    ing,
  Strained to see the last faint
    sight
Of the great ship, sailing west-
    ward,
  Down the track of evening
    light.

XXXV.

None were lonely though, — one
    sorrow
  Drew that evening heart to
    heart;
Only far from all the others
  One lone woman stood apart.

There was something in the fig-
    ure,
  Tall and slender, standing
    there,
That I knew — yet no, I doubt-
    ed —
  That forlorn and helpless air;
When a gleam of sunset glory
  Showed her yellow braided
    hair.

XXXVI.

It was Milly: ere I sought her,
  One who knew her, standing
    by,
Said, "Her people sailed from
    Ireland,
  And she stayed, but none knew
    why.
They were strong; in that far
    country
  Work such men were sure to
    find;
They had offered to take Milly,
  Pressed her often, and been
    kind;
They had taken the young chil-
    dren,
  Only she was left behind.

XXXVII.

"Michael, too, was with them·
    doubly
  Had his fame been cleared by
    time;
For the murderer, lately dying,
  Had confessed and owned the
    crime:

And yet Milly, none knew where-
fore,
Broke her plighted troth to
him ;
Parted, too, with all her loved
ones
For some strange and selfish
whim." . . .
O, my heart was sore for Milly,
And I felt my eyes grow dim.

XXXVIII.

She is still in Ireland ; dwelling
Near the old place, and alone ;
Just the same kind, loving spirit,
But the old light heart is flown.
When the humble toil is over
For her scanty daily bread,
Then she turns to nurse the
suffering,
Or to pray beside the dead :
Many, many thankful blessings
Fall each day upon her head.

XXXIX.

There is no distress or sorrow
Milly does not try to cheer ;
There is never fever raging
But you always find her near ;
And she knows — at least I think
so —
That I guess her secret pain,
Why her Love and why her Sor-
row
Need be purified from stain,
Need in special consecration
Be restored to God again.

A CASTLE IN THE AIR.

I BUILT myself a castle,
So noble, grand, and fair ;
I built myself a castle,
A castle — in the air.

The fancies of my twilights
That fade in sober truth,
The longing of my sorrow,
And the vision of my youth ;

The plans of joyful futures ;
So dear they used to seem ;
The prayer that rose unbidden,
Half prayer — and half a
dream ;

The hopes that died unuttered
Within this heart of mine ; —
For all these tender treasures
My castle was the shrine.

I looked at all the castles
That rise to grace the land,
But I never saw another
So stately or so grand.

And now you see it shattered,
My castle in the air ;
It lies, a dreary ruin,
All desolate and bare.

I cannot build another,
I saw that one decay ;
And strength and heart and
courage
Died out the self-same day.

Yet still, beside that ruin,
  With hopes as deep and fond,
I waited with an infinite longing,
  Only — I look beyond.

PER PACEM AD LUCEM.

I DO not ask, O Lord, that life
    may be
  A pleasant road ;
I do not ask that Thou wouldst
    take from me
  Aught of its load ;

I do not ask that flowers should
    always spring
  Beneath my feet ;
I know too well the poison and
    the sting
  Of things too sweet.

For one thing only, Lord, dear
    Lord, I plead,
  Lead me aright —
Though strength should falter,
    and though heart should
    bleed —
  Through Peace to Light.

I do not ask, O Lord, that thou
    shouldst shed
  Full radiance here ;
Give but a ray of peace, that I
    may tread
  Without a fear.

I do not ask my cross to under-
    stand,
  My way to see ;
Better in darkness just to feel
    Thy hand
  And follow Thee.

Joy is like restless day ; but peace
    divine
  Like quiet night :
Lead me, O Lord, — till perfect
    Day shall shine,
  Through Peace to Light.

A LEGEND.

I.

THE Monk was preaching :
    strong his earnest word,
  From the abundance of his
    heart he spoke,
And the flame spread, — in every
    soul that heard
  Sorrow and love and good re-
    solve awoke : —
The poor lay Brother, ignorant
    and old,
  Thanked God that he had heard
    such words of gold.

II.

" Still let the glory, Lord, be
    thine alone," —
  So prayed the Monk, his heart
    absorbed in praise :

"Thine be the glory: if my hands have sown
The harvest ripened in Thy mercy's rays,
It was Thy blessing, Lord, that made my word
Bring light and love to every soul that heard.

III.

" O Lord, I thank Thee that my feeble strength
Has been so blest ; that sinful hearts and cold
Were melted at my pleading, — knew at length
How sweet Thy service and how safe Thy fold :
While souls that loved Thee saw before them rise
Still holier heights of loving sacrifice."

IV.

So prayed the Monk : when suddenly he heard
An angel speaking thus :
" Know, O my Son,
Thy words had all been vain, but hearts were stirred,
And saints were edified, and sinners won,
By his, the poor lay Brother's humble aid
Who sat upon the pulpit stair and prayed."

BIRTHDAY GIFTS.

FOR A CHILD.

WHY do you look sad, my Minnie ?
Tell me, darling, — for to-day
Is the birthday of Our Lady,
And Her children should be gay.

What ? —You say that all the others,
Alice, Cyril, Effie, Paul,
All had got a gift to give Her,
Only you had none at all.

Well, dear, that does seem a pity:
Tell me how it came about
That the others bring a present,
And my Minnie comes without.

Alice has a lovely Banner,
All embroidered blue and gold : —
Then you know that sister Alice
Is so clever and so old.

Cyril has his two camellias ;
One deep red, and one pure white:
They will stand at Benediction
On the Altar steps to-night.

Effie, steady little Effie,
Stitching many an hour away,
She has clothed a little orphan
All in honor of to-day.

With the skill the good Nuns
 taught her
Angela herself has made
Two tall stems of such real lilies,
 They do all but smell — and
 fade.

Then with look of grave im-
 portance
Comes our quiet little Paul,
With the myrtle from his gar-
 den : —
 He himself is not as tall.

Even Baby Agnes, kneeling
 With half-shy, half-solemn air,
Held up one sweet rose to Mary,
 Lisping out her tiny prayer.

Well, my Minnie, say, how was
 it ?
 Shall I guess ? I think I
 know
All the griefs. Well, I will
 count them : —
 First, your rose-tree would not
 blow:

Then the fines have been so many
 All the pennies melt away ;
Then for work — I know my
 Minnie
Cares so very much for play,

That these little clumsy fingers
 Scarcely yet have learnt to sew,
Still less all the skilful fancies
 Angela and Alice know.

Yet my Minnie can't be treated
 Quite as Baby was to-day,
When Mamma or Alice gave her
 Something just to give away.

Well, my darling, there are many
 Who have neither time nor
 skill,
Gold nor silver, yet they offer
 Gifts to Mary if they will.

There are ways — Our Lady
 knows them,
 And Her children all should
 know
How to find a flower for Mary
 Underneath the deepest snow ;

How to make a lovely garland,
 Winter though it be and cold ;
How to buy the rarest offering,
 Costing — something — but
 not gold ;

How to buy, and buy it dearly,
 Gifts that She will love to take ;
Nor to grudge the cost, but give it
 Cheerfully for Mary's sake.

Does that seem so strange, my
 darling ?
 Nay, dear, it is nothing new ;
All can give Her noble pres-
 ents, —
 Shall I tell you of a few ?

What were those the Magi offered,
 Frankincense and gold and
 myrrh : —

Minnie thinks that Saints and
Monarchs
Are quite different from her !

. . . Sometimes it is hard to listen
To a word unkind or cold
And to smile a loving answer ;
Do it — and you give Her
Gold.

Thoughts of Her in work or
playtime,
Those small grains of incense
rare,
Cast upon a burning censer,
Rise in perfumed clouds of
prayer.

There are sometimes bitter fan-
cies,
Little murmurs that will stir
Even a loving heart ; — but crush
them
And you give Our Lady myrrh.

Give your little crosses to her,
Which each day, each hour
befall ;
They remind Her of Her Jesus,
So she loves them best of all.

Some seem very poor and worth-
less,
Yet however small and slight,
Given to her by one who loves
her,
They are precious in her sight.

One may be so hard to carry
That your hands will bleed
and smart : —
Go and take it to Her Altar,
Go and place it in her heart;

Check your tears and try to love
it,
Love it as His sacred will :
So you set the cross with jewels,
Make your gift more precious
still.

There are souls — alas ! too
many —
Who forget that Jesus died,
Who forget that sin forever
Is the lance to pierce His side.

Hearts that turn away from Je-
sus ;
Sins that scourge Him and be-
tray ;
Cold and cruel souls that even
Crucify Him day by day.

Ah ! poor sinners ! Mary loves
them,
And she knows no royal gem
Half so noble or so precious
As the prayer you say for
them ;

Or resign some little pleasure
Give it her instead, to win
Help for some poor soul in peril
Grace for some poor heart in
sin,

Mercy for poor sinners, — plead-
ing
   For their souls as for your
   own ; —
So you make a crown of jewels
   Fit to lay before Her throne.

Flowers, — why I should never
finish
   If I tried to count them too, —
If I told you how to know them,
   In what garden-plot they grew.

Yet I think my darling guesses
   They are emblems, and we
   trace
In the rarest and the loveliest
   Acts of love and gifts of grace.

Modest violets, meek snow-drops,
   Holy lilies white and pure,
Faithful tendrils — herbs for heal-
ing —
   If they only would endure !

And they will, — such flowers
fade not ;
   They are not of mortal birth ;
And such garlands given to Mary
   Die not like the gifts of Earth.

Well, my Minnie, can you tell
me
   You have still no gift to lay
At the feet of your dear Mother,
   Any hour, any day ?

Give Her now — to-day — forever,
   One great gift, — the first, the
   best, —
Give your heart to Her, and ask
her
   How to give her all the rest.

A BEGGAR.

I BEG of you, I beg of you, my
   brothers,
   For my need is very sore ;
Not for gold and not for silver
   do I ask you,
   But for something even more :
From the depths of your hearts
   pity let it be —
     Pray for me.

I beg of you whose robes of ra-
   diant whiteness
   Have been kept without a
   stain ;
Of you who, stung to death by
   serpent Pleasure,
   Found the healing Angel
   Pain :
Whether holy or forgiven you
   may be —
     Pray for me.

I beg of you calm souls whose
   wondering pity
   Looks at paths you never trod :

I beg of you who suffer — for all
   sorrow
Must be very near to God —
And the need is even greater
   than you see —
     Pray for me.

I beg of you, O children, for He
   loves you,
And He loves your prayers the
   best :
Fold your little hands together,
   and ask Jesus
That the weary may have rest,
That a bird caught in a net may
   be set free —
     Pray for me.

I beg of you who stand before
   the Altar,
Whose anointed hands up-
   raise
All the sin and all the sorrow of
   the Ages,
All the love and all the praise,
And the glory which was always
   and shall be —
     Pray for me.

I beg of you — of you who
   through Life's battle
Our dear Lord has set apart,
That while we who love the peril
   are made captives,
   Still the Church may have its
   Heart
Which is fettered that our souls
   may be set free —
     Pray for me.

I beg of you, I beg of you, my
   brothers,
For an alms this very day ;
I am standing on your doorstep
   as a Beggar
Who will not be turned away,
And the Charity you give my
   soul shall be —
     Pray for me !

————

LINKS WITH HEAVEN.

Our God in Heaven, from that
   holy place,
To each of us an Angel guide
   has given ;
But Mothers of dead children
   have more grace, —
For they give Angels to their
   God and Heaven.

How can a Mother's heart feel
   cold or weary
Knowing her dearer self safe,
   happy, warm ?
How can she feel her road too
   dark or dreary,
Who knows her treasure sheltered from the storm ?

How can she sin ? Our hearts
   may be unheeding,
Our God forgot, our holy
   Saints defied ;

But can a mother hear her dead
  child pleading,
And thrust those little angel
  hands aside ?

Those little hands stretched down
  to draw her ever
Nearer to God by mother
  love : — we all
Are blind and weak, yet surely
  she can never,
With such a stake in Heaven,
  fail or fall.

She knows that when the mighty
  Angels raise
Chorus in Heaven, one little
  silver tone
Is hers forever, that one little
  praise,
One little happy voice, is all
  her own.

We may not see her sacred crown
  of honor,
But all the Angels flitting to
  and fro
Pause smiling as they pass, —
  they look upon her
As mother of an angel whom
  they know,

One whom they left nestled at
  Mary's feet, —
The children's place in Heaven, — who softly sings

A little chant to please them, slow
  and sweet,
Or smiling strokes their little
  folded wings ;

Or gives them Her white lilies
  or Her beads
To play with : — yet, in spite
  of flower or song,
They often lift a wistful look that
  pleads
And asks Her why their mother stays so long.

Then our dear Queen makes answer she will call
Her very soon : meanwhile they
  are beguiled
To wait and listen while She tells
  them all
A story of Her Jesus as a child.

Ah, Saints in Heaven may pray
  with earnest will
And pity for their weak and
  erring brothers :
Yet there is prayer in Heaven
  more tender still, —
The little Children pleading
  for their Mothers.

HOMELESS.

It is cold, dark midnight, yet listen
To that patter of tiny feet !

Is it one of your dogs, fair lady,
　Who whines in the bleak cold
　　street ?
Is it one of your silken spaniels
　Shut out in the snow and the
　　sleet ?

My dogs sleep warm in their bas-
　kets,
　Safe from the darkness and
　　snow ;
All the beasts in our Christian
　England,
　Find pity wherever they go —
(Those are only the homeless
　children
　Who are wandering to and fro).

Look out in the gusty darkness,—
　I have seen it again and again,
That shadow, that flits so slowly
　Up and down past the window-
　　pane : —
It is surely some criminal lurk-
　ing
　Out there in the frozen rain ?

Nay, our criminals all are shel-
　tered,
　They are pitied and taught
　　and fed :
That is only a sister-woman
　Who has got neither food nor
　　bed, —

And the Night cries, " Sin to be
　living,"
And the River cries, " Sin to
　be dead."

Look out at that farthest corner
　Where the wall stands blank
　　and bare : —
Can that be a pack which a Ped-
　ler
　Has left and forgotten there ?
His goods lying out unsheltered
　Will be spoilt by the damp
　　night-air.

Nay ; — goods in our thrifty
　England
　Are not left to lie and grow
　　rotten,
For each man knows the market
　value
　Of silk or woollen or cotton. . .
But in counting the riches of Eng-
　land
　I think our Poor are forgotten.

Our Beasts and our Thieves and
　our Chattels
　Have weight for good or for ill;
But the Poor are only His image,
　His presence, His word, His
　　will ; —
And so Lazarus lies at our door-
　step
　And Dives neglects him still.

INDEX OF FIRST LINES

A little changeling spirit, 157.
A little longer yet — a little longer, 74.
A little past the village, 45.
A smiling look she had, a figure slight, 32.
A sorrow, wet with early tears, 71.
A trinket made like a Heart, dear, 185.
All the fluttering wishes, 82.
All yesterday I was spinning, 40.
An ancient enemy have I, 75.
Angels of light, spread your bright wings and keep, 221.
Are we not Nobles? we who trace, 220.
Arise! this day shall shine, 49.
As strangers, you and I are here, 86.
Ave Maria! bright and pure, 215.

Back, ye Phantoms of the Past, 80.
Be strong to hope, O Heart, 30.
Before I trust my fate to thee, 14.
Bless God, ye happy Lands, 210.
Blue against the bluer heavens, 144.

Calm the city lay in midnight silence, 226.
Can you open that ebony Casket, 179.
Child, do not fear, 95.

Dear, I tried to write you such a letter, 160.
Dear, set the casement open, 205.
Deep within my heart of hearts, dear, 187.

Dim shadows gather thickly round, and up the misty stair they climb, 79.
Do not cheat thy Heart and tell her, 8.
Do not crouch to-day, and worship, 41.
Do you grieve no costly offering, 60.
Dwells within the soul of every Artist, 96.

Farewell, O dream of mine, 57.
Fret not, poor soul : while doubt and fear, 215.
From this fair point of present bliss, 98.

Girt round with rugged mountains, 54.
Give us our daily Bread, 214.
Gloomy and black are the cypress-trees, 88.
God gave a gift to Earth : a child, 31.
God's world is bathed in beauty, 123.
Golden days — where are they, 145.

Hark ! the hours are softly calling, 183.
Hast thou o'er the clear heaven of thy soul, 94.
He was the first always : Fortune, 114.
How many a mighty ship, 202.
How pure, and frail, and white, 208.
Hush ! I cannot bear to see thee, 29.
Hush ! speak low ; tread softly, 119.

I am fading from you, 217.
I am footsore and very weary, 60.
I beg of you, I beg of you, my brothers, 244.
I built myself a castle, 239.
I can scarcely hear, she murmured, 91.
I do not ask, O Lord, that life may be, 240.
I had a Message to send her, 142.
I have a bitter Thought, a Snake, 153.
I have seen a fiercer tempest, 19.
I saw a Ruler take his stand, 15.
I see a spirit by thy side, 6.
I think if thou couldst know, 159.

I was with my lady when she died, 124.
I will not let you say a Woman's part, 176.
I wonder did you ever count, 189.
If in my soul, dear, 133.
If in the fight my arm was strong, 159.
If the dread day that calls thee hence, 83.
In joy, in pain, in sorrow, 207.
In the outer Court I was singing, 185.
In the wood where shadows are deepest, 122.
Is my darling tired already, 9.
It is a dreary evening, 50.
It is cold, dark midnight, yet listen, 246.
It is not because your heart is mine — mine only, 97.
It was midnight when I listened, 137.

Judge not ; the workings of his brain, 7.
Just when the red June Roses blow, 139.

Last night, when weary silence fell on all, 72.
Let me count my treasures, 27.
Let thy gold be cast in the furnace, 25.
Let us throw more logs on the fire, 26.
Like dreary prison walls, 114.
Linger, I cried, O radiant Time ! thy power, 188.
Linger, O gentle Time, 19.
Lingering fade the rays of daylight, and the listening air is chilly, 146.
Listen, friend, and I will tell you, 135.
Look, this little golden Heart, 186.
Loud roared the Tempest, 120.

Many, if God should make them kings, 117.
Moan, O ye Autumn Winds, 42.
Mother of grace and mercy, 214.
Mourn, O rejoicing heart, 41.
My God, I thank Thee who hast made, 80.
My Life you ask of ? why, you know, 62.

" Never again ! " vow hearts when reunited, 143.

No name to bid us know, 42.
Not a sound is heard in the Convent, 182.
Nothing is our own : we hold our pleasures, 175.
Nothing resting in its own completeness, 53.
Nothing stirs the sunny silence, 165.

O mighty Mother, hearken ! for thy foes, 216.
O, to have dwelt in Bethlehem, 212.
One by one the sands are flowing, 8.
Our God in Heaven, from that holy place, 245.
Over an ancient scroll I bent, 17.

Place your hands in mine, dear, 116.

Rise ! for the day is passing, 25.

Seated one day at the Organ, 119.
See the rivers flowing, 50.
Shine, ye stars of heaven, 28.
Since I have no lands or houses, 132.
So you think you love me, do you, 99.
Some words are played on golden strings, 101.
Sow with a generous hand, 57.
Spare her at least : look, you have taken from me, 16.
Spare her, O cruel England, 208.
Spread, spread thy silver wings, O Dove, 135.
Stand this way — move near the window, 6.
Starry Crowns of Heaven, 131.
Still the angel stars are shining, 5.
Strew before our Lady's Picture, 218.
Strive ; yet I do not promise, 41.

The boats are out, and the storm is high, 216.
The bond that links our souls together, 52.
The clouds are fleeting by, father, 93.
The Earth is so bleak and deserted, 211.
The feast is spread through England, 71.
The fettered Spirits linger, 178.

The Heart ? — Yes, I wore it, 186.
The House is all deserted, 170.
The King's three daughters stood on the terrace, 173.
The lights extinguished, by the hearth I leant, 105.
The Monk was preaching ; strong his earnest word, 240.
The moon that now is shining, 219.
The shadows of the evening hours, 184.
The stars are gleaming, 181.
The Studio is deserted, 168.
The tempest rages wild and high, 58.
The tender, delicate Flowers, 77.
The way is long and dreary, 53.
The wind went forth o'er land and sea, 172.
There are many shrines of Our Lady, 222.
There are more things in Heaven and Earth than we, 164.
There are times when all these terrors, 231.
There is a deep and subtle snare, 118.
Thou hast done well, perhaps, 48.
Thou hast done well to kneel and say, 155,
Though he lived and died among us, 18.
Through the blue and frosty heavens, 1.
Through the wide world thy children raise, 204.
To fight the battle of the Cross, Christ's chosen ones are sent, 199.
Trust him little who doth raise, 153.
Trust me, no mere skill of subtle tracery, 138.
Two stranger youths in the Far West, 90.

We ask for Peace, O Lord, 83.
We must not doubt, or fear, or dread, that love for life is only given,
115.
Well — the links are broken, 187.
What is it you ask me, darling, 89.
What is Life, father ? A Battle, my child, 24.
What lack the valleys and mountains, 62.
What wouldst thou have, O soul, 202.
When the bright stars came out last night, 92.
When the weariness of Life is ended, 97.
Where are the swallows fled, 16.

Where I am, the halls are gilded, 81.
Where the golden corn is bending, 87.
Where the little babbling streamlet, 158.
Wherefore dwell so sad and lonely, 28.
While the gray mists of early dawn, 174.
Who is the Angel that cometh, 133.
Why do you look sad, my Minnie, 241.
Why shouldst thou fear the beautiful angel, Death, 39.
Why wilt thou make bright music, 49.
Will she come to me, little Effie, 162.
With echoing steps the worshippers, 43.
Within the kingdom of my Soul, 154.
Without one bitter feeling let us part, 78.
Words are lighter than the cloud-foam, 59.

Yes, dear, our Love is slain, 154.
Yes, I was sad and anxious, 121.
Yes, it looked dark and dreary, 165.
You have taken back the promise, 61.
You wonder that my tears should flow, 48.
You write and think of me, my friend, with pity, 140.

INDEX OF TITLES

A Little Longer, 74.
Angel of Death, The, 39.
Angel's Bidding, The, 182.
Angel's Story, The, 1.
Angels, Listening, 144.
Angels, Ministering, 221.
Annunciation, The, 208.
Appeal, An, 208.
Army of the Lord, The, 199.

Be Strong, 30.
Because, 97.
Beggar, A, 244.
Beyond, 115.
Birthday Gifts, 241.
Borrowed Thoughts, 153.
Bride's Dream, The, 181.

Carver's Lesson, The, 138.
Castle in the Air, A, 239.
Chain, A, 52.
Changeling, A, 157.
Changes, 41.
Chant, A, 133.
Chaplet of Flowers, A, 205.
CHAPLET OF VERSES, A, 191.
Christmas Carol, A, 219.
Christmas Flowers, 211.
Church in 1849, The, 216.
Cleansing Fires, 25.
Comfort, 94.
Comforter, A, 162.
Confido et Conquiesco, 215.
Contrast, A, 179.
Cradle-song of the Poor, The, 29.
Crown of Sorrow, A, 71.

Dark Side, The, 48.
Dead Past, A, 16.
Desire, A, 212.
Discouraged, 158.
Doubting Heart, A, 16.

Dream, A, 40.
Dream-Life, 135.

Echoes, 5.
Envy, 114.
Evening Chant, 218.
Evening Hymn, 184.
Expectation, 173.

False Genius, A, 6.
Farewell, A, 57.
Fidelis, 61.
First Sorrow, A, 49.
Fishers of Men, 216.
For the Future, 189.
Friend Sorrow, 8.
From . . . 154.
From "Lavater," 153.
From "Lost Alice," 154.
From "Phantastes," 153.

Give, 50.
Give me thy Heart, 43.
Give Place, 131.
God's Gifts, 31.
Golden Days, 145.
Golden Gate, The, 79.
Golden Words, 101.
Grief, 75.

Hearts, 185.
Home at Last, 95.
Homeless, 246.
Homeless Poor, The, 226.
Home-sickness, 81.
Homeward Bound, 19.
Hours, 92.
Hush ! 91.

Ideal, An, 174.
If thou couldst Know, 159.
Illusion, 87.

In the Wood, 122.
Incompleteness, 53.
Inner Chamber, The, 185.

Jubilee of 1850, The, 210.
Judge not, 7.

King and Slave, 133.
Knight-Errant, A, 18.
Kyrie Eleison, 207.

Lament for the Summer, A, 42.
Legend, A, 240.
Legend of Bregenz, A, 54.
Legend of Provence, A, 105.
LEGENDS AND LYRICS, 1, 103.
Lesson of the War, The, 71.
Letter, A, 160.
Life and Death, 24.
Life in Death and Death in Life, 83.
Light and Shade, 155.
Linger, O Gentle Time, 19.
Links with Heaven, 245.
Listening Angels, 144.
Little Longer, A, 74.
Lost Chord, A, 119.
Love Token, A, 60.

Maximus, 117.
Milly's Expiation, 231.
Ministering Angels, 221.
Murmurs, 49.
My Journal, 50.
My Picture, 6.
My Picture Gallery, 140.
My Will, 132.

Names of our Lady, The, 204.
Never again, 143.
New Mother, A, 124.
Now, 25.

Old Year's Blessing, The, 217.
One by One, 8.
Optimus, 118.
Ora pro Me, 215.
Our Daily Bread, 214.
Our Dead, 175.
Our Titles, 220.
Over the Mountain, 114.

Parting, A, 78.
Past and Present, 188.
Peace of God, The, 83.
Per Pacem ad Lucem, 240.
Phantoms, 80.

Philip and Mildred, 146.
Pictures in the Fire, 89.
Pilgrims, The, 53.
Present, The, 41.

Recollections, 86.
Remembrance of Autumn, A, 165.
Requital, The, 120.
Rest, 135.
Rest at Evening, 97.
Retrospect, A, 98.
Returned — "Missing," 121.

Sacred Heart, The, 202.
Sailor Boy, The, 62.
Sent to Heaven, 142.
Settlers, The, 90.
Shadow, A, 62.
Shining Stars, 28.
Shrines of Mary, The, 222.
Sowing and Reaping, 57.
Spring, 183.
Star of the Sea, The, 202.
Storm, The, 58.
Story of the Faithful Soul, The, 178.
Strive, Wait, and Pray, 41.
Student, A, 17.

Thankfulness, 80.
Three Evenings in a Life, 165.
Three Roses, 139.
Three Rulers, The, 15.
Threefold, 214.
Tomb in Ghent, A, 32.
Too Late, 119.
Treasures, 27.
Triumph of Time, The, 77.
True Honors, 9.
True or False, 99.
Tryst with Death, A, 60.
Two Interpreters, The, 93.
Two Loves, 187.
Two Spirits, The, 72.
Two Worlds, 123.
Tyrant and the Captive, The, 137.

Unexpressed, 96.
Unknown Grave, The, 42.
Unseen, 164.

Vision, A, 88.
Voice of the Wind, The, 26.
Voices of the Past, 48.

Waiting, 28.
Warning, A, 116.

Warrior to his Dead Bride, The, 159.
Wayside Inn, The, 45.
Wind, The, 172.
Wishes, 82.

Woman's Answer, A, 176.
Woman's Last Word, A, 187.
Woman's Question, A, 14.
Words, 59.

www.ingramcontent.com/pod-product-compliance
Lightning Source LLC
Chambersburg PA
CBHW021056030726
47496CB00006B/1866